S...

HAVE...
OF 46 GREAT NOVELS

OF

EROTIC DOMINATION

If you like one you will like the rest

A NEW TITLE EVERY MONTH
NOW INCLUDING EXTRA BONUS PAGES

If you like one of our books you will probably
like them all!

If you don't know which title to buy,

Write for our FREE 20 page booklet of extracts
surely the most erotic freebie yet
or leave leave your name and address on our 24hr. phone
0113 287 6255 (recording only)

For free 20 page booklet of extracts from previous
books (and, if you wish to be on our confidential
mailing list, from forthcoming monthly titles as they
are published) please write to:-

Silver Moon Readers Services
PO Box CR 25 LEEDS LS7 3TN
or
PO Box 1614 NEW YORK NY 10156

CONTENTS

Your first full length novel:-

ELISKA
von Mechtingen

BONUS PAGES

This is fiction - in real life, practice safe sex

ELISKA

BY
von MECHTINGEN

SILVER MOON BOOKS LTD
PO Box CR25 Leeds LS7 3TN

SILVER MOON BOOKS INCORPORATED
PO Box 1614 New York NY 10156

New authors welcome

Printed and bound in Great Britian

ELISKA, MARGRAVINE OF ZATORANSKY

THE THIRTY LETTERS ADDRESSED BY THE DISTIN-GUISHED GRAF HULDRYCH von MECHTINGEN TO HIS NEPHEW AT THE UNIVERSITY OF TÜBINGEN

Being an account of his mission to a Bohemian region for the Imperial Court of the Holy Roman Germanic Empire in the year 1528

INTRODUCTION

The following letters and the rough accompanying sketches - which unfortunately are too explicit to use here - were found among papers of the Semund monastery when its library was split up and relocated. It is not known how this material dating back to the early sixteenth century came to lie there, particularly in view of its indelicate contents. What is known is that the thirty letters were addressed by a certain Huldrych Martin Schonheimer, Graf von Mechtingen, to his young nephew, a law or theology student at the university of Tübingen.

The original letters are written in sixteenth century courtly Hochdeutsch with passages in Plattdeutsch or in the author's renderings of the local language and dialect. For this translation the text and names (such as Regensburg for Ratisbon, etc.) have been modernized, and irrelevant passages and those dealing solely with family matters omitted.

However coarse the text may at times seem to the modern temperament, it remains a revealing testimony of a charitable and diligent man caught in the complex web of a bygone age.

Letter the second

I have now a further surprise for you, Nephew. At supper, which was excellent and a pleasant change from the inns, we were joined by a group of three men, all remarkably handsome in different ways; one is younger than the other two and must be about thirty while his colleagues are in their early forties. This fair-haired, clean-shaven youth goes by the name of Milan and is the son of some local lord; the others wear pointed beards and carry themselves with a certain aloofness. The older of the two, Ladislav, is especially well-built with dark hair arranged with meticulous care; the second older man is somewhat less engaging but quite handsome and I understand his name is Premsyl.

They have titles of some sort but these, although the Margravine cited them, I did not catch. All three are attired with exquisite taste for a region as indigent and wretched as this. But what intrigued me was their total familiarity with the Margravine, holding her hand, kissing her cheek, with something far more than mere respect.

It was not long before I deduced that they are attached to her in a highly personal way; in other words they are her lovers. And not just one but all three... (I suppose we should not forget that our noble, if unpredictable, Landgrave Philip of Hesse himself lives in bigamy to which even your Luther closes his eyes... if you will forgive the analogy!) In addition, their endearments and caresses, while they embarrass me, do not seem to disconcert the Margravine who returns their loving gestures quite openly.

Conversation is not easy as they tend to use the colloquial dialect among themselves until Eliska urges them to turn to Plattdeutsch in which they are all proficient fortunately for me; my hostess commands excellent Hochdeutsch. She is most polite towards me, but the men seem suspicious of the mission that has brought me here.

"I rule here, Graf von Mechtingen," she declared, fixing me with narrowed eyes. "I alone demand labour of these serfs, thieves, beggars and harlots of mine. I alone levy my taxes on land, flour, bread, wine, increase tithes as I wish and order military service to protect these lazy serfs. I reward and I punish. I do not believe in what you people call tolerance. It only corrupts."

I sensed at once that I was on delicate ground, taken aback by her calm fury. I tried to lead the discussion to items that might intrigue them more, such as the recent formation of the Catholic Defensive League to counter the League of Protestant Princes. It did not interest them and so I recounted the terrible pillaging of the countryside I had witnessed on my journey and the dangerous lansquenets returning from the wars. I was, I added, appalled by the sight of vagrant women and prostitutes...

Quite suddenly the faces turned towards me. It was Milan who broke into my list of woes, his features reflecting his agreement

"There you are right, my lord," - I noted with relief the use of the correct address - "and you have put your finger upon a curse. We are plagued with whores. The gracious Margravine has done everything possible to curb illicit whoring and puts as many as can be caught to the whip immediately. But they become ever more brazen and insolent."

Eliska nodded gravely. "Indeed, this is a tremendous problem, sir. We are crowded out with vagrant illicit whores - loose females that defile my lands and defy my laws."

I saw that no one was really interested in the outside world with its foreign wars, peasant revolts and the advance of Lutheranism, not to speak of their disregard for my mission. Not even the famous eclipse of the sun in 1519 that scared us all in Nuremberg could have shaken them out of their feudal past and their hunting down of whores and witches. I regretted having even mentioned prostitutes.

I found myself wishing you were here, Nephew, to talk with me. Later, I sat down before my lancet window with a candle and wrote you this with blessings.

Your loving but weary uncle. H.

... after several days, an incident occurred that may interest you.

We were at table enjoying duckling, fresh vegetables and these dumplings that are so popular here; the conversation was more animated than at other meals since it dealt with some new serving-girls who had been taken from starving families in the countryside to work in the castle. In this connection, I should tell you that we are waited upon at table by several pretty young serving-maids who are naked to the loins; and it is difficult for me to accustom myself to their breasts swinging over the table as they bend to pour the wine or clear the plates. The Margravine looked more attractive and more relaxed than usual, embracing her lovers and graciously offering me her hand to kiss.

At a certain moment we were interrupted by the entry of a masked figure, his head covered with a canvas cowl pierced with eye-holes, sinister in the extreme; he wore a black short-sleeved doublet and dark hose, his codpiece buttoned tight over the bulge of his genitals. A sword swung from his baldric or belt. The hall fell silent as the man leaned towards the Gräfin's ear; she listened quietly and then, releasing the hand of her nearest lover, rose and went out of the hall with her servant.

I enquired of Ladislav the reason for the interruption.

"Ah, that is Jakub, the Margravine's trusted senior bailiff," he told me. "It seems that a whore has been found using a brothel illegally. I need hardly explain how gravely the Margravine views this, for the brothels in the town are her own personal property. You see, sir, many of our menfolk have either been tempted into your Imperial armies or incorporated by force and this, together with the recent peasant revolts, has left countless women without support. To survive, they sell themselves to any soldier, peasant or vagrant who can spare a coin. Here we maintain that prostitutes should work only in our brothels. That is what a whorehouse is for, my lord, is it not?"

He paused before adding: "Moreover all this brings in a healthy income to the castle."

Not being an expert in whoremongering, I let him continue.

"The Zatoransky brothel alone employs some two to three dozen harlots - the number varies and sometimes we have to send out a posse to bring in more females from the countryside. They are almost invariably stalwart hardy creatures, hard-working in bed and fairly obedient. Most girls are only too grateful to find a roof and a morsel to eat. The main stew here is run by a brothelmaster and his bawd of a wife who make a good living out of their tavern."

I was tempted to mention that Luther had achieved the closure of all such establishments in cities like Ulm, Nuremberg and Augsburg but I think I was probably wise to desist.

"Ah, sir," Ladislav sighed, "these vaginas are Satan's doorways."

I was about to discuss this - you know how I love theological argument - when Eliska returned, her eyes flashing, leaving Jakub at the door.

"Gentlemen," she said, "I am told that some brazen slut is fornicating without a licence in my brothel. This she has managed through the connivance of one of my legal whores. What is more, the bitch is a vagrant from a distant part of my lands and not even from Zatoransky." She paused to allow the enormity of the crime to impress itself on us, before adding: "I have therefore given orders for the two sluts to be brought up to the vault and put in chains. It will be for us to decide on the precise sentence we wish to pronounce on the illicit whore."

Her lovers nodded while Eliska turned to her servant. "Carry out the arrests forthwith. Order Sebastian to whip the conniving whore while we are at Vespers. Then bind her open in the stalls for general use. She will be returned to work tomorrow. Order Sebastian to prepare the illegal bitch for sentencing and the full ceremony of the Three Sessions."

In a whisper I asked Ladislav who this Sebastian was. Apparently he is the chief flagellator of the castle, a task inherited from his late father who had worked for the Margrave and died with him. Ladislav added that Eliska had had the youth's tongue torn out to ensure he can keep a secret. He is now twenty-six and never leaves the castle dungeons.

"Graf von Mechtingen," the Margravine said, smiling at me,

"I should be honoured if you, as an emissary of our newly found noble Emperor and our guest, would accompany my bailiffs to witness my justice being done and testify to the proper arrest of these sluts."

I felt uncomfortable at both invitations, but out of deference agreed, which I shall probably regret. It is not always easy to respect hospitality at the same time as the terms of my mission. And above all I am cautious not to offend my hostess in any way.

So I rose and followed the cowled servant down the long passages until we came to a room within the guardhouse in the great gate. A second hooded individual sat at the table, writing laboriously with a quill. In the centre of the chamber stood a dirty ragged-clothed fellow in clogs, turning his felt hat nervously round in his hands.

Jakub offered me a chair and then sprawled out on another, ordering the man to repeat his testimony which was in fact a denunciation. Despite the dialect I gathered that a woman whom he had never seen before and certainly not one of his whores, was fornicating (his was a rougher term) in his tavern-brothel. The man using her seemed to be some officer in the Imperial lansquenets. At this I became uneasy but the bailiffs, as if reading my diplomatic fears, confirmed that as such, the officer was beyond the jurisdiction of Zatoransky.

How was it that they were using the brothel? Jakub queried. The innkeeper muttered that he and his wife had been misled by the officer who wished merely to pass the night there. The girl had then been introduced secretly by one of the whores, who was bribed to do so. (I thought it more likely that the innkeeper and his bawd had accepted the bribe, if bribe there was; but I kept well away from this primitive show of justice.)

The man was rewarded with a few kreutzer - our own coin is frequently used here along with Venetian money. As I saw it, one of the regular whores had indeed connived to allow the unknown woman and her lansquenet to use the room. As the girl was not part of the brothel, the case for the bailiffs was clear. The ragged informer was kicked out of the guardroom, grasping his precious and well-earned coins.

In the mild afternoon, therefore, we mounted our horses to descend into the town. Hans asked, as he saddled my mare Zenon, if he was needed; I preferred to leave him playing dice with a couple of pikemen. Anyway, I do not want him too involved here with brothels...

As we were preparing in the yard, Milan, the youngest of the Margravine's lovers, sauntered up to me in his gorgeous brown velvet doublet and Italian silks.

"This is a perfect opportunity, sir, for you to appreciate some of the problems we discussed at table," he said. "These females are incorrigible."

As I mounted, with Hans holding my stirrup iron, I remarked: "You speak only of females. Surely there must be male culprits also, are there not?"

"The castle deals only with the female," he replied, patting Zenon's neck. "It is the female that interests the Margravine and us. Male offenders - and there are many - are dealt with by the ecclesiastical and secular authorities in the town. This applies to males in the castle also. So, dear lord, make sure you bring back a couple of well-favoured bitches to provide us with a little pleasure in the dungeons. We thrive on new flesh."

On this note we set off down the path, the two bailiffs and I. The Spring weather was superb and it was a joy to be out of the grim castle, to be under the blue sky with its swallows and to be amid the flowering broom - so different from the dank corridors, the flapping tapestries, stags' heads and threatening weapons frozen on the cold walls. As I breathed the air, I saw Premsyl on horseback with a hawk on his wrist, a hawk hooded like my strange companions. And like falcons, I thought, they too descend upon their prey.

As we arrived in front of the inn, townsfolk knelt or bowed obsequiously, some crossing themselves at the sight of the dreaded bailiffs. Although a small crowd gathered round the door of the stew, I sensed in it the abject fear and deference born out of the menace of communal reprisals for any infringement of the castle's laws.

The building is a poor thatched affair but boasting an upper floor, rare in these parts. Above the entry is nailed a crude wooden escutcheon that depicts, in case of any doubt, an erect phallus and testicles. Beneath it the squint-eyed bawd, her head wrapped in a filthy wimple, was gesticulating towards the windows above. Behind her, still unsure of himself, the brothel keeper continued to turn his hat in his shaking hands.

The bailiffs dismounted and I followed them in.

Led by the bawd, we mounted the rotten stairs. At the end of the passage, she eased open a door, nodding towards the room. Silently we peered inside.

Dear Nephew, you know me well enough by now and so will forgive me if in my letters I am straightforward. Moreover, only if I give you the raw detail can you understand the perplexing atmosphere that prevails here and in which I have to work.

Kneeling on a bed in a disarray of soiled sheets, a bearded man with handsome, rugged but well-cut features was clasping an exceptionally beautiful young woman against his body; she was straddled over his muscular thighs, her legs locked round his loins, her arms encircling his neck. They were both naked. The girl was in profile and thus displayed the rich curves of her flesh, shining with sweat. Her skin was uncommonly pale for peasant stock, which is usually swarthy and rough.

As the bodies met and parted, the man's glistening shaft was clearly visible as it thrust upwards into the woman's matted sex-hair. She moaned with pleasure, kissing her man lasciviously, arching backwards to let him take her swollen nipples between his lips and teeth. Now and then he would withdraw his sex from hers and friction the erect clitoris directly with the straining purple head; then he would slide into her again.

Suddenly the girl orgasmed. Binding herself to her lover, she came with overlapping waves of spasms, her cries filling the room as the man let her shoulders fall to the bed where she lay exhausted, drenched with sweat and shining with the discharge of her liquids over her belly and thighs.

I was able to calm the bailiffs, who were anxious to make the arrest. The girl could not escape them, I said. And my rank and influence with their Mistress probably awed them. And so they hesitated. At the same time we all marvelled at the perfection of the copulation and - I admit it, Nephew, for my part - we tacitly agreed to let the couple continue their mad, erotic ecstasy.

After a pause, the girl rose from the sheets and, grasping the erection, drew her man down to the foot of the bed where she splayed him out and knelt between the thighs. There she commenced a smooth, regular masturbation along the entire length of the superb erection before swallowing the shaft into her throat The fellatio gathered in intensity as the girl probed into her man, tugging at the testicles while the man seized the girl's hair, wrenching her towards him, plunging deeper and more passionately into her lips until he was ready.

He came with a long guttural cry as the scalding pent-up sperm pulsed, jet after jet, into the waiting gullet. The girl milked as much of the semen as possible out of the penis until the man was emptied and drained into her. Then she fell across his loins, caressing the sagging penis and the hot body very slowly, lovingly.

Without reference to me, the group burst into the room. As I followed I noticed the lansquenet's clothes lying in a heap with the girl's few rags and above them the man's sword - well out of reach of its owner. It was the second bailiff, Bohumil, who seized the girl, binding her arms behind her rump with a leather thong and bending her backwards to show all her dazzling nudity.

She was about twenty-three, superbly built with well-formed breasts and prominent nipples still engorged from the copulation; her flat belly swept down from the ribs to the thighs and the rich pubic hair from which the labia protruded, sensually soaked. The buttocks were hung high and, despite being clenched now, predicted full and rounded gluteal cheeks.

It was her face that intrigued me: very soft and lovely with high cheek bones, a wide sensual mouth - the lips still smeared with semen - and dark eyes, the whole framed by short auburn hair.

She stood with her eyes closed in an attitude of total resignation, or rather submission. Well might she be cowed, I thought, for she lies in the terrible power of Zatoransky. I pitied her with a strange pang in my heart.

"By order of the gracious Margravine," Jakub announced

through his cowl that lent his voice an ominous, distant note, "this whore is arrested for illicit fornication."

The lansquenet broke in, using Plattdeutsch, as he stood awkwardly hiding his genitals and nakedness: "But she is my mistress! You have no right. I have paid for the room."

The bailiff waved the protest curtly aside: "The slut is unlicensed and practising as a vagrant whore in an official brothel of the Margravine of Zatoransky! As such, the scum will have to pay for it. Moreover, we have here a witness of the Imperial court who resides as guest of the Margravine." He pointed to me. "The whore must be taken to the castle."

The naked girl's mouth opened slightly as she sighed and looked at her lover. The man then turned to me.

"Sir, I ask you to intercede on our behalf. This is outrageous. She is my legal mistress."

Before I could consider an answer or suggest an intercession with my hostess, the bailiff intervened and cried: "You paid this whore, did you not?"

"Surely," he replied. "She is in sore need and it is natural I should give her money. She has lost both parents and a brother. She has no man, no home. I am her protector and I have taken her as my mistress." He was furious but prudent also, for his position was indeed unenviable.

"Then how does this slag of a whore come to be naked in a brothel?" Jakub shouted.

"She is not a whore!" the officer cried back. "I have the right to fuck my woman where I like. Anyway, we were helped by a girl who works here - and she I have paid to go with my man next door."

I winced at his ingenuousness, knowing what awaited the girl, and the innkeeper turned pale, muttering: "I know nothing of all this, your lordships and may it please you both bitches should be arrested and put to the whip."

"They will be, don't you fret, man," Jakub said. "And you had better watch your mouth." Then he turned to the lansquenet, as Bohumil began to hustle the girl out. "If this whore means so much to you, she can be collected in three weeks time outside the castle gates, unless she is condemned to work in the brothels. As an officer of the Imperial power, you are free to depart, sir. Those are my orders."

I noticed the respectful 'sir' and felt the bailiff certainty knew his job. To be discovered in a stew with an unlicensed woman, whore or not, was a delicate matter, and the prospect of recovering his alleged mistress was sufficient to mollify the officer. He did not seem to be prepared to argue further. He kissed the girl and swore he would claim her.

Pale with terror, the girl was thrown out into the passage while Bohumil carried out the arrest in the adjacent room; it was done rapidly, without discussion. A young prostitute with long fair hair and a pretty figure was roughly dragged from under the lansquenet's subordinate who was using her fiercely. Both were paralysed with fright at the sight of the masked intruder. The girl was hauled off the bed and pushed down the stairs behind the first prisoner. Both were now to be driven naked up to the castle.

The other inmates of the house cowered in the corners as the girls were roped for the ascent The crowd outside fell silent and there was no reaction to the arrests.

At supper not one of my hosts even mentioned these happenings but talked of hunting throughout the meal. I must end here for I have a busy day tomorrow and must prepare.

My love to you and to your dearest mother.

Your trusting uncle, Huldrych

Letter the fourth

This letter begins with a number of personal and family concerns after which the text continues:

...reverting to the happenings of yesterday, I should add that the lansquenet's woman was thrown over one of the bailiffs' horses and bound obscenely, belly up, thighs parted and roped securely by arms and legs; the other girl was made to walk up at the end of a leather rein, receiving a stroke of the whip to hasten her on; and thus we arrived at the drawbridge over the slimy moat

Hans greeted me and took charge of my mare Zenon; she had enjoyed the outing more than I, for she had remained outside the dismal stew as behoves the noble lady that she is. Hans stared at the naked women being led across the courtyard but the castle servants did not seem to take much notice except for an occasional glance of trepidation. The bailiffs thrust their charges down some steps on the far side of the yard and with an unsavoury degree of curiosity I followed them.

They had been taken into a vaulted chamber, the roof being supported by stout columns of stone - not unlike the crypt in the Dom at Bamberg, the one above which stand the carved horseman and the tomb of the Emperor and his Cunigunde, that unfortunate woman, unjustly accused of adultery only to prove her innocence by walking the white-hot coals. The vault here is lit by several tallow candles, for little or no light filters down.

Both girls were made to kneel, wrists tied behind them, each facing a pair of columns. The bailiffs first positioned the long-haired whore: arms outflung and manacled with tough leather straps linked to chains reaching to the summit of each column. The girl, totally nude, stood teetering on the tips of her toes before the legs were likewise pulled apart and chained. Then she hung.

The same procedure applied to the lansquenet's girl until the two pale bodies were spread and drawn to the full reach of their limbs; they looked frail and vulnerable but immensely beautiful as the muscles tightened, the breasts began to rear in search of breath. The only sound was a short gasp as the body responded to the traction and the sexes were exposed. I was able to compare the bodies: the legitimate whore (if you allow the term) with her long corn-coloured hair, was more slender, with smaller breasts and buttocks. The lansquenet's mistress (if you agree with that term too) is of stronger build, with heavier breasts, large ripe nipples and longer limbs. At the loins the sex-labia protrude proudly through the matted auburn triangle of thick hair. Both sexes were still wet from copulation.

The bailiffs went about their work efficiently, almost indifferently, as they hauled and bound, ensuring that each female was fully stretched and exposed. The two nudes were crucified as if floating aloft.

While the men were refreshing themselves with small beer taken from an alcove, they were the first to catch the sound of high heels. Rapidly they regained their places beside their charges as the Margravine entered. Her gown swirling about her riding boots, her breasts and cheeks powered white, she looked more menacing than ever. She did not seem to notice my presence, perhaps because I was in a sombre corner, but more likely because her entire attention was devoted to the naked bodies before her.

She inspected each thoroughly, weighing the buttocks as if to gauge the elasticity, chafing the nipples into erection and splaying each of the sexes with the fingers of her kid gloves. She spent a greater time on the lansquenet's female than on the whore, pulling on the sex labia here, probing into the body there.

Then her order came.

"Flush the sperm out them and wash down the flesh. Then oil it well."

To Jakub's question, in his local accent, whether the armpits should be scraped clean, her answer was curt. "I would order it if I required it, man. Just obey! I need all the hair these sluts have on them - in the state in which they fuck."

She pointed to the long-haired whore.

"This slut will be flagellated tonight where she hangs, during Vespers. Order Sebastian to scourge her properly, front and back and especially the buttock-meat, after which she will be exposed in the slave stalls below, chained open for general use through the night. Any castle males deserving merit and recompense may use her. And in any manner they wish. Thereafter, she will be returned to her brothel to work, chained to her bed by the neck for a week. Further, you will see to it that she receives thirty lashes at the close of the week, tied naked over the whipping frame in the brothel in front of all inmates."

The bailiffs bowed low as they accompanied their Mistress to the other prisoner.

Eliska contemplated the hanging body for a long moment, turning round it to view each portion of flesh. She was evidently highly satisfied with what she saw. Bohumil had begun to wash down the body and had brought forward a bowl of scented oil for the subsequent anointment, oil that enhanced the body erotically and facilitated flagellation.

"This one will hang here," she commanded, "to enjoy the scourging of her slut of an ally. After Vespers you will deliver her to Sebastian below to be prepared for the ritual of the Three Sessions. I require her in perfect condition. Is this clear?"

She suddenly turned to me in the shadows. Her eyes were bright with excitement.

"Come, my dear friend." Her long graceful arms were stretched out to me in their dark crimson gloves. "Let us go up together."

As we mounted a stairway leading to the main hall, she confided in me: "As you see, my lord, I have to administer justice at all hours. At least, once cleaned and oiled - almost a waste of fragrances - these sluts will present an immaculate exterior despite the filth in their souls. And that, I shall see to it, will be whipped out of them."

To avoid having to comment on her metaphysics, I remarked that the whip seemed to constitute the main remedy for offences here.

"Indeed," she concurred, "there is nothing as conclusive as the scourge applied to a naked female body. I do not, my lord, countenance torture of any kind here - no ugly racks, iron brodequins, strappado or the wheel. They are simply repulsive and permanently damaging and, above all, ungratifying to the spectator. And I refuse to have blood drawn from my girls. What, I ask you, is more erotic than a stark naked female receiving the lash? And there is no girl who cannot recover quickly from a flagellation." She paused before adding: "I would remind you, sir, that these females have been brought up on the whip from childhood. They are inured to it. Some, if not most, accept it willingly and even react to the erotic - or should one not say sexual? - stimulus it arouses."

"Are you victims always females?" I asked, despite Milan's earlier explanations.

"They are not victims but common sluts whose flesh has been or may be misled by lust and the Devil. But you are right. I take it upon myself, as a woman, to purge the most obdurate devil out of a woman's body; it never fails. I know how to deal with the female body. Now, as to males - I have of course dealt with them too, naked and excited - if there is need for correction, I prefer to delegate this to the authorities in the town or to the Bishop. No, it is the female that I set out to save and purify. And it follows that in so doing, I and my companions deserve compensation. And this we receive in the act itself. For whipping a nude female is indeed pleasurable."

I felt she was utterly sincere and meant what she said.

As we drew near to the chapel, she added softly: "I am sure you will enjoy the preparation of this illicit whore tonight, and thus you will see my loyal flagellator at work. And of course I trust you will honour me at the sessions themselves."

She descended the silken kerchief over her magnificent breasts and led me into the dismal chapel before I could answer.

The service was officiated by an aged priest, confessor to the deceased Margrave and now to his widow; he droned through the office in atrocious Latin and yet there was something human about the man as he blessed the congregation. This consisted mainly of women with very few men. I took them to be handmaidens, overseers, seamstresses, kitchen maids, scullery slaves and other menials; I caught sight of the young girls who served at table, their breasts now demurely covered. The Margravine sat alone in front on the south of the aisle, her three lovers behind her.

After the muttered blessing - which I felt we all sorely needed - we filed out behind the Margravine while the servants dropped to their knees, bowing to her. Ladislav apologized to me for the quality of the service.

"This elderly monk is all the Margravine requires, you know, sir. He does his duty, does not frequent brothels nor use the serving wenches as so many local priests do. The Bishop, whom you will soon meet, I trust, permits the castle to live as the Margravine wishes and decrees. He is most cooperative in granting full absolution and in selling indulgences very cheaply. He fully supports our crusade to salvage sinful and lusting females and sometimes honours us by coming to watch them being whipped naked in our ceremonies."

I admit to being really confused, Nephew, by the relations these people have with the Church, but I hold my tongue.

During the supper, excellent as usual, an incident took place which is worth recounting if only to stress the strange reactions of these noble hosts of mine.

One of the serving-girls - a very pretty serf, naked to the waist as usual - suddenly tripped, her bare feet catching in the carpets. She spilt the whole contents of a beaker of wine over the young Milan whom she was serving; it ran over the table and down into his lap. Milan sprang to his feet and turned on the petrified culprit with a torrent of abuse in local dialect. The girl, whose name I gathered is Tereza, turned white with fear.

"You foul, slovenly bitch of a whore!" he shouted. "You dirty strumpet." And a few more insults I had difficulty in following.

I was taken aback at the man's fury and the Margravine seemed to share his anger but her voice was controlled as her eyes narrowed. I started to help to mop up the wine as the second servant was called to the scene. The Margravine waved me back.

She addressed the wretched girl. "I have been watching you for some time," she hissed. "You are given the honour of waiting at my high table merely because the bailiffs selected you from among the rabble downstairs, because they think you have attractive breasts, you little scum! But you are lazy, careless and provocative - you have even the effrontery to look me in the

21

eyes."

The wench immediately dropped her terrified gaze to the carpets where the wine continued to trickle. Like the wine, my heart bled for her.

"You will pay dearly for this," Eliska said coldly. "Drop your skirt girl!"

To my consternation - for, after all, the scene was being enacted before an emissary of His Imperial Majesty - Tereza undid the cord that held her only garment to her hips (I have noticed that females never wear drawers here) and let it fall. She stood completely naked before us, trying to shield the narrow triangle of fair hair over her sex from our view.

"Stand straight, scullion!" It was Milan who shouted, at which Tereza joined her hands behind her back, jutting out her sharp breasts. She was trembling but looked so lovely.

"Send for Jakub!" Eliska turned to the second serving girl who stood quivering in a corner, as far away as possible from her companion, and now fled at once.

Eliska then addressed the table. "As you see, the bailiffs do their best to provide handsome girls with good firm breasts to serve here, but what do we get in return? I have had my eye on this bitch and her pert habits. This is the way she chooses to repay me for my generosity. I have taken her in as an orphan, fed her, clothed her and sheltered her ungrateful body. Well, her naked body you see before you will now pay for the favours she owes. it will taste the whip as few sluts have tasted it recently."

She spoke with venom as Jakub in his cowl hurried into the hall, obviously fully alerted to the situation. He seized the girl by the arms, bending her backwards viciously.

"Has this slut been pierced?" Eliska enquired brusquely. Her man nodded, squeezing a nipple to show the small insertion hole in the umber flesh.

"Yes, gracious lady, a month ago, along with the other slaves from the six villages," the reply came, precise with intimate knowledge of the bodies that fell to the man's charge. "She can be ringed again for bondage and flogging immediately, if that is your wish, gracious lady." The man took an evident delight in his duties.

"I shall decide later," the gracious lady replied. "Meanwhile take her to the slave stalls below and suspend her by the legs next to the whore."

Jakub bowed ceremoniously. Grasping the fallen skirt, he hurried the girl out towards whatever the slave stalls might be. After this extraordinary scene, Nephew, I was at a loss how to continue the discussion. Milan continued to wipe down his breeches and seemed content with the culprit's dismissal. It was Ladislav who sensed my embarrassment

"Ah, our sweet Gräfin," he aid with a smile, "she can be harsh. But a serf is a serf, a slut is a slut, and this one has been running risks for some time."

"Perhaps," I replied, twisting some bread between my fingers, "but an accident is an accident." As he did not respond, I asked what was implied by piercing and ringing.

"Let me explain," Ladislav volunteered. "The Margravine has made it a rule that any serf or servant - I speak of females, of course - who commits an offence here in the castle is usually, but not always, handed over to Sebastian to have her nipples, clitoris hood and the folds of the sex, and sometimes the navel, pierced for the insertion of rings. It is then by these rings, apart from the wrists, ankles and throat, that the woman is attached for whipping. If no further condemnation occurs during the month that follows, the rings are removed, as is the case of this slut. To be honest, I do not recall why this particular girl was ringed."

"To cleanse her?" I offered, trying not to sound sardonic.

It was here that the Margravine intervened: "Graf von Mechtingen, you may be surprised at my severity. You see, we do not live in your sophisticated parts, although your revolts, massacres and destruction of abbeys and convents in the Black Forest, in Thuringia or wherever, are hardly reassuring. But here I demand the strictest possible discipline among my serfs and servants. Women must remain pure." She paused and then added: "If they are serfs and servants."

It was Premsyl's turn to enlighten me. "Yes, such women must be purified with the whip. This is done in the privacy of the castle, sir. We disagree entirely with public whippings; they are not exemplary and only offer the victim notoriety and sympathy, as well as exciting the uneducated onlooker to lust and depravity."

At that point Eliska rose to leave the hall and reiterated her invitation to me.

"My lord, you saw a whore arrested in flagrante delicto" (I had to admire her Latin) "and she is to be prepared by my man tonight. I think it would be instructive of our methods if you were to witness this preparation as well as the actual sessions. Please feel free to wander through the dungeons and slave stalls. Apart from one or two rather special places, we have no secrets from you, my dear lord."

As she left the great hall with her lovers, I found myself confronted with the second serving girl who stood motionless before me. It was clear that she had been told to place herself at my service. As I have absolutely no desire to become entangled in the habits of this place, I dismissed the girl, but not before she made it plain to me in her local words that I could use her body in any way I wished and take the whip to her if that be my desire. I just hope that Hans is not being tempted in this sort of way!

Greetings from this vale of tears!

Huldrych

Letter the fifth

My work proceeds far better than expected and I have found time to study the way the place is run. I begin to know the immense castle better: the library and music room, the bedrooms leading off the long corridor behind heavy tapestries, the dining hall, council room and countless other chambers.

But so far I did not know the subterranean regions.

Armed with the Margravine's authority, I therefore decided to explore. Holding my candlestick above my head, I wandered through the maze of passages and galleries.

"You no doubt seek the preparation chamber, my lord," came the rough accent. Despite his cowl, I recognized Jakub and, glad of his company, walked with him. I took the opportunity of asking him if his current prisoners did not have names.

His reply was straightforward. "The brothel whore is called Marja. She works her body hard and with profit. She was scourged in the vault during Vespers. Thirty-three lashes. She's used to a thick whip, and even fucks well afterwards."

I pretended to ignore the language. "And the illicit whore?" I asked.

"She is not from Zatoransky, sir. She's called Maryska. She is about to be prepared for a full ceremony. After preparation she will join the other two - that is, the whore Marja and the slut Tereza - in the stalls and all three will be used by us and selected men deserving recompense for good service."

Jakub now unlocked a heavy door studded with nails and we entered an oval chamber lit by two candles in wall sconces. There, crouching naked on the flagstones, her arms bound behind her, knelt Maryska - I call her by her name now, for at least she is entitled to this if to nothing else. Her beautiful body glistened with oils as her breasts rose and fell rapidly with fear; yet she seemed totally resigned, submissive and docile as she waited.

Then slowly in the hollow silence and in the odour of sweat and candle tallow, Sebastian entered. He was naked except for a pair of black velvet slippers, a leather belt round the waist and straps round each wrist. In his hand, as if it were his wand of office, he held a whip. He is certainly a magnificently handsome youth, muscular and well-built, his chest, belly and crotch covered with dark hair above a heavy set of genitals, momentarily dormant and swinging ponderously against his thighs as he walked.

Jakub then delivered his charge to the young man.

"By order of the gracious Margravine, this whore is to be prepared for the ceremony of the Three Sessions - pierced, ringed, manacled and chained. After preparation, the whore will be committed to the stalls for use. You will be informed of the time for her presentation for the first session. Proceed!"

Jakub, his duty performed, bowed to me and departed, leaving me with the naked couple, each looking at the other in silence.

The girl was now made to kneel before the man. This she did almost willingly as if she knew that any resistance was not only futile but dangerous for her body. I found myself wondering if she was not conscious of the power her nakedness exerted on the youth, and if she herself was not excited by the powerful nude man before her.

As Sebastian looked down at the superb body kneeling obediently at his feet, his penis began to swell. Slowly it rose, the foreskin withdrawing gradually from the scarlet head, until it stood throbbing in full erection. The girl watched the growth in silence, passing her tongue now and then over her lips.

The scene was suddenly disturbed by the arrival of no one less than Eliska. Her heels echoing in the chamber, she approached the couple and to my astonishment took hold of her servant's erection; gently she ran her gloved hand from the tip to the base several times, looking attentively at her victim. What she said to her servant was more or less a repetition of Jakub's order except that she insisted in having both - both, she repeated - both flanges of flesh on either side of the sex pierced and ringed together rather than just single lips.

Her orders seemed to be routine. The man, flattered by the sliding hand on his prick, nodded. And then Eliska was gone as suddenly as she had appeared. She did not seem even to notice me.

Sebastian guided the girl into an adjoining chamber. This is a far larger room, also lit by large candles that threw grotesque shadows on the walls. The furnishings startled me. Two massive oak frames stood at one end, loaded with instruments and implements: whips and scourges of many sorts, plaited thongs with braided tips, coils of leather ending in waxed cords, thin flat lengths of horse leather, riding crops, bunches of short slender ropes. Suspended among them from the crossbars were iron tongs, shafts in the form of a penis and an array of iron spheres on lengths of chain similar to our infamous Morgensterns used as flailing maces in battle, each spike honed to a glittering point.

In front to this stood a heavy bench, such as those used by carpenters; at an angle on its surface was bolted a stout rod bound in leather. As if aware of what was required of her, Maryska lifted herself on to the bench and, belly down, edged towards the shaft until it was grazing her sex. With a sharp thrust on the buttocks, Sebastian drove the loins downwards and, with a gasp that filled the chamber, Maryska was impaled.

As the rod slid into her, her breasts crushed down on to the bench, the head hanging over the end. The wrists were still bound and obviously no additional bondage was required while Sebastian buckled broad manacles of black, well-used leather to the wrists and ankles, each strap armed with several rings.

This done, the man spent a long moment examining the superb curves of the raised rump, passing his hands over the flesh, between the cheeks and down the tensed thighs. When satisfied, he urged the girl off the spigot and made her kneel to receive the studded neck strap and a purple band of velvet tied over the eyes. As Ladislav had put it earlier when describing how they desired to have slaves presented, the girl from now on would be blind, attacked by unseen forces, invisible scourges and anonymous hands and sexes which took pains to purge her body of its lust and sin.

Next the girl was dragged to a crossbar where she was hauled aloft by the ankles to a beam overhead, limbs parted and wrists secured below. The breasts were then lifted and placed on the bar. At that moment an elderly woman entered carrying a tray of pots. This was Radka. Slowly and deliberately she anointed the sex and the nipples, rubbing unguents into the tender, supple flesh; later I learned she concocts these herself from herbs and they are powerful enough to render the organs insensible, dulling the pain and disinfecting. What strange and wise measures these monsters take in their cruelty!

After a long smearing of her potions, the old hag fingered one of the girl's nipples and the sex lips, after which she nodded to Sebastian that the victim was ready. I do not wish to dismay you with a description of the piercing and the insertion and clipping of the shining metal rings, but in the process Radka smeared more preparations over the breasts and genitals while Maryska only groaned, hardly moving in her bondage.

Then, gathering her jars and pots, the old woman left without a word but with almost exaggerated politeness, bowed to me in passing. All is ceremony here - even in the dungeons! May God help us.

The body now glinted with the five bright rings firmly embedded in the large nipples, the rich labia and the fold of the clitoris hood among the auburn hairs of the crotch.

I thought the preparation was over but this was not to be. Far from it. The man released Maryska and dragged her, swaying unsteadily after the shock of her suspension and piercing, to a huge sloping beam of timber to which he bound her, arms above the head, legs drawn backwards. Just as in the vault, the body was revealed in all its perfection, the belly concave from the projecting ridge of the ribs down to the bulge of the pubic mound, below which the sex was splayed wide open. It was into this now that Sebastian thrust a stout smooth wooden shaft, probably, I thought, to ready it for his own. Then he throttled the breasts at the root with straps, making them swell to their utmost volume and the nipples protrude upwards with their new rings. Armed with a hook, he then tested each nipple-ring, tugging steadily to ensure it was securely embedded. Here for the first time Maryska tossed her head and filled the chamber with a hoarse cry as the organs distended.

Content with his work, the man stood back to contemplate the beauty who lay in his total power; after caressing his sex for a long, luxurious moment he released the breasts and removed the shaft from the vagina.

Seated in a chair I had found in the shadows, I instinctively felt that the moment of the man's reward or recompense had come. And indeed I was right. He straddled over the body where it lay, still bound to the beam, and drove his erection deep into it. Maryska sucked in her breath with a long hiss and almost immediately her loins began to writhe and heave as the oldest act of all was performed. Very soon she was thumping her rump violently against the timber, thrashing her head from side to side and moaning and, after several minutes of being rammed and battered, she shrieked and came.

Sebastian remained within her for as long as the orgasm and its aftermath lasted. He withdrew slowly, unbound the body and dragged the limp girl to the side of the beam, binding her wrists behind her and seating himself on the upper end of the timber. The woman went to her knees at once and, guided by a throat chain, sought the erection as if desperate to satisfy her all-powerful master. The fellatio was fierce and long with Maryska sucking and licking with animal avidity until the vein-ribbed prick sprang from the lips to splash its turbid jets of boiling grey semen in lumps over Maryska's face and neck. The man emptied the shaft with the grip of his fist, groaning with contentment.

It was then that I left, amazed that the girl could orgasm so soon after piercing but relieved that she had been pleasured. I had had my first experience of the Zatoransky dungeons. On my way back to my solitary chamber, a gust of night air blew out my candle and, as your dear mother used to say, that is never a good omen. I fell asleep to the sound of croaking frogs and the nightjars and dreamt of nothing I can recall. A good omen?

I send you my blessings. Embrace you mother for me. It is no use your writing, even by Imperial messenger, if you could get one, for letters will not reach me here before my departure which will be, God willing, in about a month from now.

And then home.

Huldrych, your loving uncle

Letter the sixth

(Several pages of this letter are lost. The text takes up at the third page)

...and so the work advances slowly. The cooperation has been better than I anticipated except for the local convents where the Mothers Superior seem reluctant to help. I shall seek the Margravine's advice. The visits to the priories, on the other hand, have been fruitful. I have now two despatches ready for my masters in Nuremberg.

If I am not out riding and visiting with Hans and the guards, I work in my room where I frequently dine alone, pleading my labours. My meals are brought to me by a delicious, dark-haired serf girl, naked, as usual, down to the edge of her pubic hair, which is the required dress. This one is the replacement for Tereza and is full of smiles. I wonder how long she will last? And thinking back to Tereza, now and then when I am in the courtyard, taking the night air, I can catch the muffled sound of screams from the vault below and the hiss and crack of the scourge on flesh as some miserable wench is flogged for some terrible crime - like slamming a door or talking during Vespers...

The same evening, after a stroll among the fragrant boxwood hedges in the castle garden, I decided to explore more of the underworld. There are some thirty steps down which give an idea of the depth of some of the cellars. At one point I saw a great iron-hinged door, firmly locked, which I deduced was the fateful dungeon where the sex-torture - as they sometimes term it - takes place. To the right stretched a dark corridor which I took, following my instinct of direction (which you yourself admired in me when we got lost in the back streets of Heidelberg one night!). Thus I happened on what they call the slave stalls themselves.

These are a series of rough wooden partitions not unlike a stable except that no animal could be kept down here; each stall has a stone slab across its width. You can imagine my surprise, although I half expected it, to find three of the stalls occupied by females, naked and chained. In the first, the beautiful Tereza was hanging by the ankles, legs apart, her arms bound behind her, so that her head hung at the level of a man's loins, which was to be shown a moment later.

The girl was breathing rapidly on account of the suspension she was enduring. Yet she had not been put to the whip - at least, not yet - for her skin was pristine and free of lash welts. I felt relieved on her account, this little spiller of wine.

In the adjacent stall, her buttocks perched on the extremity of the ledge, the whore Marja was stretched by a chain from the neck to a large ring in the wall behind. Her thighs were wide open, chained to the base of the partitions on each side and purple whip marks over her hips bore testimony to the flagellation she had received in the vault. She sat motionless, her eyes closed, her fair hair cascading down her back.

To my further surprise, I recognized immediately the third female from her blindfold and body rings. Maryska's legs were chained to the metal circles in her sex labia, causing her to sit in cruel tension. I noticed that each partition post had a slender whip hooked to it, ready for instant use on recalcitrant flesh or to satisfy a sudden whim.

As I advanced further with my candle, I heard footsteps approaching and I withdrew into the shadows as Bohumil entered. Without taking note of my presence or feigning to ignore me, he approached Tereza's nudity, entirely at his disposal.

He caressed her body from top to bottom - the belly, buttocks, inner thighs and then the sex - and all at once opened his codpiece and brought out a pulsating erection. He thrust the head into the girl's mouth and, as her lips encircled the pole obediently, lunged in deep. Tereza gagged at each penetration but managed to perform a superb fellatio, despite her position. After some minutes I thought one or both must orgasm - particularly when the man rubbed his rough cowl against the open labia and clitoris.

But Bohumil withdrew, leaving Tereza panting, gasping. He moved to Marja. Here he plunged directly into her sex, butting her body against the wall. It was she, experienced prostitute that she is, who accelerated the rhythm, seeking the man's discharge and possibly her own.

31

But she too was left craving. Restraining himself, the man shifted over to Maryska where he relieved the distended sex of the leg chains, lifted the thighs round his waist and took her violently, wrenching the labia rings apart as he penetrated. This copulation was different. Bohumil thumped into Maryska with savage lust; I could hear the bodies slapping together as the man plundered the loins relentlessly. After what seemed like an eternity, Maryska let out a long, hoarse cry, arching herself backwards as if to drag the penis into her. She orgasmed uncontrollably. The man continued until he too was ready. The powerful pulses of hot rich sperm sluiced over the girl's belly and ribs as Bohumil withdrew and spent madly from his clenched hand.

Fully satisfied, Bohumil fastened his codpiece, unchained Maryska and, taking his lantern, led her to the far door of the chamber. The girl looked magnificent as she walked, her body shining with the scented oil over which the opaque semen slid slowly down towards the pubis. The chamber was pungent with odours: sweat, sperm, leather and tallow. Leaving the two other nudes, the couple quit the stalls and I concluded that the girl was now being taken to her cell where she would dwell for her weeks of 'cleansing'.

What perplexed me in watching the scene just enacted was the total subservience of the women and their apparent readiness, even eagerness, to cooperate sexually with their gaolers despite the bondage imposed. Also the fact that the bailiff must have been aware of my presence and yet performed without hesitation before me.

I began to wonder what Maryska's cell was like; my curiosity was aroused. But first I returned to my quarters and, after sorting out my papers in my usual meticulous manner, wrote this interminable letter to you, to whom, since I have no one civilized here to confide in, I send my blessings and love.

Your uncle in God, Huldrych

Letter the seventh

In my tours of duty the next day, I was shocked at the poverty, destitution and profligacy that abound here. The numbers of beggars and of desperate women and young girls deprived of their menfolk, offering themselves openly, even on the streets and byways, sometimes persuades me to understand the Margravine's personal crusade; but her correctives do not leave much choice to a vagrant, starving female: it is simple and coercive - the brothel or the whip.

Despite her questionable sense of justice - and her lusts, which do not concern me as a visitor and guest - Eliska is a remarkably able person; not only is she a widow but has inherited a benighted realm. She carries out frequent personal visits of inspection as far as the Palatinate border and so maintains contact with her domains, devoting attention to both the ecclesiastical and secular arms. With regard to the first, she pays lip service to the Bishop, abbots and priesthood, including monasteries and nunneries - where, I am told, she looks with envy on some of the younger and more attractive nuns who could just as well be working for her at the castle.

Here one dwells in a world of fear, of angels and devils, of cunning recompense and crude retribution, all wrapped up in mystical terror; but then, as we all well know, Luther himself became a monk after being scared by a bolt of lightning. 'Good works' in the name of God are popular - and beating these naked women is among them.

I could not plead overwork the next evening when invited to attend the ceremony in the dungeon. It would have been blunt discourtesy. I had to don a cowl, like those worn by the bailiffs, and a robe, and descend the steps after Jakub who had been sent to escort me.

The dungeon consists of a vast windowless space paved with flagstones and spanned by heavy oak beams. The place is heated somehow. In fact it is rather stifling, especially when one wears these heavy clothes. At one end is a raised dais covered with a rich carpet on which stand several chairs, and candles burn incessantly, giving off a strange perfume. Chains and rings hang everywhere between the numerous pillars supporting the roof. By the left wall presides a long rough table ladened with a huge array of whips, greased and ready for use.

Before the dais lies a massive cross of hewn timber, its head resting on blocks. To the right rears a sort of gallows, bolted to a platform, with crossbars at its head and halfway down. Further to the right, wedged into the ground, a stake stands, rising to about the height of a man's belly, its tip rounded off; a stout chain hangs above it. There are several other appliances but I had not the time to study them. Perhaps just as well...

The Margravine entered with her lovers, who took their places on the dais. Eliska looked very striking in her flowing velvet robe, high boots and coif, her breasts standing out bare from the tight bodice. The men were, like me, shrouded in hood and cloak. We all stood in an eerie silence. And then Eliska rang a little silver bell in her gloved and jewelled hand. I was to learn that each act of the ceremony is governed by this silver bell.

From the entry at the head of the stairway Sebastian appeared with Maryska before him. Both were naked and Maryska was loaded with ceremonial chains as she felt her way blindly down the steps. Very slowly the couple entered the dungeon where the girl was now to suffer - for the good of her soul!

They halted in front of the dais. There Maryska was thrust to her knees, made to bow to the ground and then, after having her lower chains removed, bent backwards to reveal her marvellous body to the company. My hosts now rose and approached the blindfolded victim while Eliska quite unashamedly caressed her lovers' sexes between the folds of their cloaks. Ladislav - to judge from the voice - unrolled a parchment and read out what I realized was the sentence.

The terms were in the local tongue, but I gathered the gist only too well. After a tedious preamble citing the Margravine's acute sense of justice and a passing reference to the Emperor (probably for my benefit), the list of tortures - or rather cleansing flagellations - followed. Taken *in flagrante delicto*, fornicating illicitly in the principal Zatoransky brothel, property of the gracious Gräfin Eliska Helena, the whore was condemned to be flagellated naked in a ritual of three sessions, each session having three sequences.

The precise postures, number of lashes and specific instruments of flagellation were stipulated. I could not follow the detail, but Maryska's open mouth and blanched complexion under her blindfold showed that she understood only too well. Certain items I did grasp, such as crucifixion, impalements, breast gallows, suspensions.

Certain sequences were to be performed by the Margravine herself, others by her counsellors, the rest by the official flogger.

Ladislav's colourless reading finally concluded and Brother Ignatius was ushered in. In a faint voice he blessed the instruments of flagellation on the table, as well as most of the appliances, and finally sprinkled holy water over the trembling Maryska, before he hurriedly left.

The silver bell sounded and we took our seats, I feeling less like an Imperial envoy than ever before in my life, and hoping I could escape future sessions.

While Eliska played openly and lasciviously with her lovers, Maryska was bound to the cross, stretched out so erotically that it cut my breath - the oiled body with its curves and muscles yielded to her master's gestures and I sensed that she had been thoroughly excited prior to her entry.

Sebastian hooked a spiked Morgenstern sphere to each genital ring and left them on the floor between the lower arms of the cross. At a further tinkle of the bell, the cross was raised upright by means of chains and ratchets until the girl hung helplessly stretched. She clenched her teeth as the man began to bind her breasts by the rings. It was almost overpowering to watch the man, with his enormous erection pulsing and dragging over Maryska's flesh, working on the nude in silence.

Once the body had been fully harnessed to the cross, Eliska herself advanced, a slender leather whip in hand. She took her stance and began to whip. She scourged from the breasts to the upper thighs. I did not count the stokes nor Maryska's groans. I do not think that the body was much hurt; rather it was the suspension and the shock of exposure in this aura of frightening ceremony that combined with the scourging to paralyse the girl.

Then Maryska was left to hang, her flesh bearing the pattern of the whip. She seemed to have had the breath taken out of her, as she sagged in her bondage.

It had been an extraordinary sight - the imperious, lustful, avenging countess whipping her naked whore-slave whose glittering body writhed and twisted on the rough timber under the smart of the lash. What had surprised me above all was the stamina of the girl, her fortitude under the whip, refusing to cry out, accepting her fate. But for how long would her pluck last?

At a further ring of the bell, the cross was lowered and the body released only to be dragged across to two heavy chains that hung menacingly from a beam. Immediately, allowing the girl no respite, Sebastian made her lie belly down on the flagstones while her ankle straps were attached to the dangling links. Slowly and with the help of another ratchet, Sebastian raised the body until it hung, head down, swinging from the beam, legs parted wide.

The wrists were now chained outwards as Eliska approached to relish her victim for the second sequence. She examined the open sex, tugging in the rings with her gloved fingers and at the same time sliding her other hand up and down her man's magnificent straining penis, now streaming with trails of liquid. Satisfied with the girl's posture, Eliska returned to her seat and sounded her bell.

I was now to see Sebastian at work. He came forward with a stout length of leather in his hand, which he greased anew before taking his place to the side of the nude. He brought the lash down across the offered rump.

Maryska heaved in her chains with a long groan as the leather curled round the bulge of the buttock and bit into the sex. At each stroke the man snatched the tip away from the crotch so that the terminal fang sliced into the slit. After some dozen strokes, the man changed sides and whipped from the right. Now the rump was receiving the main force of the stroke. The girl moaned at each lash but little more and I had to acknowledge this peasant resistance again. She was fighting her persecutors in her own silent way.

While the flogging rose to its crescendo, Eliska offered herself to her lovers, swaying between them as they caressed her sex and clitoris and she, turning her jewelled rings inwards on her fingers to enhance her grip on their pricks, masturbated them rapidly. One by one they orgasmed, she first, crying out with her head thrown back while the lovers ejaculated their heavy loads of sperm over the chairs and floor.

Finally Maryska's whipping was over. She was lowered and lay sprawling before Sebastian, his erection still hard and dripping freely. My hostess and her lovers stumbled back to their seats to recover their spirits. They drank deeply from wine offered by almost naked serving girls who had entered just at the end of the second flagellation. While refreshing ourselves and discussing the sequence - an exchange that I tried hard to avoid - Maryska was being prepared for the third and last episode of punishment.

She was chained between two columns, her ankles bound tightly together and the arms outflung above until she was on the utmost reach of her toes, presenting her entire nudity to the scourge. Sebastian caressed the taut body for a while, holding his long plaited whip ready until the silver bell commanded him to commence. He lifted the scourge and with the other hand began to frig the bursting shaft of flesh, veins and gristle that reared from his crotch.

Then the scourge fell.

Sebastian devoted great attention as to where his thong struck, working down from the breasts and ribs, over the concave belly to the loins. He concentrated this time on the upper thighs, ensuring that the blows landed across the lower belly and pubic mound. The rump received many new lashes that only served to increase the damage already inflicted. Maryska jerked and twisted her body to ride the scourge but her chains allowed her little latitude. The leather thudded into her ever more viciously as she began to cry out, her resistance conquered. Then she broke down in a long, anguished shriek and sank from the wrists. Sebastian cleaned off his scourge carefully and replaced it among the others on the instrument table. He turned towards his Mistress who nodded.

The exhausted whipped body was lowered as Eliska began

to move to the stairway with her lovers. Maryska, sobbing silently, passed her hands, free for once, over the welts on her loins and waited, trembling, gently soothing her erect clitoris as if the whipping had so excited her that her body demanded relief. Could this be so?

For the first time during the session, Eliska addressed her faithful whipmaster.

"You have performed well. Before returning the whore to her cell, you may use her as you wish as your usual recompense. See to it that the slut cleans up the flagstones." Then she turned to me. "My dear lord, feel free to continue with my man, if that is your wish. If you will excuse me and my friends, we will retire."

With a delicious smile, she left the dungeon, anxious no doubt to share her bed after the excitement, and I found myself alone with the naked pair.

Sebastian seized the girl, pulling her to where the group had stood during the sequence, and thrust her to her knees, pressing her head down and guiding her mouth to the still glittering traces of sperm. In the presence of the dumb man, Maryska seemed to understand all his orders readily and she had heard the Margravine's imperious command. Obediently she began to lick the semen from the stone floor, searching blindly and desperately for the viscous remains with her freed hands. After cleaning up one area, she was dragged by the man to another spot and he stood beside her to ensure that every trace was collected. Now and then he brought the lash down over the raised buttocks to hasten the task since his dripping erection, straining from the root, sorely needed attention, particularly as it was further stimulated by the sight of the heavy folds of the girl's sex with its dangling rings.

Finally the man was satisfied and drew Maryska to her feet. To my surprise, I saw the two bodies cleave to each other, fondling each other's genitals and kissing greedily. The girl moved as if she was about to kneel before the great erection and take it into her mouth, but Sebastian pushed her over to a wooden platform on the far side of the dungeon. This was equipped with a pair of posts bolted to it and a low bench.

With deliberate movements, the man laid the girl down over the plank, her buttocks firmly upon it, and opened the legs one by one, attaching the ankle straps to chains at the summit of each post. This done, he secured the wrists tightly to a bar on the platform beyond the girl's head. The body was totally stretched. Throughout the preparation, Maryska had seemed to cooperate with her torturer, proffering not the least resistance.

Still very deliberately, which was strange, considering his need, the man pulled the labia rings to each side, chaining them to pegs in the bench, designed obviously for just this purpose. In this way, the vagina was opened to its maximum reach ready to receive the coming thrust of a man who could barely restrain himself longer.

Then commenced one of the most penetrating, hungriest and violent copulations it is possible to imagine. The man entered the crimson slit, gleaming with liquids, with one lunge, and then battered the woman's crotch with a rage of primitive lust. The coupling lasted for far longer than I had anticipated and the woman seemed to enjoy it with every sinew and nerve in her body, despite - or, the thought crossed my mind, because of - the stringent bondage wrenching her limbs.

I decided to leave them alone with their recompenses and had begun to mount the steps when a long, high-pitched cry, as if from someone being knifed, filled the dungeon. Maryska orgasmed in utter abandonment, thrashing her body in its chains, her muscles quivering while she tugged at the restraining posts. She screamed as if her life was being torn from her entrails; she seemed to come in several successive avalanches of fulfilment, each fiercer than the last, and then slumped back as if dead.

Sebastian continued to enjoy the drenched sex and was still pounding when I left them. Once he had filled her, he would certainly play with her body and then, probably reluctantly but according to orders, return her to her cell and to the care of the bailiffs who, in turn, would...

But no. Enough, Nephew, of this, the first session. It was clear to me my hosts had derived immense lascivious pleasure in watching a naked female being whipped in chains. But what was more intriguing for me was the clear impression that, despite the obvious pain of the lash, Maryska had not been averse to the session.

Or I imagining?

I am sorry to have tried your patience with this long letter, Nephew, but I want you to understand the behaviour of these people. These letters are naturally only for your eyes. It would never do to let them be seen by your parents - my sister would not forgive me for sharing such enormities with you! So destroy them when read.

Huldrych

Letter the eighth

I have to admit, Nephew, that it took me some time to get over the effect Maryska's flagellation had on me: the vision of her oiled curves flashing in the candlelight as her nude body writhed, jerked and stretched with each slash of the whip, the rump clenching into hard muscle as it defended itself, the pelvis thrusting forward, parting the sex, the breasts swinging, the flesh sweating, the inner thighs awash with liquids, and the throat dry from her groans and muted cries - all this eroticism is new for me.

What troubles me a little is the contradiction in these hosts of mine - I almost said hypocrisy, but this would not be just. They claim they are meting out punishment to profligate females, illegal prostitutes, lesbians and so on, in order to 'cleanse' them. And yet at the same time they enjoy it thoroughly. Young serving girls are put to the whip in front of them, even in the Gräfin's own bedchamber, for the least misdemeanour; if a culprit is not readily available, a girl is sent for, stripped by the bailiffs and put to the whip before them for nothing. This, in my opinion, makes a mockery of justice. But I cannot say so.

Further, I am told that showing mercy for what they call 'lecherous flesh' is a weakness and an insult to the community. In fact Eliska has all her own domestics - handmaidens, serving girls, kitchen slaves and occasionally even overseers - whipped before her at some time or other in the firm conviction that she is thereby protecting them from temptation, carnal lusts and the wiles of Satan who works within them. Hence the belief that such purgation (especially with a tough leather lash) can 'save' a female and restore her to a state of virginal grace. Like the Virgin. Except that there are no virgins here.

The contradiction lies in the erotic excitement my hosts derive from the process, a process in which a docile female is flogged naked in the seclusion of private vaults and dungeons. All reserved for the privileged. No one appears to acknowledge...

(Here there is a break of two lost pages in the MS, after which the text continues)

...and my work has not suffered from the disturbances in the area. These sometimes require the presence of all the armed guards and Landsknechte of the castle to help in quelling local risings and carry out some hangings at the town gibbet.

Among recent news is the fact that the Bishop is indolent and fornicates freely, keeping three or four mistresses in his residence. Less and less do I desire to meet with him, particularly since Premsyl divulged to me one evening that the holy man regularly entrusts his female servants and mistresses to the Margravine for severe correction. The two discuss precisely how the females are to be given the whip or some specific sex-torture and when. It is then performed here at the castle in something called the Red Cellar by Sebastian in the exclusive presence of the Margravine and the Bishop, the latter insisting on attending his servants' mortifications. Much, you see, Nephew, goes on here.

Speaking of the Bishop, I have now inspected the land tenure records and revenues of almost every monastery and the extensive episcopal territories and have managed even to visit the Premonstratensian abbey which was not easy. A truly dismal place but one I could not criticize.

On the other hand, I still have difficulties with the nunneries and the large convent of St. Ursula where I gather debauchery is rife. Here again, in addition to penance, frequent punishments are administered with, this time, a knotted scourge for which the nun is stripped naked. Really, Nephew, flagellation is so common here that one wonders if there is one woman who has not undergone it. Brother Ignatius, who talks to me whenever the Margravine is not nearby (he has scant love for her but knows her secrets), informs me that these nunneries are forced by Eliska to shelter many destitute or loose women to save them from starvation. These wretched women, however, are subject to the strictest possible discipline and - once again - the whip is more frequently worshipped than the cross. The unfortunate man is called upon, here too, to bless the instruments.

What would you do, were you here?

Your loving uncle, Huldrych

Letter the ninth

It was a mild late Spring afternoon in the shrubbery of the castle gardens. I was reading over the text of my third report to Nuremberg, due to leave by rider on the morrow, when Ladislav came and sat next to me on my bench. Among what he had to say there was something that disturbed me.

It seems that Tereza (the wine spiller, you remember?) had been released after her long suspension in the stalls. She had been returned to work in the sculleries and apparently my own servant Hans was forever hovering around the girl; this was being noticed by the overseers and the bailiffs.

Now, of course, Hans as my servant enjoys a certain immunity, but I was filled with consternation. I did not blame him at all for being attracted to this exquisite creature, but with Hans I can never tell what may happen. I have warned him to observe the decorum befitting my mission but here he was fatally taken with the good looks of a castle slave. No doubt also, he probably needed to sleep with someone as I refused him the right to frequent the brothels in Zatoransky. Ladislav courteously suggested I speak to the Margravine to avoid misunderstandings.

I agreed and did so, choosing my time carefully when she seemed to be in a good humour and about to go out riding and hawking with Premsyl and her servants. With an indulgent smile she forthwith gave her permission for Hans to use the girl. Thus, Nephew, I have a well contented servant again; they sleep together and make love untiringly. The little maid seems delighted with Hans. So I am grateful to Ladislav and to the Margravine for having negotiated round a delicate situation. I shall probably have to pay for it dearly some way or another.

But to return to my moment with Ladislav on the terrace. He gave me a far clearer picture of the peculiar relationship between him, his colleagues and Eliska. After praising her beauty and energy (there he is right and no doubt included her sexual appetite!), he told me that he and the others had been her lovers even before the Margrave's death. The three companions had served together in the Bohemian armies and were inseparable. They had no qualms over sharing her - as if I had not noticed.

His discourse moved inevitably to the whip. The whip, he declared, is a great healer. "It is essential that serfs be kept on a tight rein and repressed as rigorously as possible. Our authorities do exemplary work through imprisonment, punishment, executions or, like the Margravine herself, recourse to the whip."

"Especially on females, I believe," I remarked.

"Quite. For they are the moral canker in the tree of life. The lowborn female is the worm in the rose. Sometimes there have to be executions - here we drown some in the moat, but generally there is no more effective way of dealing with these filthy peasant wenches than to flog them."

The garden was now heavy with the scent of the lilacs, beginning to bud. For a fleeting moment the castle looked almost civilized, despite the evil within it.

"Lord Ladislav," I remarked, "the role of the bailiffs and the youth Sebastian is still not very clear to me."

My host rose and we strolled towards the southern battlement. "All three men, like myself also, have sworn fidelity to the house and hence to the Margravine. Nothing would ever deter them from carrying out orders to the letter. Jakub would prefer death on the gallows or by his own hand than see Eliska affronted or defied. As to Bohumil, he is the bastard son of the late Margrave Matthlas by some chambermaid who" - he waved his hand vaguely - "disappeared suddenly. Now, as to Sebastian who, as you know, was rendered mute to safeguard secrets, his father reigned supreme before him in the dungeons; now it is he who is called upon to work on our females which he does with exquisite delicacy."

"And the other men in the castle?"

"They are few but they are all faithful - guards, equerries, servants, grooms. The Margravine has elaborated a scheme whereby they are compensated by being permitted to use castle women according to merit."

Suddenly he broached a subject that left me almost speechless. What he said, Nephew, went like this, word for word.

"The other day with the gracious Margravine, we were wondering if you yourself, my lord, would wish to select a female for your own use, either in bed or in the cellars. There are some attractive creatures among them with liquid fire between their thighs. Your mission is arduous and you must not hesitate to take advantage, my lord."

I managed a reply with some difficulty. "I thank you and my noble hostess but my Imperial masters would hardly approve, alas." It was as elegant a rejoinder as I could summon up. And it sounded conclusive. Ladislav shrugged with a smile and then frightened me with his next remark.

"You are not associated, are you, my lord, with the Lutheran conspiracy? We hear that certain circles, even in Nuremberg, favour it and its heretically strict morality!"

I wondered why he had this suspicion. Had I let slip unguarded remarks? Was my rather strict moral attitude responsible for this reaction? I vowed to be prudent in future, and I thought of you, Nephew, and your present hesitations.

"A servant of my rank in the Imperial service, sir, could hardly be a Lutheran!" I replied. And with that the subject was dropped but I was disturbed.

The following day was a very successful one again. Not only did I cover much ground, both physically and administratively, but found that my survey was almost complete for all six outlying districts. The main problems remained with the nunneries and monasteries. On these long rides I was glad to have Hans with me as well as a surly guard who did little but complain and pare his cheese with his dagger.

We ate at a dreadful inn where the beer was sour and the food rancid; moreover, the place served as a brothel and belonged to the Margravine who also owned the miserable girls working there. Several of them looked as if they were frequently beaten, and two wore rings in their nipples which stuck out bare from their breasts.

Conditions in the area are deplorable and I wonder if the official incorporation of this place into the Empire proper will improve matters. I doubt it but please do not quote me!

At one place, near a farmstead, we met a group of ragged men (some armed to my surprise with the new wheel-lock arquebus) evidently back from some campaign. There were robbers, quick-fingered pedlars and whores everywhere. What is to be done?

"Graf von Mechtingen!"

I recognized the voice of the young Milan as he came level with us, riding a fine roan mare flecked with froth from the bit, having been ridden hard.

The man was beautifully dressed and it was hard to recall the cowled figure caressing his mistress in the dungeon, watching a naked girl being whipped.

"Still spying into our domains, I see," he said - only half in jest, I felt. "Life could be worse, I suppose, under the Hungarians or Zdenek Leo..."

"Or under the Sublime Porte and its janissaries," I joked in rather bad taste.

As we rode, Milan told me several interesting things. First, that the Turkish janissaries, converted to Mahomet, were celibate throughout their service, which possibly accounted for their ferocity; celibates are uncommon here, Milan smiled. Secondly, that full serfdom in Zatoransky and the region had been enacted only forty years before, in 1487; and thirdly, that he had just been back to his father's estate held in fealty to the Margravine to inspect the local peasant girls for promising fresh domestic flesh for the castle.

Looking back at Hans, riding dutifully behind with the guard, Milan leaned towards me.

"I hear the little bitch who spilled wine over me at table has been freed and sleeps with this man of yours. The Margravine is far too lenient! The little slut should have had the skin whipped off her rump." He paused only to add a second later: "By the way, my lord, you know that the second session will be tonight for the condemned whore. You may enjoy it more than the last one."

This was the first I had heard of another session. Inexorable people with their inexorably planned sessions! I wondered if there was a way of extricating myself.

I suspect these letters of mine take much time to reach you in Tübingen. It is fortunate I have the Imperial seal to protect them; I would not want them to fall into the wrong hands. Work diligently, do not go whoring and be careful of the strong Württemberg beer.

Tell your mother I think of her.

With love, Huldrych

Letter the tenth

(The first pages of this letter are missing. The narrative takes up at this point.)

...again I was obliged to draw the detestable cowl over my head before descending the steps into the now strangely perfumed and flower-decked dungeon! Already I could hear the swish and slap of the whip in action, each stroke dragging a hoarse cry from the victim. No one seemed to notice my late arrival as I drew into the shadows behind my hosts.

What I saw before me made me catch my breath.

In the far dimly lit corner of the dungeon, Maryska's nude body, glistening with thick oils, the rump already reddened from some preliminary whipping, hung impaled by the sex on a stake. She was curved over backwards, the legs parted and chained taut to rings in the floor, the arms wrenched beneath her and bound to the foot of the stake. The strain was alleviated by a chain running from the neck strap to a huge iron ring in the beam above.

Sebastian was evidently taking particular care over this flagellation, using measured strokes with a thin lash which he laid into the nude's taut belly methodically, marking a lengthy pause between each delivery as if to ensure the full penetration of the effect into the flesh before slashing the girl again. Each cut was met by a hoarse cry from the gaping mouth, proving that Maryska's stamina and resistance were being taxed to the limit.

In full throbbing erection, the young man whipped his victim with a vicious virtuosity, leaving her time enough in which to jerk upwards, fill the chamber with her cry and slump back to await the following lash. As I watched the thin thong curl round Maryska's beautiful flanks - which encouraged my hosts to caress Eliska and themselves to the brink of orgasm - I recalled what Premsyl had told me the previous day.

"The first lashes," he had explained, "are always the worst, unless, as is the custom here, the flesh has been well prepared beforehand with a preliminary whipping to bring the girl to the summit of excitement. In any event, as the flagellation proceeds,

48

the sensitivity is dulled. The accumulation of strokes blunts the pain and, if the female has been correctly prepared, the pain and the sexual pleasure begin to merge. Impalement is one of the positions predisposed to excite the victim sexually - as long as it is applied with measure, restraint and finesse, which we insist on here - and the female can be whipped at leisure until she is even ready to spend. This is the aim of impalement. One often sees a female orgasm when split and stimulated on the pale."

The flagellation lasted a long time. Sebastian then caressed the body, rubbing in oil to soothe and damp the fire the whip had aroused. Then he carefully lifted the woman up and off the pale, laying her over his shoulder to carry her to the side of the dungeon where he laid her on the flagstones. She sprawled out before him, passing her hands over the scourged midriff and still distended sex-lips.

She looked magnificent in the glow of the candles in front of the large vases of Spring flowers; but this flagellation had been severe and Maryska continued to groan as she curled up on the stone. Transfixed by the spectacle, I had not realized that the silver bell had rung for the end of this first sequence, Eliska holding it in her mauve-gloved left hand and Milan's penis in the other.

An interval now followed during which a group of girls, this time totally naked but for few ornaments, served refreshments to the company. His wine in hand, Premsyl came up to me - I now recognize each man by the voice. He was particularly affable, enquiring about my day and my work as if there were no naked female lying on the ground, no pale standing there and no flagellator carefully cleaning off his scourges and replacing them on the table covered with other whips and intruments of sex-torture. He spoke as if we ware out riding under a blue heaven. Then suddenly he reverted to the session itself.

"The three sequences of tonight's ritual are dedicated to the whore's cunt." He used the word in dialect, and before I could react he went on. "Just as she used it in the brothel, so do we use it here - after our manner. We cleanse it. You will see the Gräfin herself in action."

The bell tinkled anew and we assembled to the right of the

49

dungeon, where Sebastian was binding the girl to a rectangular stone block, rather like a sacrifice. The wrists were chained to a floor-ring beyond the blindfolded head while the legs were raised, parted and secured to twin posts, lifting the rump clear of the stone in order to splay the sex. It was indeed the cunt, as Premsyl put it, that was now to receive the whip. In order, to quote him again, to cleanse this altar of lust once and for all...

Maryska was bound helpless, offering her cunt to the scourge; behind her, Sebastian, his erection straining and streaming like a furious animal, was selecting his whip from an array of lashes, crops, canes and knotted ropes. I had no doubt that the precise instrument had already been designated, but the man took pleasure in handling, fondling and testing the various lashes.

At last he advanced on the open thighs with a bunch of short leather thongs, slender but brutal enough to give the girl much to contend with. Sebastian laid the group of leathers like a spray of flowers on the girl's breasts and slowly drew the lash down the body, across the belly, over the triangle of thick auburn hairs and between the pouting profiles of the yawning labia.

Then he struck.

First it was the white inner thighs. Then into the lips. With a thud on the protruding flanges of flesh and the clump of wet sex-hair, the whip cut into the genitals and was greeted with a strangled cry from the gaping throat. As the leathers buried deeper into the slit, Maryska strained her loins into the air, held the posture for a moment, and then sank back to await the next inevitable stroke, which would be delivered after a long pause to allow the effect to course through her. She tugged uselessly on her wrists as she was lashed, her head swinging madly.

The whipping seemed to me to last an eternity until the labia and lower belly were crimson.

Sebastian then paused, while my hosts enjoyed themselves, shamelessly excited by the spectacle of an undefended, nude crotch under the lash. He returned to the split writhing body, now armed with a riding crop similar to that which I had seen Eliska carrying while out on horseback. It was pliant, slender, slightly rugged and tipped with a leather fang.

With slow measured strokes, he slashed into the sex, dragging the tip away between the swollen labia; as he beat the girl, the sex-rings sprang upwards with each stroke. Maryska cried out grotesquely, not for mercy but for something far more physical.

At last the final lash was delivered and Maryska, drenched in sweat, sagged in her chains. This was greeted by a cry from one of the men - the youthful Milan, I believe - as he spurted his load of sperm, aided by his mistress clenching his erection firmly; the heavy clots spread over her rich brocaded bodice, causing her simply to smile with pleasure at his eagerness.

The whipped girl was released by Sebastian and I thought there would now be a pause - which I feared in the event that I would be engaged in conversation and asked for my opinion. God forbid!

Instead I was forced to watch the naked victim drawn to her feet facing her flagellator, whose straining sex seemed to reach out for the swollen crotch. Deliberately, with almost gentle gestures, Sebastian bound the girl's arms behind her back with a thong of black leather. She stood unsteadily before him in complete submission while he drew her breasts together and joined the nipple-rings.

The flogger now brought three large candelabra with the candles already alight to the centre of the dungeon, which was suddenly haunted with strange shapes on its walls. He made the nude lie prostrate. The silver bell sounded again and the final sequence of the three whippings began.

I do not with to weary you with detail, Nephew, but I have to describe the event that followed, for you will not, I am sure, believe it.

The man attached overhead chains to each ankle-ring and spread his victim's legs wide apart as she lay before him. He then began to wind up each chain by means of two worn ratchet-wheels fixed to the far wall until, one leg after the other, the body rose from the flagstones and hung, head down, the limbs stretched out sideways to their utmost extent, revealing the whipped sex which, in turn, was forced open with special chains linked to the labia-rings and shackled tightly round the thighs. The sight was breath-taking, as erotic as it was cruel.

Now two events took place that surprised me even more. As if in sacred ritual or a Greek pastoral, Eliska delicately divested herself of her clothes, the young Milan helping her to unbutton her gown and bodice, until she stood naked, retaining only her head-dress, ruff, gloves, boots and spurs. She looked extraordinary - her breasts rose in their full majesty from the tapering thorax and below, her belly swept down sleekly to the dark pubic hair over the bulge of her sex. On either side her muscular thighs, hardened from riding, held the buttocks high and tight.

Luxuriously she ran her hands down her flanks, to the delight of her men, and slid a finger slowly between the pouting lips of her saturated sex.

My second item of astonishment was the effect the sight had on the onlookers, her lovers and the flagellator. Each uncovered himself and commenced a slow masturbation while Sebastian, holding his Mistress's clothes, presented her with the scourge - a bunch of thin leather thongs. Eliska ran the whip through her fingers and took her stance. She could hardly wait to commence.

Her powdered flesh, contrasting vividly with the oiled, sweating body of her 'whore', made her look like a fierce goddess in comparison. She seemed to have stepped from a painting of Hell.

Running the tip of her tongue over her lips, Eliska raised the lash. What followed can only justify my apprehensions as to the real nature of my noble hostess - vicious, cruel, despotic, ruthless but sumptuously erotic. She scourged obviously with intense pleasure and ingenuity: the inner thighs first received their share of lashes, leaving scarlet weals on such white flesh as Sebastian had not already marked.

Each vicious stroke added to the torments the threshing body before her had to contend with. The cries, so rare at the onset of the first session some days ago, now filled the dungeon as the thongs stung and bit the sex itself - the seat of lust that required, in Eliska's own words, proper cleansing and purification. In order no doubt to drive home the lesson, the flagellation was delivered almost languidly with regularly spaced pauses yet with a determination that caused the whip to linger each time on the oval entrance, the extremity of the thongs marking the shuddering buttocks beyond. By the end of the sequence, Eliska herself was gleaming with sweat as, breathless, she returned the instrument to her servant and, taking her gown to cover her shoulders like a cloak, made for the stairs, grasping the hand of Ladislav.

No one made a gesture to me as the group left - no doubt to spend the rest of the night in customary orgy, stimulated in every fibre by the nudity, the writhing body and the flagellations.

As she swept out of the dungeon, Eliska motioned to Sebastian who immediately wound down the quivering nude body. I waited to see what recompense he would seek.

The girl lay motionless on the stone floor, her purple blindfold soaked with tears, until Sebastian lifted her to her feet to lead her - or rather almost carry her - to the far end of the dungeon where a stout whipping post stood and which I had not yet noticed. I followed at an unobtrusive distance. To my astonishment I saw the two naked bodies cleave to each other again, kissing lasciviously, with Maryska, as if conniving with her flagellator, sliding her hand voluptuously along the huge glistening erection with its long strings of liquid.

I could hardly believe what I saw; here was a girl who, a short moment before, was crying under the whip and now had the sexual force to fondle her flagellator!

The caresses, however, did not last long. Making her kneel, Sebastian bound his victim to the post, pressing her backwards on to a rearing shaft jutting out in the form of a penis that was forced in deep between her buttocks. With a sharp cry Maryska jerked her pelvis as she was penetrated; sinking down, she let it enter her while her ankles and wrists were chained. As if he desired to remind her still of the flesh that had betrayed her, Sebastian then opened the sex-labia with hooked chains that he fastened tightly to two floor-rings. The post was clearly designed for this precise position and purpose.

I wondered if the taut body with the upstretched arms was not to be again put to the whip. Instead, when fully satisfied with her posture, the man approached her face, and, holding his erection firmly, plunged it into the open lips. There followed what I can only call a frenzy of fellatio, Maryska's head thumping against the post as the man's shaft, ridged with protruding purple veins, plundered her throat.

Soon Sebastian was grasping her hair to enhance his thrusts, making Maryska suck with all the energy remaining in her; dementedly she licked the head and testicles when the man offered her the chance. The fellatio was very different from that I had seen her perform on her soldier when she had been in control; this was imposed, cruel, frantic, without restraint.

Sebastian was receiving his reward and made the act last.

He rammed his full length into her mouth, his buttocks clenched like fists, the muscular limbs taut with effort. He came at last and spent his boiling sperm down her throat. Maryska gagged and swallowed the gift, according to castle rules. After enjoying the last suctions of the residues, the man withdrew and wiped his sex over the face, hair and blindfold.

I left them panting in the dense, pungent atmosphere of leather, chains and burning tallow inextricably mingled with the smell of flowers, flesh, sweat and sperm. As I climbed the stairs I saw one of the cowled bailiffs approach the whipping-post, possibly to take over from Sebastian. What ensued I do not know but I presume the girl was finally returned to her cell, her welts and lash marks to be cared for by Radka. For my part, I found my room again, relieved to be out of the heat of the dungeon. I sat looking pensively at the moon going down over the dark hills beyond the castle gardens.

I shall be glad when my work is completed and I can set out again on Zenon for my own garden with its sweet peas and pleasant shade, and a quiet normal life near those I love, such as you, my sister and that incomparable brother-in-law of mine. And we shall go for long walks again, maybe along the Rennsteig.

Spare a prayer for me meanwhile, and tell the parents to buy a mare not a young gelding. Think of the valuable foals to come.

Your loving uncle, Huldrych

Letter the eleventh

It has rained without ceasing and my visits to the farthest areas of the province have been less than agreeable. Presenting myself at the dwellings of local dignitaries or convents, drenched to the skin, does not seem compatible with my rank, but little can be done about that.

Hans is, as usual, most helpful, and dries my clothes before a fire he enjoys in the servants' quarters; he seems in the best of spirits, no doubt on account of his Tereza who, after a busy night in his straw palliasse, also appears happy, relaxed and quite beautiful. I just hope that nothing untoward is in wait for them; I am always suspicious, as you know, of too much contentment!

I still have not encountered the Bishop but, knowing his reputation, perhaps this is all to the good. On the other hand he is possibly apprehensive of me and of my mission. He owns enormous lands and, although these are not in question at the moment, he must be suspicious of my mandate. It is said he sleeps with two girls at a time.

On the other hand, have met Brother Ignatius on several occasions. Despite his advanced age, he is intelligent but bitter. Gradually I am learning that he bears a deep-seated grudge against the Margravine. particularly because of her way of life, her lovers and what goes on in the lower regions of the castle - and in her bedchamber. One secret that I have unearthed, by pure chance through Hans who in turn learnt it from Tereza, is that our Brother Ignatius is himself no saint or rather was no saint, for he must be too old now to fornicate; it appears that Radka, the apothecary and almoner here in the castle, has been his mistress and continues to keep him company. It seems that she is no admirer of the lady of the house either. But all this is gossip and there is nothing more unreliable than such talk. One item, however, is of interest, namely that this Radka has talked to the poor Maryska and seems to pity her.

I have been wondering if I myself could not exchange a word with Maryska - perhaps to express my sympathy, my disagreement with the severity of the sentence and my disavowal of the sexual enjoyment my hosts derive from her punishment. On the other hand I am not prepared to exculpate her as I am still uncertain of the precise facts. Somehow I do not believe her to be a professional whore or even a wandering strumpet.

To try to speak with her - if I can understand her dialect - is of course fraught with dangers and would entail a certain risk for me, leave alone a breach of a guest's protocol. Perhaps old Radka could help. In any event I decided to explore the underworld again.

And so, when all was tranquil in the castle after supper one night, I took a candle and descended the stairway. After considerable wanderings, I finally found the cell. It is a small space under a low vaulted ceiling and cut off from the main passages by a massive barred iron gate. By the light of the dim lantern within I could see Maryska lying naked on a large slab of stone, her neck chained loosely to the wall behind her. To her right a narrow opening seems to suggest that it is here her food and drink is passed to her from a room beyond, for several utensils were visible. Otherwise the cell is bare.

Maryska seemed to be in a fitful sleep, her body smeared with some ointment, possibly testimony of Radka's medicinal attention. She lay with her legs open and the rings in her sex glinted in the lantern light. With an unusual audacity, I tried the gate, only to find it was securely locked and it was useless to attempt to speak to the girl from such a distance. I looked for a long moment at the exquisite body, watching the fine breasts rise and fall; I was both fascinated by her nakedness - I admit it, Nephew - and disgusted at the treatment to which she was being subjected, however guilty she might be.

I was about to leave when I heard steps approaching along the dark passage behind me. I had no desire to be discovered here, so I doused my candle immediately, withdrawing out of sight into the dark beside the gate.

The two bailiffs appeared, carrying a hooded lantern, and passed by me within arm's reach. Strangely enough, I was quite calm since I have developed a sort of comradeship with these strange cowled individuals; but I did hold my breath until they had passed.

They unlocked the gate and entered, then stripped themselves of their hose and doublets, retaining only their felt slippers and hoods. One of the men then awakened Maryska with a sharp cut of his whip across her belly. The girl arose at once and I could sense her blindfolded terror as she was turned over on the slab. One of the men, possibly Jakub, presented his erection and drew the girl's head down towards his loins while Bohumil spread her thighs apart as she knelt obediently.

Almost simultaneously, the two shafts of tumescent flesh penetrated her, Bohumil driving into the vagina up to the hair of his lower belly, Jakub demanding the full reach of the throat. While they belaboured the girl, I was taken aback to see Maryska's hands fondling the heavy testicles and the root of Jakub's penis; indeed, she seemed to urge him on further by tugging him towards her by the sack as she sucked on him ravenously. The men used her mercilessly, pounding and driving deep into her with violent thrusts of their loins and ensuring that she delivered up to them the full depth of her sexual cavities.

Occasionally Bohumil withdrew, only to work his stiff throbbing prick into the furrow between the buttocks and there sink deep again up to the hilt, while Jakub, stripping back his foreskin, made Maryska suck on the compact, crimson head of his penis. Both the men made use of the young girl for a good half-hour until her face, throat and inner thighs were awash with their liquids and her own. Frequently Bohumil, deep in the vagina again, slapped Maryska's buttocks and back savagely, leaving dark mauve marks on her oiled flesh, crying obscenities, urging the girl to 'squeeze her whore-cunt tighter round the prick' unless she wanted the whip across it again.

I could see Maryska straining to satisfy her masters, her body now streaming with sweat, bright liquids and creamy gluten round where she was being penetrated. I thought they would never finish battering her, until Bohumil withdrew and, with a hoarse cry, spent over the back and rump, smearing the sperm into her with vicious blows of his hand. Soon after, Jakub orgasmed but within her throat, making her suck the last drops out of him.

Satisfied, they turned the woman on her back and pulled on their garments without a word; as suddenly as they had arrived, they left, slamming the gate to and locking it securely. I could hear their footsteps fading as they returned to their quarters and I was again alone with the naked beauty, stretched out as before, but now caressing her sex gently. I wondered if she was about to give herself some pleasure, but she fell asleep almost immediately while the sperm cooled and jellied beneath her.

I must have watched her for an interminable time - I could not take my eyes from her curves and sweating muscles. I half hoped that she would awake and sense my presence, but she hardly moved.

Then in the middle of the night the unexpected happened. Again carrying his lantern, Jakub returned, unlocked the gate and again commanded sex. Again he stripped, dragging the woman to the edge of the slab to splay her thighs wide. Although hardly awake, Maryska seemed to offer herself even more readily than before as Jakub sank his pulsating prick into her sex, drawing her labia aside by the rings to denude the inner walls of the vagina sheath. I did not think that a man could use a female with such lust. Still thrusting, he began to grunt, pulling the loins towards his crotch until his spasm exploded again. The sperm ejaculated as if he had not already spent a short time before; he held the shaft over Maryska and sluiced his stream of viscous lumps of hot semen over the girl's sex-hair, belly and up to the breasts.

Then, as if this was a normal pastime or passing fancy, he turned, dressed and left without a glance at the naked body, satisfied at having used the girl again but in a different manner.

Later in the night - I remained below for quite a time, as you see - I was now not surprised to see Bohumil return. This occasion was distinct from what I had witnessed.

Bohumil released the chain from Maryska's neck-strap with a key and made her squat before him as he sat on the slab. This time he did not strip but presented his erection for Maryska's mouth by unbuttoning his codpiece. I saw now the same incomparable fellatio as Maryska had performed for her soldier. She used both her hands over the man's genitals and thighs. She worked on him with exquisite technique, rolling the testicles round in her mouth, stripping the prick head bare, thrusting the tip of her tongue into the slit, biting on the stiff gristle until the bailiff was ready. Then she swallowed the shaft as the fresh load of sperm pumped and surged into her gullet.

Without a word, the man replaced the woman on her chain and slammed the gate. It was then, when all was still, that Maryska stretched herself out over the slab and parted her thighs. First she caressed her breasts, tugging gently on the nipple-rings, letting her hands wander slowly down to the auburn-haired groin where the sperm had now begun to congeal. She eased back the clitoris-ring to uncover the rigid stub of flesh from its hood, smearing it with her own viscous liquids. Then she masturbated before me. She circled her middle finger over the point, compressing it, elongating it until the pale tip became inflamed and fully erect; now and then she buried her hand in the vagina, reaching for her most secret places of excitement until suddenly her hips rose from the slab. Her entire body arched from shoulders to heels, the head straining backwards, the mouth distorted as when crying under the lash. The friction accelerated to set fire to her loins. She teetered for a moment on the brink of paroxysm, groaning as if under torture.

With a long unearthly cry, she surrendered to a series of prolonged orgasms which seemed to devastate her, crashing over her like waves of the sea covering a precious wreck of treasure that had voyaged from very far away...

Her body writhed and twisted voluptuously as the climax drowned her entrails with soft relief and her cries dwindled. She let herself slump back to the stone of her slab, curling over with both hands sealed over her ringed sex-lips; slowly she slid back into the velvet curtains of deep.

Denied orgasm by her jailors yet forced to service and gratify them through the night and probably several times a day - the girl avenged herself with a vehemence she kept for herself. It was her victory over her victors.

I left her in the flickering light of the lantern to walk back to my silent chamber. As I watched the pale dawn breaking over the eastern hills, I felt the light paid homage to her resilience.

The same sun brings you my love, Nephew.

Huldrych

Letter the twelfth

I was sitting in a despondent mood before my lancet in the late afternoon (it was too early to call for candles) when Jakub knocked on my chamber door to announce that the third session would commence after supper and that meanwhile the Margravine wished to meet with me in private.

Stroking the head of her favourite whippet, Eliska was seated at the long table in the so-called council hall, a room as solemn as the rest of the castle but graced with several high casements that do let in some light; they give out over the busy courtyard where the usual evening braziers burn as dusk closes in.

She greeted me with one of her special smiles, languid and bewitching. I noted with relief that her breasts were soberly veiled below her goffered ruff with a mantle of white muslin. She wore soft deerskin boots, without spurs for once.

She enquired what she could expect to happen now that her world was an integral part of the Empire. This I think was the reason for the meeting. I had to admit that I had no way of knowing; after all there were literally hundreds of such provinces with their princes, dukes, landgraves, margraves and bishops... Nothing much would alter, I suggested, except taxation and military recruitment. She seemed content with this and probably was just as aware as you and I of the impossibly slow and confused working of the Imperial authority, especially as Charles himself was about to leave for Spain. We spoke of such matters for a long moment and then I mentioned St. Ursula's.

"Ah, St. Ursula's." She leaned back in her chair, looking very different from the callous torturer of the dungeons below. I explained my problems in getting the prestigious convent to give me the information I needed.

"Both Milan and I have influence there and we shall intervene on your behalf," Eliska said. "You should know, sir, that our Mother Superior, Maria Magdalena, is terribly overworked. Upon my instructions, the good dame is generous enough to take in numerous poor girls, mostly of bad repute, even whores who cannot find places of work in my brothels. Like me, she takes infinite care to cleanse them and render them useful to society. I do my best to take off their charge as many polluted females as I can. Only yesterday Mother Maria was obliged to entrust to me one of her noviciates to deal with and purify. A truly ungrateful and lascivious slut of seventeen! This caitiff, this good-for-nothing, is found to be involved in a lesbian affair. You understand what I mean by that, my lord?"

My hostess sometimes treats me as if I has just dropped from the moon.

"Now, such things, alas, are rife among nuns," she went on. "It seems the slut got involved with a much older Sister, responsible for the stores and larder. Perhaps she was hungry in more senses than one."

Eliska enjoys her own jokes more than I do.

"You see our problems, sir. A young noviciate hardly out of her probationary stage desecrating her convent between the thighs of a nun ordinary!"

I tried to display concern: "Such a case, I suppose, can be referred to the Bishop if not handled within the convent itself?"

She dismissed the holy man with a curt slap on the table, upsetting my ink-horn that I had propped up among the papers.

"The Bishop? That useless whore-monger? But it is true that the convent is authorized to deal with common, everyday failings like neglect of prayer, disobedience, sloth, indolence, lethargy, slovenliness, swearing, dirtiness and clandestine masturbation..."

I thought the list would never stop. I was quite disconcerted at the last term - not shocked because nothing shocks me any more here - and lifted my eyebrows.

"Yes, masturbation," she said. "You are a man and a bachelor. You cannot know the distress and heartache this causes a noble conscientious woman like Mother Maria."

All this is unploughed virgin ground to me, if you will permit the expression, but Eliska was now launched out into one of her favorite subjects - recalcitrant females.

"All the junior nuns and noviciates sleep in large dormitories without cubicles which are reserved, like cells, for the senior Sisters. Anyone reporting a colleague abusing herself is rewarded, spiritually, by Mother Maria. The system of spies functions quite effectively in weeding out the guilty ones although, as you can guess, it is by no means easy to detect nocturnal games."

As I could not guess, I asked: "So what correction is there to curtail the practice?"

"Enforced fasting, penances of various sorts on bread and water and, of course, the whip. I have at last persuaded all three Mothers Superior to strip their culprits naked, whether for masturbation or other sins, and flog them."

The lady was now warming well to her subject.

"What more can one do, dear lady?"

"What more, sir? What more! I will tell you what more. I have ordered that any inmate convicted of clandestine self-abuse for the third time shall be roped naked to a special post in the cloister garden and whipped before the whole convent. All approve of such measures and also of those employed by St. Barbara's where Mother Emelina prefers binding her culprits to a carpenter's trestle, the four limbs tied to the diverging wooden legs and the offending genitals crushed against a neat bed of nails on the bar. My young scoundrel Milan always rides down to watch these little ceremonies but annoys us all by his pleading to have the nuns breast-whipped."

Eliska smiled indulgently, shaking her head.

"In any event the culprit is deprived of all privileges for a month after her whipping and is made to wear a leather triangle to prevent her using her clitoris. A chastity belt of sorts, allowing natural functions like any other celibacy belt. Well?"

"I suppose the same approach can apply to the lesbian you mentioned," I suggested, to revert to St. Ursula's from which I still needed information,

"I really cannot understand how these women dare take the risk," Eliska exclaimed. "It is foolhardy. We have fewer cases in the castle but many in the nunneries. As to St. Ursula's, in this particular case, the older nun will be dealt with by the Mother Superior - she has some sturdy Sisters to do the flogging for her. As to the young girl, she has been passed to me to deal with in the dungeon and I can assure you that she will not 'fall in love', as she has the effrontery to put it, with any other women after I have finished with her. You should see my bailiffs bringing a lesbian to heel! It is a shame you will have left when the sessions begin ten days from now."

I silently thanked my patron saint that I would indeed be on my way home. The Margravine interrupted my meditation.

"Yes, every now and then, my lord, I have this burden thrust upon my shoulders. The only detail I do not relish is the custom of shaving lesbian victims completely - for I think a thick pubic growth over the sex is admirable. But this is the custom and Ladislav, for one, would rather die than offend custom and ritual."

The interview was obviously coming to an end, and this encouraged me to broach certain confidential matters and present other papers to Eliska since I needed her seal which, with the help of my wax and her ring, she gave me with good grace. Then she surprised me again, as we heard the bell tolling for Vespers and were preparing to go down.

"You must not think me a prude, my dear lord," - this is about the last epithet I would have used! - "in refusing these trollops their pleasure together. To be sincere with you, I myself do not quibble over passing a night with a salacious, vigorous lesbian, strictly in private. It does provide a change from these wonderful, insatiable men of mine. But lesbian practices in a convent in my realm, no! Never!"

I am still mortified by the memory of the Imperial troops, even if unpaid, sacking Rome last year. They should have done the act here instead!

I struggle on and will be so relieved to depart. I hope the Court will recognize my work and my steadfastness under the tribulations I am bearing.

Be virtuous, dear Nephew,
Huldrych

Letter the thirteenth

I am writing this letter, after doing some drawing (I do about a dozen sketches a day), sitting in a delightful wood. Hans has made a fire of twigs with his tinder-box and flint and Tereza is with him cooking fish and onions. I wonder, watching them, if they should not marry? Brother Ignatius would suffice for the ceremony.

Now I must revert to the Margravine. First, she asked me to comment on the political situation for her benefit once again, which I was glad to do concerning Bohemia.

The Emperor had, I said, appointed members of his family as regents: his aunt Margaret of Austria to the Low Countries, his wife Isabelle of Portugal for Spain, his younger sister Mary, married to Louis II of Hungary and Bohemia, to report on those lands, while his brother, the Archduke Ferdinand, was responsible for Austria and Germany. Ferdinand had married Louis' sister, Anna, and when the childless Louis died miserably in a bog on that terrible August day in 1528, defeated by the Turks, Ferdinand was eligible, through her, as king. The Bohemian Diet however insisted that the crown was elective; and finally last year it 'elected' Ferdinand. Thus Bohemia was now an integral part of the Holy Roman Empire. Hence my mission.

Eliska listened with interest as I mentioned the Emperor's powerful and astute tutors and secretaries, and the brilliant chancellor, Mercurino de Gattinara.

"And who will be appointed for Bohemia?" she enquired. "It could be you, my lord. You now have experience of our parts. You are liked. You have my support."

I dismissed the idea with a modest gesture. "We do not have the ear of Nuremberg, dear lady. And I have neither the competence nor the language, alas."

"It might be arranged." A strange silence followed. This, to my mind, could be more than a poisoned gift. Then she reverted to her problems.

"I have the sentiment, my noble lord, that you are not yet convinced by my sincerity and resent some of my methods, such as those I use to reform fallen women in my domains. Now, I want you to understand me. It is true I enjoy the physical rewards in whatever form they take, in scourging iniquity out of these females. Their flesh must not be relinquished to the fires of hell. As you serve your Emperor, so I serve to purify my realm and" - she sought the word in Hochdeutsch - "exculpate all females from sin. In so doing, I exculpate myself from sin."

She went over again to the window and stood outlined in her slim beauty against the glow of the evening braziers below, which incidentally remind me, Nephew, of those fires we had to light to ward off the plague.

"Sin is what is thought of as sin," she remarked. "I do not know if your rigid conceptions of life allow you to follow me. I sacrifice my victims on the altar of my duty and so am sanctified in this Garden of Eden of mine."

Her face was hard as rock.

"Let me go further. This whore I am cleansing, for example, receives just and due punishment of her sinful body and constitutes for us a redemptive sacrifice. You notice she does not protest. She is as soft and yielding as silk and provides us with gratification. I do not deny ourselves - or her, for that matter - the sexual reward. It is part of the local tradition of our Flagellants. That is why I demand that she and my whip-master to be naked to recall the state of our First Parents in Eden before the Fall."

I was lost for a reply but managed a comment which did not please her. "While I admire your strivings for justice, gracious lady, can one not have some compassion for these wretched people lost in this rapidly changing world?"

Eliska stared at me with surprise. "My lord, take this female below: she is a contemptible whore, an insolent lustful whore who had defied my authority, defiled my Garden. She must be retrieved through the whip and this provides us with pleasure."

She paused.

"What is more, she derives a perverse pleasure herself, as you have witnessed." She began to gather her papers together to descend as the Angelus sounded. (By the way, Nephew, here time is reckoned by counting the hours elapsed since the Angelus.)

On the threshold of the chapel, she added: "Our next session will be rather special and even colourful. You will see my cherished companions in action, each clothed as he desires and thinks appropriate for the further cleansing of the whore. You must not miss it." She concluded with a sweet smile: "I assume you would prefer to attend in the usual robe and cowl and remain not only anonymous but passive."

The last thing I desired was to be active here! And also I wondered from whom I was still meant to hide my features! Then we took our places in the melancholy chapel as she signalled to Brother Ignatius to commence his mumbled office.

Some nights ago we were entertained by jugglers and magicians (I held tight on to the wallet at my belt) and a dancing bear. There are many bears here in the mountains, I am told. The animal was made to dance to the tune of a pipe. I gather it has been trained on heated ploughshares. Perhaps they seek to cleanse its soul...

Your loving uncle Huldrych.

Letter the fourteenth

The third session took place in extraordinary circumstances. The dungeon was stifling hot, particularly for me in my robe and hood. Yet I was relieved they had not asked me to dress up. Eliska was voluptuous in scarlet velvet and a newly starched coif and goffered ruff; her arms gloved in mauve, the fingers heavy with jewels that flashed like the spurs on her long boots. Her companions stood behind her, clad entirely differently from the way they were in the earlier sessions. Resplendent in richly embroidered bodices, high boots or fawn slippers, each wore a different satin mask; other than these few items, they were naked, their genitals well-greased and hanging before their thighs.

There was an atmosphere of ceremony, as usual, but also a strange aura of festive anticipation. Amid the odours of stone, candles and leather, I sensed a pungent smell of lilies and lilacs; bunches of purple and white branches of blossom were set out in large vases on the dais and around the cellar.

A further variation was in Maryska herself. She was led in by Sebastian held loosely on a long, glittering chain attached to her neck-strap; her shoulders and unroped arms were covered by a short purple cape reaching to her hips, her eyes encircled by a crimson blindfold, replacing the usual one, and bright earrings adorned the lobes. A jewel was buried in her navel, drawing attention to the flatness of her belly. The lips of the mouth and the areolae of the nipples glowed dark red, the pubic hair was carefully combed. Her buttocks had been reddened by a preparatory whipping - more of this later, Nephew.

She seemed to walk with a new attitude of sensuous pride as if aware of the impression her perfumed and oiled body with freshly burnished rings in her breasts and labia made on the gathering. I began to understand the erotic pleasure she evoked in her abusers.

The whole scene recalled more a gay pageant than the entry of a girl about to be whipped in bondage. It was then I realized that the session was reserved for the three lovers, as Eliska had hinted. Then something strange happened.

Standing before her Mistress, Maryska spoke for the first

time. Her voice was hoarse, and in its dialect seemed to reach us from another world.

"Gracious Mistress, to whom I belong," the words came falteringly, "I entreat you and my Masters to whip the vicious venom out of my body."

The girl hesitated.

"And?" Eliska's calm voice filled the chamber. "And?"

"And deliver me from whoredom."

Manifestly the girl had been made to learn the plea. How was it possible to humiliate a victim to this degree? To force her to beg for the whip as one begs a favour?

The only reply was the soft ringing of the bell and the ceremony commenced.

After being stripped slowly of her cape, Maryska was led to the weird gallows-like frame I had noticed in the course of the first session. It consisted of a small platform of rough-hewn planks holding two sturdy posts surmounted by an upper crossbar. A second bar traversed the frame half-way down.

Sebastian's erection throbbed rigidly as he went to work to secure Maryska. As if readily consenting to what the ritual imposed on her, she knelt and lifted her breasts to cradle them within the grasp of two thin straps riveted to the lower bar. The inner surface of the leather was ladened, I noticed, with small barbs, spurs rather than spikes, clearly designed to clench the breasts in their grip. As the soft masses were throttled, Maryska recoiled for a second and then seemed to proffer the breast flesh with pride or defiance.

Sebastian encircled the breasts as close as possible to the chest, hauling brusquely on each strap in turn until the buckle found the last hole in the leather. Maryska jolted the gallows in the shock of constriction as the flesh was wedged in; she swayed her head as she felt in her blindness the scores of minute barbs bite into the first tissue of the skin. Immediately the breasts gorged outwards, lined with swollen, blue veins, the areolae and throbbing nipples surging into capacious cones of red tumescence, to a degree that allowed one to discern behind the rings the orifice created by the piercing.

Sebastian passed his hands over the tight spheres and stiff

nipples to ensure that the utmost swelling had been attained to allow him to proceed further. He roped the wrists to the upper bar - the first time I had seen hempen cords used - and manacled the ankles well apart to the boards. Maryska was kneeling now before Eliska's altar...

It was Ladislav who leaned over to me to whisper: "The bondage straps make it inadvisable for the whore to tug at the bar while the breasts receive the riding crop. She would only rip her flesh and the Gräfin and ourselves have a horror of blood."

I attempted to move away, only to be held by my sleeve as the man went on:

"We have drawn lots and it is Milan to perform first. He cannot resist a fine pair of tight breasts and Sebastian knows precisely how he prefers them. Even the Margravine enjoys a moment of pleasure with Milan's silken whip on hers, bound with red ribbons but, of course, tonight he will use Eliska's riding crop on the whore..."

Catching the sibilant sound of her name, Eliska frowned and gestured for silence. But Ladislav had to add for my benefit: "The rump is left to the lord Premsyl and me. We infinitely prefer and advocate buttock-whipping. I must have scourged every girl in the house at some time..." Then to my distress, he added excitedly: "If you were to probe into this whore's cunt, you would discover her already awash with lust." He had no time in which to correct his language, as the silver bell tinkled through the sultry perfumes of the dungeon.

The young Milan now stepped down from the dais, grasping the Margravine's own silver-handled riding crop which I have myself seen in her hand when she was out cantering through the broom-bright meadows. I suppose this is a privilege - to use her crop.

Again the cries that arose from the girl seemed to echo pain and a sort of panting, as if she was in reach of an orgasm. Milan did not whip with strength but regularly and slowly to allow the effect to penetrate deep into the girl's nerves. The cries became long moans. Swiftly the flesh reddened, the lashes striking the crown of the breasts time after time.

I looked at the young man. He wore a gorgeous jacket of

brown satin - or was it sepia silk? - the sleeves gashed with red to match his slippers. Each arm terminated in exquisite lace ruffs, the quality of lace you find in Bruges and Ghent. His purple hose gaped wide to allow his straining penis to sway before his flat, haired belly. As he whipped, trails of bright liquid seeped from the head of the stiff monster as if it was salivating with lust.

While the slow flagellation proceeded, I saw Eliska staring with narrowed eyes, caressing herself freely, legs wide apart, holding back her climax for later.

Suddenly and quite unexpectedly, the bell rang out as Maryska sank back, jerking and moaning, held by her breast-straps. She must have received some thirty stripes.

"I do not want blood drawn, Milan," Eliska said. "That will do. You have performed well. That will do, my love."

Milan looked at his Mistress with dour surprise and ceased the flagellation.

"You should scourge from both sides, dear love. Spend a moment with Sebastian to see how he excites a pair of breasts with the tongue of the crop. There is no sense in laying into breasts as if scourging the rump which can take every type of lash. You must control your desire, my dearest. And it is best to whip with the the tip rather than the rod of the crop. But you dealt with the whore well. Now let us refresh ourselves."

Eliska closed her robe and rose. Though deprived of his flesh and disappointed, Milan did not appear to resent Eliska's remarks at all. He deposited the crop with the other whips.

We retired to where several serving girls, naked but for white hose and black lace visors, offered wine and sweetmeats. Some were ringed, some had recently received the scourge to judge by the welted buttocks and thighs, but all without exception wore round the throat a narrow band of red velvet. This, Premsyl tells me, indicates that the girl is on duty (in the dungeon, at table or in the bedchamber) and is entirely and instantly available for sex on demand; she can also be put to the whip as and when desired and even, since these are well-trained slaves, subjected to some measure of erotic sex-torture. Although the scarlet band necessarily exposes the woman to harsh handling, it is considered here as a honour and a privilege to wear it.

Eliska seized one of the girls and then bared the head of Milan's expectant erection.

"Dearest Milan! I know you need relief, but I cannot have blood drawn, even from a whore, and her breasts were about to shed. It is not your fault. In recompense, you may have this little slut to work upon, let us say on Tuesday. Not now but I promise - in my bedchamber, tied to the bedposts stark naked. You can whip her raw for an hour."

Milan looked at the trembling girl who paled, almost dropping her silver tray, her body freezing in goose-flesh. She was quite plump with fine breasts and rump and long plaits.

"Let me deal with her now!" he pleaded. Eliska ran her gloved finger along the blue veins standing out like whip-cords along his penis.

"Not now, dearest. I cannot have the ceremony disrupted, particularly when we have a guest present. Next week, *Schatz*." She used the German word that only made my embarrassment worse, having been made the pretext for the postponement. Then Eliska weakened a trifle. "Very well, then. As you badly need to spend, amuse yourself with this little blonde slut while we drink. Empty into her and come and join us."

Milan looked at the girl. Although stronger, she had something about her that recalled Dürer's Eve he painted for us in 1507 - except for her mask and hose!

Milan sought solace in the girl. He pushed her petrified body against the dungeon wall, making her drop her tray and thrusting her to her knees. As taught in training encounters with the bailiffs, she promptly reached out to grasp the heavy scrotum in one hand and the huge erection in the other. She slicked back the foreskin to begin a frantic sliding of her hand from tip to root and back again, smearing the shaft with her spittle and Milan's secretions flooding from the slit. Now and then she reached her fingers down between her sex-lips to add to the lubricants.

Taking the whole length and girth of the prick into her throat, the girl took less than thirty suctions to spare Milan any further delay. He came in hot heavy spurts some way from the girl's lips. She directed the discharge into her gaping mouth, expertly and dutifully pressing along the tube behind the testicles to empty him, milking carefully and sucking him dry. She swallowed the thick clotted sperm with a gulp as Milan wiped his penis on her golden plaits and left her kneeling, his turbulence calmed.

Joining us with a satisfied smile and kissing Eliska, he agreed with his divine Mistress.

"She sucks well and merits her red band. Her breasts are almost as inviting as the whore's over there." He showed no resentment or disappointment.

Eliska laughed, raising her glass to him. "The bailiffs inform me that she is among the best in bed, under the whip and even enjoys a taste of sex-torture if properly bound. You spend too much time with me, my love." She fondled his flagging sex. "Now drink. I promise you can have her for as long as you wish - but next week. I shall lend you my own crop, my dearest love. We must not keep Premsyl and Ladislav waiting too long. And afterwards you can fuck me for as long as you like - until daybreak..."

As we took our places again, Eliska stopped before the girl, still sitting on her heels.

"What is your name, slut?"

"Ottla and it please your Majesty." The girl now was erect on her knees, not daring to look her owner in the eyes. She was a magnificent specimen of robust peasant flesh.

"Well, you are attractive as slaves go and you suck with energy and devotion. After your flagellation next Tuesday - which I cannot spare you since you have been reported by my kitchen overseers as lazy and grossly impertinent and since you are now promised to my lord Milan, I shall have you pierced and ringed to serve me as a chambermaid. You will be clothed by Bojena in tall slippers, red hose, ribbons tied tight to hold your clumsy breasts and, of course, the scarlet neck band. For the moment I do not want manacles."

The Gräfin paused to lift the girl's head. "Tell me, have you made love to a woman?"

The blood drained from Ottla's features as she heard what seemed to be a question and a veiled accusation. All is accusation and retribution here, Nephew!

She stammered out a few words which became clear to me from Eliska's reply.

"Sleeping with your sister and fondling each other! That does not count. I mean full, voluptuous sex. You will go to Radka and ask her to explain exactly what is expected of you when you are called to service me. And I suggest you listen very carefully with those sweet ears of yours. If you prove unimaginative or clumsy, leave alone unresponsive, then I shall just have to entrust you to Sebastian for a night in his cellar."

"Oh, Mistress, please!"

"Very well then. So listen to Radka as to how you must behave. If you make love as a sex-slave should, you will come to little harm."

It was fascinating to watch and listen to this exchange; Eliska was evidently quite attracted to the servant and here she was, in the midst of a formal dungeon session, actually selecting a girl to sleep with her and participate in her nightly orgies.

"Do you frig yourself, girl?" she asked nonchalantly. Again Ottla paled like chalk.

"Never, and it please your gracious Majesty. Only when the bailiffs make me do it before them. But never by myself, I swear, not since I was brought to the castle."

"Good. Now, as agreed, you will be whipped on Tuesday after the evening Angelus and pierced in the same session. On second thoughts," here Eliska gave the girl's navel an offhand prod, "I think a ring should be pierced in here. Yes certainly. And so that means the body should be fully pierced for the eight rings: through both the inner and outer cunt lips, clitoris-hood, nipples and navel." As Eliska enumerated the points, she touched each sensuously and almost clinically. "Yes, that makes eight rings leaving aside the lobes of the ears. But on no account do I want the nose, lips or tongue touched."

I listened aghast at the dispassionate way she described how she wanted or did not want her slave to be equipped. Ottla paid heed to every word, still on her knees.

"I shall attend your flagellation on Tuesday with the lord Milan, of course, as I have promised your body to him. Then on Saturday night you will present yourself, naked but fully ringed, to Bojena, the head chambermaid, for your first night of service. Do you understand?"

Ottla bent forward and kissed the toe of her Mistress's riding boot in pure gratitude at her sudden - if frightening - graduation from a simple domestic to one of the most sought-after posts in the castle's female hierarchy. Not only now was she to serve with a dozen or so other colleagues as a chambermaid within the sanctum and enjoy the privileges this implies but also she had been selected personally by her Mistress for direct sexual duties. Such an honour was well worth a beating and a few moments of pain.

Then, as so often here, the unexpected occurred: Eliska raised the exquisite girl to her feet and, sliding her hand between the thighs to cup the bulge of the sex, planted a long kiss on the girl's quivering mouth.

"She has promise," my hostess remarked casually, "and is probably passionate and fierce in bed and reliable under the scourge." She regained her throne. "Come, let us proceed."

As we took our places, I watched Ottla join her companions against the wall; she was blushing from the crown of her head to her breasts at the distinction bestowed on her and was met with wide-eyed stares of incredulity, astonishment and possibly jealousy.

I found my chair. Before us, amid the scents of the flowers and the unfathomable smell of the dungeon and sex, Maryska stood, still blindfolded, glistening with fresh oil, stretched from her fingertips to her toes in chains, tensely awaiting the flagellation she was now to receive at the hand of Ladislav. Something told me that, despite the pain that the whip was about to bring to her flesh, the girl seemed to give herself erotically to her flagellator, conscious of her nudity and the sexual desire she stimulated in him. She awaited the scourge, lusting for that mixture of pain and pleasure she had now been taught to enjoy.

So much for now, Nephew. The Passau rider leaves tomorrow at dawn with my official reports and brings you this letter as well as one for your dear cousin Margretlin.

With your uncle's love, Huldrych

Letter the fifteenth

Having caught up with my work and not yet summoned to see the Bishop, I can resume my narration which is not easy because there are so many things happening here.

The pageantry of the session continued. Ladislav's preparations seemed to take an interminable time while he himself rather than Sebastian positioned Maryska; his fastidious attentions to the naked body contrasted curiously with the effective and almost effortless manner in which Sebastian dealt with his victims. It must also be an agonizing ordeal for the girl as she is made to wait and wait for the first hiss of the whip.

Ladislav was superb in a jet-black velvet doublet adorned with ermine at the collar and wrists and the spurs on his high riding-boots (not unlike Eliska's) gave off the same silver glitter. The handsome bearded face was half-hidden by the silken mask over his eyes, below which hung a golden chain over the broad shoulders with a pendant medallion carrying the letter E.

Maryska's rigid nakedness revealed an almost white pair of buttocks except for dark still healing streaks earlier lashings had left; but the flesh was virtually unspoiled, quite ready to receive more. The preparatory reddening had by now faded though not the effect.

But it was the state of the breasts that startled one; they were heavily marked and seemed to throb still with pain. It was the tumid nipples that Ladislav took in hand first, hooking the rings to a chain which he secured to the pillar in front of the sweating nude.

Just as he had tugged out the breasts, Ladislav now chained the sex-labia to the column. Standing back, the man tested the bondage; with a sharp tug he made Maryska jerk and totter on her toes, throwing out her rump as far as she was able to alleviate the traction on the clitoris-flesh. Then Ladislav called for his whips.

Sebastian handed him both: one consisting of a long thin length of rawhide tapering off into a tip of braided cords; the second a bunch of slender thongs of medium length. (Later Ladislav admitted to me that these were his favourites, that he had had them made specially and that he had used them on scores of naked women.)

Holding the long scourge and the chain in his left hand, the thongs in his right, Ladislav looked lasciviously at the buttocks before him, brandishing his huge erection that pulsated with craving and lust 'to strap and thrash the bitch of a whore', as he told me later. The fatal bell rang out in the silent dungeon. We sat back to watch one of the most erotic spectacles, according to my hosts, that it is possible to invent for the eye.

Each jerk of the chain held in Ladislav's hand caused Maryska to succumb to the sudden drag on the cusp of her cunt (I use the word, Nephew, since they all use it in front of me now) and as the clitoris is tugged down, the buttocks rear up towards the flagellator. At each lash of the thongs, the nates and thighs clenched and began to redden.

Ladislav flogged the oiled mounds slowly and deliberately from left to right and right to left, standing squarely behind the body as if he were about to ram in between the buttocks.

Despite at least a dozen strokes, Maryska seemed to concentrate more on the delicate balance she needed to safeguard her nipples, labia and clitoris than on fighting the lash itself. After a long silence, her first moans greeted the slash of the leathers which only encouraged the man to whip further round the thighs. He appeared to be engaged in a sacred function or duty. And he relished every moment.

After some thirty strokes, the whole rump and hip area was scarlet and I could see Eliska caressing herself gently, wistfully watching her love scourging with the same long slow strokes she herself always employed. Then Ladislav changed whips, looping the thongs over his erection, and immediately displayed his mastery with the rawhide. (I gleaned later in the session from Premsyl that his colleague had practised its use with Sebastian in the vault on an unfortunate serf-girl caught stealing and condemned to three sessions of thirty-three lashes. This contributed to his elegance and ease with the whip.)

Virtually only the extreme end of the whip was now used although occasionally the man made the plaited leather curl round the nude to lash the front of the body, avoiding the tight lateral chains and the column to which they were stretched. Regularly the vicious tip licked over the rump like an adder's forked tongue, searing a purple welt in the form of a V as it flicked again and again over the epidermis. The buttocks, particularly, reacted violently, clenching and releasing as if they had a life of their own.

Maryska began to writhe, and by the tenth or twelfth slash her cries filled the dungeon, swelling into short high-pitched screams. Whatever sexual thrill the girl was experiencing, the pain was evident and seemed to prevail. Suddenly she subsided in her fetters, scourged to the edge of her resistance. And yet the inner thighs were wet.

The already scarlet surface of the nates, and the flanks of the hips and the thighs below, were superimposed with violet forked lines furrowed into the flesh where the rawhide bit. The flagellation was one of pure virtuosity. She hung there so naked, beautiful and docile, it was as if she was begging for more of this treatment to satisfy the man's erotic quest.

Then the bell rang in Eliska's fingers.

Ladislav had finished with her, his forty strokes delivered as he had wished. Maryska's head fell forward and I saw her clenching her teeth to fight back the tears seeping from beneath her blindfold. The perfumes on her body seemed to be intensified by the sweat creeping down her flanks - the odour of leather, flesh and sex mingling with the smell of the flowers in the dungeon. I admit, Nephew, it was a strangely erotic mixture...

I turned my attention to the group. Eliska was evidently extremely excited and flushed. As she gave pleasure to both Premsyl and Milan on each side of her throne, the latter's penis swelling anew in her grasp as he watched the whipping. Caressing both men's erections, she fondled the organs lovingly, now and then sliding one into her mouth to bring it to the point of spending; as she worked on them, her lovers excited her, their fingers delving into her vagina, twisting and kneading the clitoris, then chafing the nipples, probing into her mouth and tonguing her ears.

As they kissed her open mouth, Eliska heaved in the seat and came. She orgasmed and discharged with a cry of utter ecstasy; the howl of rapture must have reached the upper chambers and even the courtyard. She fell backwards, clenching her thighs, as the two men pursued their masturbation. As if in a trance, she motioned them towards Maryska with a weak gesture; they approached the fettered body and directed their long jets of boiling sperm over the whipped rump, and as it splashed, Sebastian dutifully smeared the heavy cream over the welts until it dried like a light veil of silk.

I thought Ladislav would either make a further call on Eliska to relieve him or at least summon one of the serving-girls to empty him, but to my surprise he also turned to the exhausted victim. Slowly he parted the buttocks he had flayed to reveal the dark rose in the white unwhipped cleft, and equally slowly he thrust into the slack sphincter until his thighs were pressed against the crimson buttocks and he was firmly within.

Holding her loins by grasping the muscles of the inner thighs, he reamed the passage. Alternating deep and shallow penetrations, sometimes withdrawing from the rim to leave the sphincter gaping, awaiting the return of the shaft, Ladislav signalled to one of the serving-slaves - a young girl not unlike Ottla, a long-haired, brown-skinned beauty with broad hips and plump breasts. She curtsied low to her Mistress and to her Master who continued to thrust into the rump. She was practically nude except for the narrow neck band, white satin mask, white stockings and long red gloves reaching to her armpits. How carefully these people select and clothe their slaves. She looked superb against the dark walls of the dungeon.

For an instant I conjectured that Ladislav, still eager for a further victim, was about to lay his whip into this girl but, as if aware of what was demanded of her, she crouched low and went to work on Maryska's sex, unfastening the chains from clitoris and genitals to commence a fierce cunnilingus. Maryska stiffened and drew her breath with a gasp, then lunged forward as if to encourage the lips and tongue while behind the penetration continued to bore and thump into her.

The girl twisted her small hand into Maryska, burying it as deeply as possible, the ball of the thumb circling over the erect clitoris. The little red tongue licked and flicked over the dripping labia and joined the thumb until Maryska's loins were jolting with desperate spasms. The head had now risen, the mouth agape with hoarse groans as the orgasm that had been made to stagnate in her was ready to erupt and lay waste the entire body.

It was Ladislav, almost at the same time as Eliska behind him cried out in a wild tide of further paroxysms, who came first. With a shout of satisfaction, he emptied into Maryska; he remained inserted until the sphincter ring had squeezed the last drop out of him. It was certainly when she sensed the scalding gush enter her that Maryska's excitement towered; she thrust her cunt violently into the girl's face below, grinding herself against the lips and teeth. The orgasm shattered her body; she shuddered in her bondage, lifting herself aloft by her chains with an unearthly cry. Then she collapsed as if lifeless upon the girl beneath her, drenching the face with glittering discharge.

I was at a loss to understand how a female who had just been thoroughly flagellated could come with such lust. She hung, panting and jerking in the aftermath of one of the most intense and passionate convulsions of orgasm she had ever achieved, for by now, Nephew, I had seen many. It was as if the expiatory victim sought by her own sexuality to appease and then outdo her flogger. There ensued a long silence in the dungeon filled with the scent of lilacs. Quite incredible!

As Sebastian began to unchain his charge and prepare her for the next sequence, Eliska had regained her physical composure and regal equanimity; she was evidently well pleased with the evening so far. She raised her glass to Ladislav - and curiously to me also - and we drank to her and, at my (ironic?) toast, to the future of Zatoransky. I wondered how long her Garden of Eden was deemed to endure...

"Prepare her, Sebastian!" she said, "and let it be erotic, man! And then, my dearest ones," she turned to her men, "I need to be well fucked for the rest of the night. I cannot wait too long in my bed. Proceed, Premsyl, my lover."

Sebastian dragged Maryska to the side of the dungeon and began to prepare her for the lord Premsyl's flagellation. I shall tell you more later, Nephew.

With my blessings from this backwater of Lethe. Tell your mother I have written (not in the same vein!)

Huldrych

Letter the sixteenth

I must relate to you, before describing briefly Premsyl's turn with Maryska, what he told me the other day.

He is certainly not the most eloquent of men, but he is far from unintelligent. He tends to be morose - perhaps on account of his splenetic humour. Apart from reading and his smouldering interest in sex, particularly with Eliska who indulges and pampers him, he is an excellent falconer, a subject about which I know little or nothing.

He was out in the meadow before the castle when I came across him, a hooded hawk linked to his gloved hand and his dogs at his heels. The falcon carried a tiny silver bell on the leg above its spur and I was stupid enough to mention another silver bell, and instead of discussing falconry I found myself engaged in a familiar subject.

"You may wonder, since you mention it, why we use a bell in our rituals," Premsyl said gravely. "We desire the purification ceremony to be reminiscent of the Mass and to avoid the spoken word once the condemned victim has been prepared and is ready to be cleansed with a suitable horsewhip."

"Pray, what is meant by 'prepared' and 'preparation', my lord?" I asked. "I am aware of the piercing, ringing, oiling and chaining of your victims ..."

"Let me first give you, my noble lord, some history. There was a time when the whipmaster, Sebastian's father it was then, performed his duties clad in leather - mask, jerkin and breeches. He was part of the household and had merely use of the dungeon where grain was stored. So, victims (far, far fewer than now, I can assure you) were delivered to him as they stood, in working clothes, and only then were they stripped partiallly, if at all, to permit whipping. The females retained their head-wraps and hose. The Gräfin changed all that after the death of the Margrave - may God safeguard his soul" - we both crossed ourselves - "many things were changed and ritual flagellation was introduced. The Gräfin insists now on total nudity on the part of the victim to be cleansed as well as her flogger. We maintain this to be commendable and far more appropriate for the act of purification, both for the actors and for us as witnesses."

He paused, but after a moment went on with solicitude for my ignorance. "We now have five categories of flagellation to correct transgressions among our serfs and slaves. First, any clumsiness, tardiness, disreputable grooming or dressing, particularly on the part of females waiting on us at table, in our bedchambers or in the cellars, is dealt with by the bailiffs in the stalls, with which I believe you are familiar. That slut you saw spilling wine the other evening is an instance, although she escaped her whipping, alas, through your intervention, sir."

He sounded truly resentful. "Ah, Tereza?" I said, at which Premsyl shrugged as if such a slut had no name. Then he went on, smoothing his falcon's breast.

"The second category concerns offensive or vulgar behaviour, disrespect to us, the bailiffs or overseers, impertinence, insubordination, swearing, blasphemy and so on. Here again the stalls are used. Thirdly, cases of dishonesty, duplicity, lying or theft are severely disciplined."

Emphasizing each heading by counting on the fingers of his hand, he continued: "The fourth rank of punishment is reserved for far more important and serious cases: sexual misconduct such as illicit prostitution - as this wretched whore has had the effrontery to commit. Such cases are handled by Sebastian, as you are aware, in the dungeon proper in formal or informal ceremony and according to the sentence we decide upon. All unlawful relations fall under this category. Except a few which are subject to the last and most rigorous retribution of all."

Intrigued, I waited for details as Premsyl caressed his falcon's speckled breast and offered the bird a morsel he produced from his leather satchel.

"Attempts to escape from the castle are punished severely, of course. But also lesbian practices. The Gräfin is adamant in her hostility to the unnatural habit of women sleeping with women, at least as concerns the common herd. Alas, this happens far more frequently, sir, than you may imagine."

Premsyl then offered me a recent example.

"The convents are particularly to blame and the culprits are almost always delivered to the Gräfin to correct. Only a month ago, a Sister from our nunnery of St. Barbara over there" - he pointed over the roofs of Zatoransky towards the east - "was visiting us. She was found naked in bed with a young serving-girl in the guests' bedroom in the west tower, in fact the very chamber you occupy at present, my lord. Now, normally the nun would have been returned to her convent for correction but, with the consent of the Mother Superior and the Bishop, she was handed over to us. Both females were judged by the Gräfin and ourselves, both were pierced and ringed and underwent a full series of sessions naked, such as you are attending these days. They were also given to the bailiffs to be used in the stalls before being sent out to the fields, chained together by the neck, to labour, clothed only with a piece of sacking round the loins. I can point them out to you, if you wish, when you go riding. Otherwise you can attend their weekly flagellation in the vault, if the Gräfin agrees to the request."

I begged to be excused both spectacles, and mentioned that Eliska had already been considerate enough to describe to me some of the problems lesbians caused her. Premsyl looked surprised and alert, since he was not aware of these divulgations. He looked out over the pine woods and shook his head.

"My own solution, my lord, would be very simple. Stake out a masturbatrix naked on the bed she has defiled and flay her rump." He rose and proposed a walk. "Ah well, Hector will catch us a few hares for supper," and he stroked his hawk lovingly again.

I had hoped to escape and return to work after the breath of fresh air but, by my own doing, I was engaged now in the explanations regarding 'preparation' and could not curtail the dialogue without giving offence.

"Preparation, then, is an important chapter of our ritual," he said, as we strolled towards the conifers. "Having heard her sentence, a culprit is fully aware of what is in store for her but we insist that she is presented fully aroused sexually, despite her fear. Sebastian prepares his charge on the slab in the privacy of her cell, first by oiling and greasing the flesh at length, a sensual operation to say the least and one that excites the woman without fail. She is then prepared further by means of the quirt."

Here Premsyl interrupted himself, calling his hounds to heel and unhooding the falcon. He released him from his outstretched arm with a cry. The bird left in a tumult of wings, towered high, held its hover and plunged, to return minutes later to the wrist with a twitching hare in the scimitars of its claws. Premsyl broke the neck and thrust the prey into his gamebag. I sensed a grim affinity between what he was describing and the hawk's swift unerring ferocity.

"As I was saying, sir, the quirt, as you probably know, is a riding-whip much used out here while hunting. it has a short handle and a couple of braided strands, again quite short."

I nodded, indicating that I was acquainted with the quirt or 'cuerda', meaning cord, widely used by the Spaniards in the Low Countries and, I added, not necessarily on their horses.

"Except that here the quirt is of leather not cord," Premsyl remarked. He was right and I regretted my stupid display of Spanish.

"The quirt is used here in the castle for one particular purpose. As it is of soft leather and different from the tough whips used in sessions, it serves to stimulate and excite our female victims and ready them for what is to follow. It is laid on by the whipmaster in the privacy of the cell across the buttocks and hips without undue force. The female is made to prostrate herself over the corner of her slab, her cunt thrust firmly down against the promontory of stone. The strokes across the rump drive the clitoris into the angle of stone, splaying the flesh until the loins are brought to as high a level of sexual arousal as possible."

Murmuring to his hawk, he spied out the ground before us for movements and then went on.

"As you know, sir, the buttock-meat is the easiest portion of the female body to stimulate sexually with the whip." As I did not know, Nephew, I let him continue. "The girl grinds into the slab as she is whipped - or 'prepared' - slowly. The loins become lit with fire and desire, the breasts also scraping their nipples until the flesh is throbbing with lust. You must remember also that the female is stark naked and is also excited by the noise of the quirt on her nudity. All this never fails to bring her close to orgasm."

I concede that he described the process eloquently.

"Our man Sebastian is an artist in taking a naked female to the height of sexual arousal, leaving her trembling on the precipice of orgasm. On no account is she permitted to come. She is then presented to the gathering, trembling, the rump scarlet; all she asks for is to be fucked. Such is the work of the quirt," he ended conclusively.

After a further lethal flight Hector brought back another hare which was stuffed into the satchel. Premsyl had now warmed to his subject.

"As I say, the quirt is used without force." Here he enlarged on points made to me earlier during my stay and which, I think, I recounted to you in an earlier letter. "Once the flesh has been properly prepared, the full flagellation can be administered. The lash or crop makes the nerves in the flesh or epidermis" - I was impressed by his command of modern terms in German - "contract and regain their former state a moment later. It is this that creates pain. But if correctly aroused beforehand, the sensitivity of the flesh decreases rapidly and is replaced by a mixture of pain and sexual pleasure. The greater the arousal, the longer can be the scourging and the less the pain. A strange cloud of erotic lust and pleasure blurs the pain; now the one prevails, now the other. As you will now have seen in our sessions, the lash is laid on the naked female with slow, regular, well-spaced strokes to ensure the thong reaches down into the nerves. While the flesh begins to flare up in red and purple stripes, the cunt is also kindled like a fire being stoked. After all, sir, the centre of sexual lust is the cunt; in sex it is the cunt that is fucked. Flagellation and fornication are twin sisters..."

I saw his language was becoming coloured, unseemly and rather wild, despite his saturnine disposition; I admit that I followed his reasoning with difficulty.

On my way back to the drawbridge, I wondered if Maryska, Marja, Tereza (spared for once), Ottla and the beautiful young nun, Zdenka, and so many countless others would confirm, as they writhed naked under the whips and thongs, the pleasurable emotions described by my lord Premsyl. After all, it was their flesh that burned in pain.

In time of plague, you recall, Nephew, we invoke St. Anthony and St. Sebastian. The latter not a propitious name here; whom can one invoke to spare these girls from the lash held or commanded by Eliska's hand in its Venetian glove of expensive kid?

What cheers me, however, is that today I received by rider from Regensburg my papers of safe-conduct for the octroi and customs at the Palatinate and Bavarian borders. The Margravine is to provide an escort to the confines of her lands. The sooner I conclude my work, the sooner we can ride out under that awesome portcullis that I never wish to see again. (I say 'we' but I have still to ask the Gräfin if I can take Tereza with us. I hate to ask a favour of her. And when best to approach her?)

Huldrych

Letter the seventeenth

The third session finished in the small hours of the morning with Premsyl's whipping of Maryska. Like Ladislav, he had an unquenchable appetite for naked buttocks and therefore his victim was again positioned to display her rump. Sebastian stretched her arms and legs well apart, making her stand on tiptoe, curved forward in a long, slender arc of lubricious flesh. Again her most delicate parts were chained to maintain her body still. Tottering on her toes, Maryska strained to protect her extremities from damage.

She looked exquisite, still exhibiting some self-confidence although she seemed languid and physically extenuated after the two first floggings. Sebastian began oiling the area again, sensuously massaging her as Maryska swayed and groaned with wild erotic pleasure. Then the man thrust his hands between the thighs to lubricate the distended crotch, frictioning the clitoris and the viscid inner walls of the vagina. Sporadic jerks of the loins testified to the effect; the girl's head swung from side to side, her mouth beginning to gasp as her entrails were brought to full sexual arousal. From where I stood I could plainly see the stub of the clitoris erect between Sebastian's fingers. The victim was ready.

Premsyl was masked in dark mauve, matching the colour of such other clothes as he wore: a brief jacket, heavily embroidered, and tight hose, no doubt from Italy from where most of their beautiful garments come. Dressed like this with his genitals swinging free before him, the man looked so different from his usual daily appearance. Then he produced from his doublet his whip: a thin length of supple leather hafted in an intricate handle of carved ivory - obviously his own.

For an interminable moment Premsyl whipped the girl from the armpits to the thigh muscles, laying the lash each time a finger's breadth lower than the previous streak. He did not flog too hard but tended to snap away the tip, causing Maryska to cry at each sting; the buttocks, however, received their full ration of heavy strokes, adding to the damage done by Ladislav. Now and then, and I believe purposely, Premsyl let his whip strike the chain holding the cunt and nipples, at which Maryska's groans filled the chamber.

I have to say, Nephew, that of all the scourgings I have witnessed here, this was the most dexterous, skilful and, if you will allow the term, most erotically done. Despite her cries, I believe the girl tolerated it with strange acceptance and voluptuousness, to judge from the liberal trail of liquid squandered by her cunt and glinting between her legs.

When the silver bell sounded, Maryska had slumped forward and I saw that my hosts were again enjoying each other; Eliska was lying back in her throne, her legs dangling over the arms, her sex opened wide with sperm seeping from the lips. More trickles of bright semen ran down her brocaded bodice. Milan and Ladislav were using the serving-girls to clean off their penises with their lips and kerchiefs. Premsyl approached his divine Mistress and straddled her where she sat. Turning inwards the facets of her precious-stoned rings on her fingers, Eliska took her lover's erection firmly in hand, holding the testicles tightly, her forefinger reaching behind to excite him further and to enjoy the imminent rush of the sperm along the hidden pathway between the thighs as the ejaculation burst. Using both hands and with her mouth over the head, Eliska masturbated and sucked with fury.

When Premsyl cried out, she directed the repeated spurts towards her breasts. The sperm arched out and Eliska emptied him, smearing the grey clots over her skin, until her breasts dazzled with the lucent juice. She sucked her fingers, closed her eyes and ran her hand over the lips of her cunt.

When the session was over, I was inevitably drawn into conversation, this time by Eliska herself.

"A stimulating session, my lord," she remarked, flushed and pleased, the discharge now dry over her chest like a diaphanous film, with a translucent drop about to fall from the tip of her left breast. "I find inexpressible pleasure in these duties, not only through the fulfilments they give me but in the thought that I am helping this whore to emerge at last from the curse and hell of illicit prostitution."

She drank deeply from her glass.

"You know, my lord, you should not be surprised if this whore is reluctant to leave us. She is fed, sheltered, cared for, enjoys plentiful sex and later will find friends of her sort here, now that her whippings are coming to an end. She cannot now envisage living without me. She has become a slave. She has become so used to the lash that later I will be able to have her undergo her routine weekly scourging standing without chains. Yes, she has become one of us."

Ladislav endorsed his Mistress's view. "The Margravine is right. The whore will find it an imposition, for instance, to wear clothes again. Rather than wander in rags and clogs or barefoot in that thankless, cruel, harsh and unreal world out there, she will beg to be taken back into our all-embracing care and bridled again as a slave. At the least the Margravine may in her humane benevolence find her a place in one of the brothels."

I nodded understandingly and meditated what her soldier, the lansquenet officer, if he still existed, would think of such a prospect were he here in this pernicious cellar of vipers to hear the conversation.

Although Sebastian had not participated in the whipping as such, he was nevertheless rewarded, as is the custom here. While we had been talking and drinking, he had slung Maryska by the arms and legs like a sack, belly down. As if to affirm her courage and assent, she managed to keep her head high, her earrings sparkling between her stretched upper arms. At the further ring of the bell, Sebastian began to load the body with weights, a Morgenstern for each of Maryska's five body rings. As the flesh jerked downwards with the traction of the irons, the girl drew her breath in with a hiss of pain, fighting tenaciously against the vertical pull on her tenderest parts.

From a nearby bench, the man selected a stout leather-bound stump in the form of a penis, about twice the size of his own throbbing erection. He prised apart the buttocks, still scalding from the double scourging, and screwed the head of the shaft into the narrow entry, lubricating it with his dripping liquids until Maryska was plugged deep and tight. I concluded this impalement was designed to excite the victim rather than to supplement her suffering; Maryska heaved in her chains, gasping as she contended with the sheer size of the thing.

Arching his loins forward and forcing her head and fettered neck back by holding her by the hair, Sebastian fed his erection into Maryska's mouth. The regular stabbing plunge of the tumescence made Maryska choke and gag helplessly as the monster reached into the recesses of her throat. Desperately she performed the fellatio as best she could, sucking savagely, compressing the meat with her lips and teeth to enhance the gratification she had, at all costs, to give to her master. Only now and then, when the sex was withdrawn to relish a re-entry, was the girl able to catch her breath and swallow the gathering liquids and saliva; even then her tongue flicked out like a lizard's to lick the head, once she had gulped in air... Maryska worked on the penis with a sort of ecstatic sexual frenzy - as she had done with her soldier, but then free and unchained. Her body was bathed in sweat as she sucked ravenously, the lapping being the sole sound in the silence of the dungeon.

Suddenly the man's buttocks clenched, his head fell back and the pent-up pulsations of sperm surged into the throat. In the fury of the orgasm, the man wrenched Maryska's head backwards to enjoy the full depth of the gullet; he held her there until he had finished sluicing into the throat and even then remained within her. Maryska fought and choked in her struggle to swallow the sluggish deluge, her cheeks gorged. Sebastian held her as if about to snap the neck. Then he withdrew with a jerk.

Maryska's head lunged forward. The choking mouth opened with the release. And the hot sperm, still turbid, thick, opaque, slithered out over her lip and chin to the flagstones, where it splattered in glittering clots.

An even deeper hush fell over the dungeon, transfixing the audience; even Eliska, I saw, caught her breath. Something had disturbed the ceremony.

Instantly I realized, recalling an earlier exchange I had had with Milan, the terrible fault, the appalling transgression which the retching, choking Maryska had committed. Failure to swallow down the full load of an ejaculation during a formal session was deemed not only an insult to the male concerned but also a presumptuous affront to the Margravine herself and to the sanctity of the ceremony.

Dissatisfied rather than shocked, the group began to leave the dungeon, each member bowing courteously to me. As I followed, catching sight of Maryska being unchained and made to lick up the wasted semen, the lord Milan took my arm.

"An execrable end to a session, sir!" he lamented. "The slovenly whore will have to pay for this. She has insulted her whipmaster's manhood and will do penance..."

"In what form, pray?" I asked, about to protest that she was prevented from swallowing by the way he had held her head; I thought better of it and do not want to be accused of commiserating with the girl. "What penance more can she possibly endure?"

"Oh, but it is his right," Milan replied. "He will take her to a special cell of his, we call it the Red Cellar, and deal with her. Sebastian himself has fashioned all the contraptions, gear and instruments there. The Margravine does not like us to spend time there, reserving it for herself and special friends. Rather unfair, I consider."

He smiled, then Eliska turned round.

"Graf von Mechtingen, do not listen to this sweet boy! He is never satisfied. And do not worry about the whore. She is in expert hands. And she will orgasm countless times before the night is out, for Sebastian is not as inhuman as he seems."

She took Milan's arm. 'Come, take me to that bed of feathers and make heavenly love to me."

I wandered back to my chamber across the bars of moonlight in the great corridors and soon was between my coarse linen sheets, wondering what was happening to Maryska. Again I felt so out of place here, so ingenuous, rather like a shorn sheep among wolves and, as I fell asleep to the hooting of the owls (and, believe it or not, a nightingale!), I comforted myself by presuming that if God had not wanted them shorn, He would not have created sheep.

My love to you, my dear student,
Your uncle Huldrych

Two items of interest today, as I send off this letter. First, the characters of my hosts seem to fit the four humours well. Secondly, Radka says that she 'trusts' me. Why?

Letter the eighteenth

I mentioned the old woman Radka in my last letter. Well, oddly, she has begun to play a strange role in my existence here. I think she confides in me not only because of our ages but because she trusts me. But I do not wish to become too familiar and I am staying aloof (as befits my station); above all I must be careful to avoid her connivances. Despite her humble origins, she is an intelligent if wary woman; she has worked here in the castle all her life and I suspect she has sympathies with the sects, possibly the Taborites since she spoke one day of John Zizka, their leader a century ago, who preached common property, free love and so on. The name still lives on.

In the course of the next days, between my journeys to towns and villages in the outlying countryside, I saw much of the woman. At one moment, as I was poring over my revenue figures in my chamber, I saw Radka picking herbs in the terrace garden below. She made a sign to me and I went down, taking the chance to stretch my legs and, to be honest, Nephew, to talk to someone.

I have found Radka to be a mine of information.

While she collected fronds of plants for her medical concoctions, she imparted to me some extraordinary things. Obviously she heartily detests the Margravine and the lovers and yearns for the times of the old Margrave. This hatred is shared by several of the overseers and by the scores of servants in the castle - but does not compare with the loathing in the hearts of the serfs in the Zatoransky domains, hence the perpetual rumours of revolt. On the other hand, the Margravine is adored by her all-powerful bailiffs, the Landsknechte and guards who enjoy great privileges, not least among which is ready access to any slave-girl they fancy. As to Sebastian, who is rarely seen, he is feared as Satan is feared.

The starving peasants and the servile rabble in Zatoransky seethe in the feudal grip of the castle, monasteries and local landowners. The whole situation reminds me vividly of our great unprisings of 1525 at home.

May God save us from that!

"Most of the serfs exist on groats and dried beans mixed with winter grass," Radka told me, picking her camomile and chervil, "while the royal table here is loaded with pork, beef, boar, venison, poultry, duck, goose, quail, chicken, vegetables, fish -"

Her list petered out at last. I then asked about the destitution I saw around.

"Conditions have grown worse since the Margravine increased taxes fourfold. The serfs have to pay more or work harder for salt, corn (which they have to grind in the Margravine's mill against payment), bread (which they are not allowed to bake for themselves), beans, butter, meat (once a month if they are lucky), wood (no felling or gathering without permission from the bailiffs) and all cloth for clothing. Infringements are punished with the utmost severity - males in the town prison, females in the castle, as you know." She paused and then added: "My lord, the Great Whore of Babylon controls all you see around you. Except your lordship, your man Hans and your horses."

"Tell me about the servants," I said.

"Servants? They are slaves, sir - orphans, widows, destitutes, young girls. My Ignatius says that girls are hauled up here 'to be trained for service', but the phrase must be taken *cum grano salis*. We all know what will happen to them, particularly if they are pretty and well-proportioned. Their fate is almost worse than living in misery in this impoverished province except that they are fed, sheltered and clothed."

I recalled Ladislav's similar words a day or so ago, as Radka added: "Clothed unless they are naked for whipping."

Then she stood up and faced me. "My lord, if you will come with me tonight, I shall show you the Great Whore of Babylon, who owns us, at work. I shall knock four times on your door. Go now, dear lord. Do not let her see us too much together. She is a fiend."

That evening, after my long ride out to Librec and the surroundings, supper was a gay affair with Ladislav particularly truculent and Eliska in the best of spirits, teasing me with a pleasant humour. When they had retired, I listened to the music played by the two minstrels and drank my wine, before going to my room. The light tapping came soon after.

I followed Radka silently up the stairs to the long corridor above with curtained rooms leading off. She stopped at one heavily brocaded curtain and signalled to me to peer in.

In the very centre of the luxurious chamber - evidently Eliska's own - four naked bodies were engaged in passionate, intense sex. The candlelight identified them clearly: Ladislav lay prostrate on a low table, fully penetrated in Eliska's vagina as she knelt, clothed only in her riding-boots and spurs, above him. Premsyl, sweating before Eliska's face, was using her mouth with long, slow strokes in and out of the lips that encircled him. Behind her, the fiery young Milan had grasped her around the hips and was plunging deep between the buttocks. All four seemed to move with a preordained rhythm, well-practised and smooth.

The scene was enacted in silence except for the panting and groaning and the sound of lapping and suction as the Margravine of Zatoransky enjoyed three men in her at once.

Beyond, the Margravine's bed stood in complete disarray and a heap of clothing lay on the carpet, among which I noticed Eliska's wimple and starched cowl, discarded for the first time. Indeed now I saw her dark hair straggling around her face as she worked on Premsyl's prick. She looked like an animal, lustful and sleek and beautiful. It was then that Radka whispered in my ear, as she drew me away from the tapestry, "Our Great Whore of Babylon, my lord."

Swiftly we descended the stairs, I somehow feeling ill at ease and remorseful at this eavesdropping on people who are after all my hosts and...

(At this point one or more pages are missing. The text then continues:-)

... I entertained Radka with various stories, describing to her the sea which, of course, she has never set eyes upon and which I enjoyed so much during my mission to the Low Countries. I then recounted the recent voyage of discovery to the other side of the world, which she had difficulty in believing. In return she told me about a nearby lake where the carp are as 'big as dogs'. She also mentioned the moat round Zatoransky castle since we were talking of water; she affirmed that she knew of women being thrown into the slimy depths and sent to their forefathers in this way. No one here knows how to swim. Why people were drowned in this moat, I could not get out of her.

We also talked of my male hosts and I explained how they could be considered in terms of the four humours. The lord Ladislav, for instance, is sanguine, full-blooded, positive in everything and with a balanced, agreeable nature. His allegiance to his Mistress is typical of this sort of character. Milan, I went on, is of course our choleric, easy to anger, spontaneous and when irate, uncontrollable and even dangerous. He can be capable of cruelty and ruthlessness, I suspect; this Radka confirmed in words I do not wish to repeat here. She particularly loathes this young, vain lecher.

It was Radka herself, enjoying the game, who depicted the lord Premsyl: a man tending to melancholy, who rarely smiles and keeps much to himself. At the same time, he can be selfish and, under his severe exterior, thoroughly relishes his privileges, his hunting, dining and the sex he has with Eliska; it is he apparently who coldly draws up the terms of punishment to be visited on females who fall into their clutches.

"And the Margravine?" I asked Radka provocatively. What she said I translate into my own terms which you will understand, Nephew. Thus, Eliska is phlegmatic. Not easily disturbed or ruffled even before severe challenges; determined in her decisions and duties and quite unforgiving, hard and sharp as a steel sword; never satisfied and forever seeking new pleasures in a calculated manner, capable of immense cruelty and terrible revenge and all carried out with cold composure.

"If you want further evidence of her hypocrisy and deceit," Radka said as we entered the main door, "let me take you, like the other night, to her chamber again. What you will see there tonight even the Last Judgement is insufficient to condemn. You know, my lord, that a misguided young nun from St. Ursula's or St. Barbara's - I do not recall which - has been taken making lesbian love. She will be shaved - that is my task, sir - and ringed and put to the whip in full session thereafter. But meanwhile, sir, she is being used shamelessly. If she is not chained in the vault, she is up in the bedchamber of our Great Whore of Babylon. It is worth your trouble to see it, my lord, for I feel you do not believe me." She paused. "Like the other night, I shall come for you in your room when the evening meal is over."

I went with her again along the dark passages until we were before the weighty tapestry. Long groans of pleasure could be plainly heard beyond and I was sure they came from Eliska. Conscious of my risk, I parted the curtain.

The first thing I saw in the pale glow of Eliska's chamber, lit by a few candles, was a chair with its back towards me. Then I recognized Ladislav, seated and watching the spectacle being enacted before him. Stretched completely naked over the bed, Eliska lay writhing, one arm flung up beyond her tangled hair, her thighs thrown out wide. She trembled as she grasped the edge of the bed; her cries were soft and continuous.

Between her legs knelt a nude girl, her head shaved, her wrists tied behind her back, licking Eliska's cunt, spearing deep into the vagina and working her tongue luxuriously and quite unrestrainedly over the clitoris and swollen labia. Now and then the teeth bit the flesh and extended it lasciviously before returning to suck the erect white clitoris.

I cannot repeat here the expletives that issued out of Eliska's mouth; they would blunt my quill. As she pressed the girl's head into her groin, she called for more tongue, more suction, more liquid, ordering her to move here to the inner thigh, there to the buttock-cleft, cursing the young nun for a whore, a bitch at its bowl, a lesbian slut.

Eliska's voice was hoarse and unearthly as she rolled on the bed, the girl sucking the sex-hair into peaks wet with saliva and which she held between her teeth, tugging at them to excite the woman to whom she now belonged. She seemed to work on Eliska with that same passion as Maryska used on her flogger - as if to commend herself and curry favour.

Eliska was like an animal thwarted of food until she began to sense the storm of her orgasm taking form within her; then she gave herself totally to the slobbering lips labouring on her labia. But at the supreme instant, she cried out to Ladislav.

"The whore's killing me... Fuck me, fuck me while she sucks me. Quick. I'm coming!"

Ladislav rose and, thrusting the young girl aside, entered Eliska until the pubic hair of both was one. The girl pressed her face into Eliska's belly, flicking her tongue anew over the spear of flesh and biting the huge shaft that fucked just below it

The orgasm reduced Eliska to a rigid corpse while her muscles jerked as if continuing the paroxysm. After a moment, during which Ladislav plunged into her deeper, Eliska said in little more than a whisper: "Lay the slut over me and fuck her - she needs a man in her. Fuck her, Ladislav, tear her apart! Plough deep into her, the dirty lesbian."

He pulled the girl to him, laid her back over his Mistress and exchanged one sex for another, ramming into the girl before withdrawing to slide again into Eliska's dripping vagina. The girl's tied hands reached down and astutely caressed the cunt beneath them, cooperating with the copulation. Then Ladislav emptied into the girl. He did so with a roar of pleasure, and Eliska wound her hands round the hips of the girl above her to stretch the lips apart; then she crushed the clitoris between her fingers, extending the point upwards only to roll it viciously in her grasp until the lesbian surrendered herself entirely, arching back over her Mistress as the orgasm came. At the same time, the girl turned her head towards Eliska's mouth to enjoy the thin lips and tongue. They kissed voraciously, drowning the cries of the girl as she jerked her loins uncontrollably.

Ladislav withdrew slowly, long lines of sperm linking the huge head of the penis to the slit he had used. Eliska eased the girl off her body.

"Tie the slut to the bedpost, my love," she said, still prostrate on the bed, "and whip her for coming so quickly."

Willingly the man took the girl to the end of the bed, untied her wrists and placed her in bondage, the arms reaching to the top of the bedpost. She stood palpitating, her breasts heaving, the belly withdrawn with lumps of semen dropping from the cunt.

I saw Ladislav select a whip from a side closet. There must

have been some twenty whips available among which hung a thin lash armed with tails of braided leather at its extremity. Neatly he laid the whip across the breasts at least six times and then flagellated the bulging ribs and descended to the pubic mound. There he laid the whip on her flesh with a violence I had not yet seen. The girl writhed and screamed as the tongue of the leather marked her skin with purple fangs; she was obviously not yet used to the whip as Maryska was. The flagellation ceased suddenly as Eliska spoke, dragging her nails over the superb buttocks as if to mark the girl - who is called Zdenka, I hear - as her own.

"This lesbian must be introduced into our midst. She sucks well. She takes the whip well, her flesh will be kept for our use over the next weeks. She will be whipped by Sebastian to the very edge of her resistance. I need flesh like this. We shall see to it that she is kept naked, ready for flagellation several times a day until she is ready for the ceremony where she will certainly distinguish herself, I am sure."

She turned to Ladislav. "You whip well, my love, but I still have to have her pierced and ringed and whipped by Sebastian. Is her cunt acceptable?"

Ladislav smiled. "She was or seemed a virgin and tight as a fist over my erection."

"So much the better," Eliska replied. "in a week or so she will be like a whore, open and fully acquainted with erections. So far she has only enjoyed fingers, lips and tongues and the thrust of a woman's hip-bone. Now she will learn what it is to fuck, suck and open her buttocks for what a female is made for. She is an admirable addition to our slaves."

With this, Eliska rose and tugged on a bell-rope. Almost immediately, Bohumil appeared, as if he had been waiting for the call; bowing low, he untied the naked girl.

"Have this creature oiled, shaved and ringed for bondage. I need her available for my service until we order her to be brought for flagellation in the dungeon. You may use her in the cells but I require her to be fully chained. And I wish her breasts to be throttled so that, when she comes before us, we can observe how her nipples react." Eliska paused a moment before saying:

"The breasts of a lesbian need special treatment."

At this point, I withdrew from the curtain to creep back to my chamber, agreeing with Radka that I was indeed in the presence of her Great Whore of Babylon.

I said this in a whisper at which Radka promised me further evidence of evil.

"Come with me tomorrow night my dear lord, and I shall show you much more," she announced with hatred. Such invitations leave me in two minds.

In this desperate atmosphere of carnality, I went to bed and wrote you this letter, Nephew.

May God preserve us, Huldrych

Letter the nineteenth

After a long ride through the outlying districts, where I was able to complete my survey of the secular lands of Zatoransky, I was, thanks to Radka, shown something that you, dear Nephew, will not believe.

After supper she came, as usual, to my chamber and led me down to the infamous bowels of the castle, to the so-called Red Cellar - why is it called red? Possibly because of the colour of the flesh that is scourged crimson there? It is a very secret place, open to few to view. We looked through a small vent in the wall.

Maryska was being punished for having refused her flagellator's ejaculation, She was suspended by the wrists in shackles, naked and blindfolded as always, above a gigantic leather-covered wooden penis bolted to a block. Sebastian, by means of a chain running over an overhead wheel, was lowering the body on to the shaft which impaled her vagina, then raising it again.

The cunt was distended time after time by the shaft, as if to remind the girl that this narrow secret slit was the reason of her undoing and had become the centre of interest for her torturers. Maryska muttered strangely each time the rod bored into her; it was then I noticed that, for the first time, she was gagged. Why this was imposed on her, while she was allowed to cry out during her main whippings, I still cannot guess, unless it was to increase her sense of submission.

Finally, after innumerable impalements on the huge artificial penis, Sebastian whipped the girl's buttocks with a short lash and then used a pair of iron tongs to play with her nipples until they were red and swollen. But as was the custom, no blood was allowed to be drawn from the slits of the nipples; they merely elongated to twice their normal length like bruised fruits on the summit of the breasts.

This sex-torture seemed totally divorced from the sentence to which the 'whore' had been condemned and I realized that, once in the Red Cellar, a victim is entirely at the mercy of the whipmaster to use her as he wishes. No rules apply as to how a female is treated here, it is a mere private interlude.

And yet to recall Eliska's comment on the way Sebastian uses his victims, the man had some trace of humanity in him. Having played with the naked body, Sebastian now proceeded to pay attention to the clitoris itself in order to provide the groaning, over stimulated female with a modicum of pleasure. He removed the girl's gag and closed in on her in order to grind the pommel of his whip into the cusp of the sex.

Maryska responded immediately, despite the treatment she had endured. Although impaled, she jerked her loins with tremendous force as her clitoris rose with the masturbation, the ring pressed flat against her belly. Her body became rigid, her bound legs reaching out, the head hung back, as the orgasm gathered. Then it exploded. She screamed and let her loins ride the blissful rasp of the whip-handle as the climax from the clitoris set fire to her whole being, radiating out to her limbs and every tissue, vein and muscle. Then she sank on the shaft plunged within her loins; she hung, sweating and panting, while the residue of the orgasm consumed the totality of her naked body. Her head fell forwards as if she had lost consciousness or at least any awareness of her anatomy.

Thus she paid for her inability to swallow her flagellator's gift and yet was permitted to orgasm. How strange! How could she, I asked myself, attain such sexual heights while under such physical stress? I even whispered this to Radka.

"Ah, my dear lord, she suffers perhaps but the thrill in her cunt is very great The Peitschmeister knows well how to balance pain and pleasure, ordeal and orgasm. She is enjoying it, dear sir, They form a team, both naked, crazed with sex. it is the Great Whore who is evil. Not these two. One enjoys working on a nude victim, the other enjoys being worked upon by a handsome, nude flagellator with a big cock. This is normal. What is not normal is the Great Whore, sir!"

Not having expected such a torrent of homely comment, I nodded to Radka and took my leave, while she continued to watch the events within, cursing her Mistress, her sworn enemy, Eliska. For Radka, as far as Zatoransky was concerned, Satan was not male but female.

I went to my bed bewildered, weary and utterly confused

over the nature of human behaviour here. Before falling asleep, I recalled that Radka had threatened me with yet a further sight of our Great Whore. Yet another!

(After a hiatus, the MS continues but on different paper and in different ink)

Two nights later, with Radka and at her express bidding, I parted the curtains at the side of Eliska's bedchamber. What I saw surprised me more than anything else I had witnessed. Let me try to describe it, with the help also of my inadequate sketch which I beg of you to destroy along with these letters.

Eliska was spread and bound with slender crimson thongs to the posts at the end of her bed. Except for her riding-boots, she was completely naked, her white arms and legs outstretched, her superb body taut and shining in the flickering glow of the candles; her breasts bulged forward, jolting under the effect of what her lovers were doing to her. Beneath her and between her parted thighs, one of the men - I believe it was Premsyl to judge by his hair - was firmly inserted in her sex, Eliska thrusting down on him to the extent her bonds allowed.

Standing on the bed before her face was Milan, his hands on his hips, plunging a vein-ribbed erection into Eliska's throat while she sucked insatiably on the monster, her lips retaining the foreskin back to enable her to concentrate directly on the sensitive rim of the bloated purple glans.

Behind her sweating nudity, Ladislav - I deduced this from the size of the penis that swung before his loins - was lashing his woman's buttocks with a bunch of soft thongs that I took to be strips of fine kid. Compared with the strokes laid upon Maryska's flesh, the whip seemed almost gentle, but it was quite adequate to heat up and mark the magnificent rump clenching in pain and pleasure at each blow.

Eliska's eyes were closed, her mouth half-open with sexual pleasure as she was penetrated and whipped; only occasionally did a cry issue from her gullet, a hoarse, deep shout of erotic delight. I watched for a long moment until the men exchanged positions, as if each was eager to give and receive to the utmost reach of ecstasy. It was a cry from Eliska that caused them to release her. They fell together on the feather bed where each man continued to belabour one of the three orifices in turn.

I never thought, Nephew, a woman could be used with such force; she lay writhing and panting, her arms caressing her lovers in a sort of wild abandon of frenzied sex. Then, with a simultaneity of practised masters, the three erections were ready for the climax of the scene. Kneeling round their undulating Mistress, the men withdrew and frigged strongly. The loads of scalding opaque sperm shot out from the slits, splattering over Eliska's body until she looked as if glued with it - like a wasp in amber. Eliska spread the lumps of heavy liquid over her entire torso and then masturbated violently before them as if her life depended on the magic energy of her orgasm. Slowly the group subsided into the sheets.

A short while later Ladislav tugged on a bell rope at the head of the bed which brought to their side a handsome, middle-aged woman clad only in a short skirt. Carefully she wiped down Eliska's breasts and belly, passing a lace cloth over the cunt, pubic mound and inner thighs; then she bent over, her fine dugs swinging above the bodies, to clean off the liquids from each man's dwindling erection. As if this was insufficient for her Mistress and Masters, the woman licked each of the four sexes until the last trace of sperm had been cleared. She then covered the bodies with fresh sheets and left them to their rest.

"That is the senior bedchamber overseer, Bojena," Radka whispered to me, "a famous whore who rules her domain and her underlings with ferocity. She fucks with Jakub when not on duty here. A true bitch! Beware of her, sir! She reports all to the Great Whore."

With that I returned to my room, bewildered and yet thankful to Radka for having shown me the depths to which this hostess of mine is capable of descending. I decided in the future not to agree to any further clandestine pilgrimages of this sort. These orgies of self-gratification among my hosts, although they are amazing to watch, are not my business, and I am taking risks that I should rather not run.

I might mention that I offered a Venetian ducat to the old

Radka for her pains, informing her of my decision, but she refused it haughtily. "Pieces of silver lost a man once, my noble lord," she announced with biblical simplicity. "Let us rely on revenge."

The next day I was entertained to a festive supper of goose, dumplings, cabbage and apple sauce, which you know I relish, and for once I enjoyed the conversation which, for a change, did not include the treatment of serfs and slaves but rather dealt with the invention of Gutenberg whereby characters and letters are now printed with ink. And, as with Radka, there was talk about the great voyages of the Empire's captains and the discovery of the New World. We avoided all mention of Luther and the Speyer Decree of Toleration; I am very prudent now. Evidently my hosts are aware that the end of my mission draws close and they wonder what will be the result of my reports to Nuremberg. If they only knew of the contents of my letters to you, Nephew!

Another thing: the goat cheese here is admirable and I intend before my departure to see it made down in Zatoransky. I wish you could taste it.

It is Ascension Day and beautiful weather for once. Everyone seems content in the castle - except no doubt Maryska in her cell, Ottla who awaits her piercing, ringing and flagellation, and the lovely lesbian nun, Zdenka, who also is under preparation for a full session of cleansing.

During Mass, Brother Ignatius seemed highly agitated for some reason; is it because of the revolts that seem to be brewing, or his customary hatred of Eliska or is it something else? I shall tell you more later, for indeed it is something else... And something very serious, something intimately connected with his meek compliance before the wiles of our old Radka.

May your studies advance with success,
Huldrych

Good news! Eliska has agreed to let Tereza go with Hans. I offered to pay for her. "She's not worth a Venetian ducat!" she said. "Tell your man to ride her with a sharp spur and give her the whip twice a week." I ask you! Hans couldn't wield a whip if he tried!

Letter the twentieth

Before I recount the frightening new developments that have come to complicate my life and which the old Radka imparted to me, you should know about some of Ladislav's remarks. I had rather reluctantly and unwisely agreed to his accompanying me and Hans, instead of the surly guard, on one of my visits to Beremec where another minor convent is situated and where I could complete my land and serf survey.

Among his stories, which I admit are fascinating, he said that the local sects of the Flagellants, now forbidden but of which he naturally, if secretly, approves, held Venus, the goddess of spiritual and sexual love, to be their goddess.

If this is true, it is no wonder they have been pursued as heretics and burnt alive! Further, he recounted that some defrocked priest from Wallachia beyond the Danube was spreading the rumour that St. Ann's rich aunt, St. Elizabeth, was made pregnant by John the Baptist! How such dreadful tales get about is totally beyond me, but they demonstrate the state of credulity rife in these parts. How far Nuremberg, Dürer, the Court and you seem to be from me...

As we rode through the fine forests of evergreens and aspens, he repeated the fact that over a third of all the lands is owned by the Church and that it, as well as the nobility, had the right to arrogate village and seigneurial cases to be tried in their own courts. This is, of course, irregular - just as irregular as the Gräfin Eliska judging and sentencing females in her castle. What is frightful is the persistent use of the *Ex abrupto* procedures by the Church, and incidentally by the Bishop here, whereby suspects can be tortured and whipped before being read the indictment.

Even the Margravine, Ladislav protested, does not go this far in her dealings with female serfs, servants and wayward whores. Every woman is told beforehand why she is to be stripped and flagellated. Cold comfort, I thought to myself. Cold comfort for the poor girls writhing and screaming in chains below.

He firmly contends that we are now entering what he terms the Age of the Spirit, the very threshold of the Last Judgement.

If only he could have read my thoughts, Nephew! For Zatoransky, with its castle and such miserable, cruel places as this Beremec would certainly not survive that Judgement. To make conversation, I informed him that the Spaniards who now rule the earth consider their venture into the New World as the Last Crusade and that they have been chosen to bring this Last Age he mentioned to fruition prior to the ending of the world; Columbus himself, I hinted, was considered to be a Joachimite messiah, seeking to purify the Church as a leader of the Crusade, yet employed by Their Most Catholic Majesties.

We duly arrived at the grim convent of St. Agatha; its sole enlivening feature were the fresh lilies of the valley of our new month of May growing in the inner court. Here I was able to consult the copy of the census of all households in the area, including the muster rolls of local men available for the wars; Eliska retains the original but never told me so!

Again the counting of females is more difficult since so many are beggars, destitute vagrants or whores, apart from the few living in homes as wives, offspring or elders.

The mention of females prompts me to repeat what I learnt anew at this convent - it was a chilling confirmation. Apparently several young nuns have, under Eliska's dictates, been handed over to the castle for the usual 'cleansing' for misconduct - which, of course, implies sentencing, flesh-piercing and ringing and whipping. Then I was shown, with Ladislav in close attendance, how these inmates are treated on their return as an example to others.

The old Mother Superior took us to a small court, surrounded by arched walks; in the centre stood a massive, much-worn wooden post.

"On the return of a culprit from the castle," she explained in the most casual manner possible, "I have her scourged again before my assembled Sisters. As the body-rings are always retained by the castle, I dispense with them, my noble lords, and merely have a stout nail driven through the hole in the hardened nipple and thus fasten the sinner's breasts to each side of the stake, the wrists locked to the nape of the neck. It provides a convenient and highly educative posture and the buttocks can be scourged at leisure. I find it has an admirable effect on my women, as well as on the delinquent herself."

I was astounded but even more so when the old Superior added: "It was the idea of our gracious Margravine Eliska Helena, whom may God bless" - we duly crossed ourselves - "for taking such care of women in her realm. I am sure your noble lordships approve also of our simple methods. I wish to retain your lordships to a simple meal - we are a poor and needy establishment - after which, if you so desire, I can arrange to have a young Sister of ours stripped, nailed and flogged. I have one in the cells at this moment, as it happens."

I politely declined both invitations. Ladislav, on the other hand, showed distinct interest and began questioning the old witch about the type of scourge used, the number of lashes, whether the victims were gagged, blindfolded and so on. Before I could put a stop to this. the Lady made it clear that the unfortunate Sister in question had been pierced and that it was no trouble whatsoever, if her Lordships would stay. Finally, controlling Ladislav with a hand on his sleeve, we took our leave, receiving a fulsome blessing at the porch.

During our return ride, while fording a stream, I noticed more of these threatening bands of ruffians, beggars and idle serfs - what your Luther, Nephew (I say 'your' only to tease you again) calls the 'murdering hordes'; among them, to my consternation, were heavily armed lansquenets, some sporting the Imperial eagle, who probably have never been paid and now roam the countryside for booty, food and women.

It is truly strange to think of rebellion against authority here among these lovely orchards, pine forests and pear blossom. The Gräfin does not yet seem aware of any danger. In this so-called Garden of Eden of Eliska's, no one seems worried, least of all Ladislav who continues to annoy me with his regrets at not having witnessed the proffered flagellation at the gloomy nunnery.

My thoughts are often black here, and when crossing the dismal, clogged-up moat round the castle, I had to look down in case there should appear a green and slimy face of some woeful victim floating there.

On arrival back I found flags and pennants flying to greet

presumably the month of May rather than me. In the midst flapped the great silver E for Eliska. I gave Hans orders to start preparing for our departure the following week. I agreed that Tereza should ride with him astraddle and not side-saddle; we would look for a donkey or a mule for her once out of Bohemia. I do not wish to crave favours of the Margravine, having already achieved my ends regarding Tereza herself.

As I dismounted and entrusted my faithful Zenon to Hans, I was met by Brother Ignatius. I could have fared better without this, particularly when I learned what he had to say.

"My noble, esteemed Lord, a word, I pray."

We walked to the garden. "I learn, sir," he said, "that a certain noble officer of the Imperial lansquenets - possibly a Lutheran - is stirring up revolt near the town. But above all," and here he drew close to me so that I could share his secret and his foul breath, for his teeth are badly decayed, "it seems he is claiming some female or other held prisoner here."

Maryska's soldier! My heart missed a beat and I saw trouble looming. And I hate trouble, as you know.

"The man has fought on the side of John of Wartemburg, sir, against our Zdenek of Rozmital, our supreme burgrave, to whom our sinful Gräfin - may God soak her soul in pitch! - owes allegiance."

I had to try to understand what this implied. First, here was Eliska's own private confessor, a man who had the effrontery to curse his Mistress before God. Then, the man was citing the Wartemburg prince, allied closely to the Hussite movement in Prague and here and therefore against Rome. I decided to abridge the discussion.

"We shall discuss this later, Brother," I declared and went in to prepare for supper. All the same, these few words obviously had a sequel. I had misgivings over involvement.

I decided to raise the matter at table, Nephew. Eliska looked more seductive, more lovely than ever, almost regal, wearing a neck-band of precious stones set in black velvet that displayed her fine throat to advantage. What a strange, beautiful creature she is indeed, her proud breasts powdered white with the nipples deeply rouged with some pigment. When I mentioned the

Wartemburgs, she merely brushed off my remarks with a superb gesture of a jewelled hand - that hand that wielded the whip so effectively! No one seemed to have the slightest notion of the outside world: the French duplicity, the English leanings towards a breach with Rome, the rapid spread of the thinking of Luther who was now hidden safely in the Wartburg.

Recalling the bands of ruffians I had seen with Ladislav, I mentioned that the Bishop of Bamberg, your beautiful Bamberg, Nephew, confronted with huge peasant disquiet, had agreed to the peasants' terms. Evidently they could not digest this.

It was Eliska, naturally, who replied, pausing over her pottage.

"Graf von Mechtingen", she narrowed her lovely eyes, "you may not agree with everything you see here nor with everything I do, but I envisage no change. I am aware that reform abounds in your parts of the Empire, including cowardly lip-service to the grotesque heresy of the creature Luther and his supporters. For my part I find it difficult to choose between him and the Turk."

I nearly choked and was excused a reply to her sinister jest by the arrival of a huge carp dressed with leeks, brought in, as usual, by two attractive half-naked maidens. Now, as you know, carp is among my favorite dishes; I just prayed that it had not come out of the dreaded moat!

Eliska went on, once served. "I rule here, my noble lord, as I am destined to rule. If I have to double" (she meant, of course, fivefold) "tithes, taxes and enforced labour, keeping my serfs bent to the earth and putting lazy whores to the whip to purify my lands, what happens in your Gotha or elsewhere does not concern us here. You can say this to your masters." Then she added to my surprise: 'Lex dura sed lex.'

Well, as you know, I have problems with her laws but kept my mouth shut. We then discussed how best to fish carp from the depths. Just as well, for I was in deep waters...

I retired to bed beneath a sinking moon which is never a commendable sign in the cosmos according to you dear mother. And, alas, she would have been right, for events followed all too quickly. I shall write again tomorrow if I have the time, for you must know all, however distressing.

Do not omit to burn these letters. They are only for your education, to understand this evil world.

Huldrych

Letter the twenty-first

As I expected, Brother Ignatius caught up with me the next day near the stables while I was on my way to inspect Zenon's newly-shed hooves with the blacksmith and ensure that Hans had started to give her oats for the long ride home.

In his scapula and hood, the man gave me alarming news.

"A general revolt is brewing, my dear lord. Like beer. I tell you this because Radka and I trust you although you are closely linked to the satanic woman and, in a manner of speaking, are cautioning with your august presence her devilish sessions below. But we are aware of the delicate position the monster places you - like ourselves."

The veiled threat disturbed me. I therefore pressed him to tell me what was on his mind.

"You should fight against the wiles of this werewolf and her Beelzebub lovers. Beware!"

Reluctant to be singled out in this way, I reminded him that it was he who heard the avowals of the Gräfin in the privacy of the confessional; it was he who blessed the instruments of flagellation prior to the scourging of a naked - and probably innocent - girl in the dungeons. And I added, astutely I thought, that it was none other than his Radka who was charged with tending to the victims after sex-torture and whipping.

"True, my lord. But we are obliged to officiate, just as you are obliged to attend the sessions below. But I know you will honour my trust." He held my sleeve to say: "Radka and I have decided to liberate this girl in the cells before it is too late."

"Too late for what? They are not going to whip her to death, as far as I am aware."

"True, my lord," he repeated. "They never flagellate beyond a certain point and she is robust even if she is now completely in their power. I have seen so many females put to the whip that I cannot count them, but they almost all survive - only one or two to my knowledge were flogged to death, and that for very special reasons. But this one we have decided to save anyway."

"For her sake or on behalf of someone else?" I asked pointedly.

111

"Both, my gracious lord," came the frank response. "She has a lover who has vowed to save her before she is thrown into the brothels. He is prepared to commit the greatest crime of all - to attack the castle with a band of serfs he has gathered over the last weeks. The castle will be sacked. We shall be massacred. Including you noble self, of that there is little doubt."

"It cannot come to that!"

"You think not, dear lord? Then you have not witnessed the revolts here three years ago when we lost our noble Margrave who was stern but just, human and God-fearing. Now with this black angel from Hell with her Lucifers..."

I drew him further into the shelter of the stables. "What do you intend, Brother?"

"Our plan is simple. Radka has the keys to the cells. While the bailiffs are at their supper and the household at Vespers, which I shall prolong as best I can, Radka will release her, clothe her in my second cassock and lead her out."

"To where?"

"To her lansquenet, sir. He awaits his woman near the moat."

Suddenly all became clear to me. The only item missing was the price the lansquenet must have promised to the two accomplices. I did not raise the matter since the answer, if not the amount, was obvious in Brother Ignatius' eyes.

"And your alibi?" I asked. "How will you and your lady escape detection?"

"With your august permission, I shall be with you immediately after Vespers, walking in the shrubbery, taking the night air. God will protect Radka. She will never be suspected."

"And the bailiffs?"

"At supper, my lord."

"And Sebastian?"

"He will be busy with a vagrant whore called Vasskia from somewhere in the east, who has been found in the town. She is to receive thirty-two lashes, impaled, by express order of the Margravine. This will take time, my lord."

I then asked him what role I could possibly play in this dangerous scheme.

"You, with your position and influence, can calm the Gräfin.

Considering the revolt that threatens, you can persuade her to forget the incident."

Nephew, I agreed. Why, I really do not know, but I agreed. The thought of Maryska in chains, the courage of these old people in the face of the indomitable Eliska and the determined love shown by the lansquenet, all made me think I could, with my rank and power of persuasion, convince the awesome Margravine. The least I could do was to try.

Brother Ignatius looked at me as if I were a saint descended on earth again. For the first time he smiled, revealing his rotten teeth. "Thank you, my dear lord." And he kissed my hand. "Radka thanks you. We all thank you. Maryska too."

Going back to my chamber, feeling holy, I wondered at myself. Of course, the whole stratagem fell apart almost from the start. And for two reasons that were simultaneous. I shall try to outline them both for you. It was because of these rather than owing to my pusillanimity that I came out unscathed. I shall tell you more tomorrow, for it is worth the recounting.

I wish I were in Tübingen to discuss Desiderius Erasmus with you. Meanwhile, pray for me, my boy, although by the time you receive this letter, I shall either be dead or a hero. Or both.

Your loving uncle, Huldrych

What happened is this, as far as I can gather. Radka went to the cell, opened the gate, released Maryska, removed her blindfold, comforting her with the voice the girl knew so well and led her into the passage and finally to the threshold leading to the vault. After taking some steps, Maryska stopped, despite Radka's urgings that her man was waiting for her.

But, bewildered by the candles and the flickering of the brazier fires beyond in the courtyard, petrified by the heavy cassock offered to her, the poor girl refused to move a step further into a foreign world with which she had now no affinity. Some strange loyalty had been beaten and tortured into her; her world was the cell, the chains, darkness, the nightly hiss of the whip across her flesh and repeated ejaculations into her body as the men bored into her. Every waking moment of her recent existence was conditioned now by the relentless use made of her nude body. She had been broken, she had relinquished her will and become a docile sex slave, chained to serve.

Outside lay forced labour, the brothels, misery; within these stone walls she was fed, sheltered and even cared for by Radka's administrations. She was conscious of the pain as she was lashed but it was mixed with strange pleasures. Moreover, she was allowed to orgasm freely many times a night, even during the long sessions of sex torture in the dungeon. She had been transformed into a slave by her Mistress to whom she was now inescapably bound in a limbo of sexual lust that took on ever-changing patterns as she was helplessly used in a delirium of sex, sweat, sperm and perfumes.

This seemed to be the first reason why the plan failed. Maryska was incapable of liberating herself. Without voicing it, she had become a consenting participant.

The second cause of the miscarriage was fortuitous to say the least, but contributed directly to the crisis. It was Ignatius who told me how their luck had veered.

Apparently during the service in the chapel, a young scullery maid, who had been in slavery for only a few days, working among the slops and the pigsty, had refused to perform certain duties ordered by the overseer in charge. The girl had become involved in a fight. She was immediately handed over to Bojena, chief of the bedchamber, who happened to be in the area when the incident took place.

From where I stood in the garden alone, for Ignatius had left me in haste, I saw the girl, screaming, struggling and kicking, being hauled from the dunghill into the courtyard and forced forward by the bailiffs towards the fatal vault. She could not have been more than seventeen, well-built to judge from the flailing legs throwing her smock aside; a solid creature and very attractive as such serfs can be, with pale features and a freckled complexion under a red mop of cropped hair; her cheeks and arms were covered with light, auburn down.

She was being dragged across the cobbled yard in the light of the braziers by the two bailiffs, disturbed from their supper, and it took both of them, together with the brawny Bojena, to subdue her as she fought like a wild animal. She tore at the bailiffs' cowls and doublets, yelling curses and blasphemies, her eyes blazing with fury.

It was obvious to me that the girl was going to be punished in the most terrible manner for her disobedience and resistance. I could almost hear the plaited leather whips lashing her. As the vixen was lugged forward, a small crowd gathered to watch, while faces appeared out of the upper casements, although it is a common spectacle to see a slave taken to the vault, usually for flagellation. But contrary to the usual female docility, here I was witnessing a fierce crazed creature bent on selling herself dearly.

Poor deluded wench!

Finally they were able to rush her down the steps of the vault and I followed out of mere interest, not knowing if Radka's scheme was still valid. I was in time to see the girl being stretched in fetters between the same set of columns that had held Marja weeks before. The legs thrashed and struggled in every direction until she was spread and bound, her limbs drawn tight by the two men hauling on the chains with such a force that it seemed to dislocate the four joints. The body became completely rigid in bondage.

Bohumil then slashed open the girl's smock from armpit to

hem, using the trencher with which evidently he had been cutting up his meal when interrupted. He ripped the rough sacking from the body, swearing at the victim, until he had her totally denuded.

What we had before us was one of the most erotic sights imaginable of the naked feminine physique. I had become so accustomed to docile, almost consenting, female bodies, that this wild demonstration of sheer nudity seemed out of keeping in the confines of Zatoransky. These protestations, I knew, she would have to pay for.

How can I describe to you, Nephew, this nude in bondage? Her limbs were slim but muscular as they strained outwards to the shackles, the tendons taut and quivering from the shock of the sudden extension. The pubic mound with its triangle of bright fair hair, wet and matted from the sweat that ran down the body, protruded superbly above the pouting umber labia that closed tight over the young cunt and clitoris; above, the belly curved upwards from the bulge of the genitals and the sharp points of the hip-bones to the arched limits of the ribcage in a sweep of white flesh, interrupted only by the dark deeply-sunk navel.

The breasts were by no means large compared with Maryska's, but knowing my hosts and particularly Milan with his fixation, there was ample flesh hanging there to be tortured and beaten to their satisfaction. With the traction of the arms, the nipples pointed upwards as if begging for the grip and twist of iron tongs and piercing instruments, while in the drenched armpits a pleasant crop of fair hair stood out invitingly.

But it was the nature of her nipples that was special, particularly in such a young female: the stiff teats had risen upon enormously swollen purple areolae, providing a second contour to the volume of the breasts. I hardly dared to think of Milan again; these nipples were made for him and his lust. How long would it be before he would be left alone for an hour with his canes and instruments before this spread beauty?

The girl had sweated profusely in the fury of her combat with her jailors, which only accentuated the symmetry and gleam of the curving flesh and muscles. To the rear, the small buttocks were clenched tight below the twin dimples on either side of the spine.

While the obscenities began to fade under the force of the spreading, the girl was still able to spit at Bojena. With that, the woman gripped the girl's upturned freckled nose, causing the neck tendons to tighten and the veins to distend, until, gasping for air, she opened her mouth wide. Bojena crammed into the gullet a ball of material torn from the girl's smock and the voice was stilled.

Then she was ready. Ready for the inevitable scourge.

Bohumil brought down his six-thonged whip over the slender thighs and cunt with full-blooded force. I do not think Maryska ever received a stroke as brutal as this. The girl heaved herself up by the wrist-chains and fell back. It took some ten well-placed lashes to turn the flesh from the thorax to the thighs to bright crimson. Then Jakub began to flog the buttocks with equal ferocity, The thud and slap of the thongs echoed through the vault while Bojena, nodding her head at each stroke, urged the men to flog harder. This they did, from breasts to the knees, from the shoulder-blades to the fat of the rear thighs, the rump receiving most of the punishment and, on Bohumil's side, the belly and breasts.

Then, in turn, the flagellators whipped upwards between the thighs, lash after lash, until the whips, wet with the girl's sweat and fluids, had made the cunt swell visibly. The nude must have received some thirty or forty lashes before her head dropped and she surrendered to her masters, scourged finally into submission.

It was much later, while talking to Milan - who naturally had the girl to himself nightly for breast whipping and a little breast torture - that I learned this was the first time the girl had been stripped naked and flagellated. And certainly not the last! Milan also confided to me that Eliska had agreed to his using the breast-gallows - where I had seen Maryska's breasts throttled and cropped with Milan's riding whip some nights before. Apparently he was given permission to whip the girl's breasts, amuse himself with a pair of iron tongs on her nipples, and even lead her round the cellars and into the chapel for penance tied by the roots of the breasts and laid naked over the altar steps. Eliska, he claimed, enjoyed watching his performances to such a degree that this particular slave was allowed into the bedchamber to be displayed, scourged and used mercilessly between the bedposts. Milan also admitted that she was by far the best flesh he had had the advantage of whipping for weeks and that also she now fucked well.

It is, of course, very rare that a kitchen scullion gains such a privilege. It seems that she became docile after three nights of the whip and is now kept naked with a riding crop tied round her neck temporarily in a special cell near the dungeon for immediate use. The bailiffs, however, are not permitted to use her in any way; and so far she has not encountered Sebastian.

So much for a young girl who becomes involved in fight near the dung heap!

This is merely to explain the second cause of the failure to liberate Maryska. For, by sheer chance, the need to whip the young scullion slave brought the bailiffs from their supper to the very scene of the abortive escape. It was Bojena's quick eye, while the girl was receiving the whip, that caught sight of Maryska's trembling body standing alone on the far threshold of the vault, for Radka had rapidly disappeared as the struggling group rushed the scullion down. Thus it was Bojena who realized the situation and raised the alarm. It was then that the whipping ceased and the bailiffs turned, amazed, to see Maryska before them, unchained.

They closed in on the numbed, paralysed nude standing where Radka had left her; staring apathetically at the scene before her and beyond, the far light of the braziers in the courtyard beckoning her to freedom, only a stone's throw away but too late.

From where I now stood on the lower steps of the vault, I was no longer looking at the gagged girl under the whip but at Maryska. She was pathetically beautiful in her panic and confusion, lost without her chains and cell; I could see her uncovered face plainly with its dark circles under the eyes bearing witness to the fatigue and endless sufferings, tortures, sexual ordeals and orgasms.

Within minutes the whole castle was in an uproar, roosting hens scattering, sows woken from their fat sleep and screaming shrilly among their piglets and peelings, and figures crowding the courtyard, outlined against the flaming braziers. A sudden ominous rattle of great chains rang out as the drawbridge slammed shut. It was all very appropriate as a way in which to greet the failure to free a whore from the clutches of the Margravine of Zatoransky. It was like the thud of doom.

The bailiffs flung Maryska to the steps leading to the upper regions. The scourges, still hot from flogging the young redhead, slashed over her flesh as she was bound. Jakub hooked a chain seized from a nearby column to Maryska's left nipple-ring which he tugged on mercilessly. Bohumil rapidly chained the ankles while the clitoris-ring was swiftly clipped to a further length of chain. With whips lashing her loins, she was hauled back to her cell and the iron gate crashed to as she was again locked in her natural habitat.

The chattering crowds of servants were dispersed by Bojena's shout, and as I emerged from the dreadful vault I saw flashes of lightning in the night sky, as if, like the drawbridge, they also saluted the recapture of a miserable female who had failed to free herself from Hell.

Beyond I could see Jakub dutifully mounting the main steps of the castle to report to his Mistress, Radka's Great Whore of Babylon. But Radka was nowhere to be seen, well concealed from the place of crisis, from the lightning and, more importantly perhaps, from the impending fury of Eliska's eyes. No seraphs, Nephew, were flying tonight in the tense air above Zatoransky Castle. At least I could see none.

I feel so weary, so weary,
Huldrych, with affection

Letter the twenty-third

Later in this inauspicious day, we were summoned to the dungeon once again.

The appearance of Eliska was quite startling. Milan, standing next to me, leaned over. "When she is dressed like this," he whispered, "it means deep trouble for her victim."

There was excitement hidden in his words.

Indeed she was magnificent. The tight bodice of dark carmine velvet clinging to her body enhanced the prominence of her bare breasts with their rigid nipples painted purple to the very edge of the broad areolae. The flared skirts, gashed with crimson pleats, parted as she strode in, disclosing the high riding-boots topped by the bands of thigh flesh like porcelain leading up to the rich triangle of dark pubic hair. In her grasp swung an evil looking three-thonged whip, its handle glinting with precious stones set into the worn leather haft, each jewel flashing in rhythm with the rings on the gloved fingers and the sparkle of her jangling spurs.

Her lips were thinner, more compressed than customary; the pale features seemed lit only by a fire of fury smouldering in the narrowed eyes. This fire appeared to redouble when she halted to watch her wretched, trembling victim being manhandled down the dungeon steps.

The air was charged with anticipation and menace. All talking suddenly ceased as we took our usual station behind and around Eliska, our cowls adding to the sinister sight that now met Maryska's unbound eyes. As if in a state of shock, the superbly naked girl stared at the spectacle. Down the length of the dungeon she could now take in those grim, dark appliances that her body knew well but which she had never seen - the huge crucifix, the impaling stake, the breast-gallows, the slabs, the dangling iron chains, all cast their flickering shadows on the walls in the light of the tallow candles.

Even more terrible was the figure of the woman who had total dominion over her, surrounded by the group of her insatiable lovers who attended merely to be excited by the sight of a naked body writhing beneath the scourge. Then there was this stranger, myself, whom she had seen at the moment of her arrest in the brothel and who had declined to intervene on her behalf; and who never seemed to take part in the erotic proceedings.

Behind her, twisting her arms, were the bailiffs, those ruffians who used her body unceasingly night and day. All that was missing from this hellish array was the silent flogger whose whip hand she had learnt to fear but whose penis provided her with endless pleasures.

This absence was abruptly remedied.

Summoned by Eliska through Radka - of all people! - Sebastian entered as the bailiffs thrust Maryska down the steps. Eliska drew the whipmaster to her side and seized his already erect, pulsating shaft to caress it from the purple head to the hair of the flat belly. Maryska watched the long strings of liquid extend from the eye of the penis; no doubt she experienced again the uncontrollable desire to feel it thrusting up into her...

I too looked at the immense organ and its veins standing out thick as cords. It was encircled and laced from the rim of the glans to behind the testicles with a lattice of thin leather thongs, heavily knotted down its length and around the girth. This, Milan explained to me in hushed tones, was worn for very special sexual duties in the cellar below, being particularly employed in dealing with lesbians sent for full cleansing. Although the thongs and knots were designed to increase the friction and penetration of the vagina, it also served, Milan added, to provide unexpected sensations of pleasure as the cunt became accustomed to it. (My hosts, Nephew, no longer use circumlocutions when speaking of sex and take no heed of my embarrassment.) This mixture of pain and pleasure, I recall, was also Premsyl's theory, and I think I mentioned it to you.

I understand that the thongs are worn when dealing, as I say, with condemned lesbians in order to introduce them rapidly to the proper and regular use of the vagina by males, once its soft furrows have been ploughed up by Sebastian and the lesbian well whipped to drive home the lesson.

To return to the scene, it was not difficult to see that the man had been called to the dungeon from the cellar below while well advanced in some disciplinary and sexual duties of this sort, to judge by the erection and the caked residues upon its length. Milan told me that, in fact, a young convent lesbian was in the process of being broken in, after which she would be subjected to a series of ceremonial cleansing sessions of flagellation similar to those to which Maryska had been sentenced. I found myself wondering whether this might not be the tender, nubile nun Zdenka with the shaven head whom Eliska had enjoyed with such ecstasy the other night.

We now had time to admire Maryska, unblindfolded for once; she was poignantly beautiful in her submissive posture which might well be construed as an admission of guilt by her tormentors. There was an aura of fear and fatigue about her; the eyes, after their long concealment, were drained of colour and life, underscored with deep dark circles, bearing witness to the shock of the abortive liberation that had been forced on her and to the prolonged flagellations, the incessant chaining and use made of her body to slake the sexual thirst of her overseers. Unexpectedly, her flesh now seemed pristine and almost unmarked.

A sheen of sweat, mixed with the residues of oil, shone over the thorax, seeping from the armpits and no doubt her sex was drenched as it always is when awaiting the scourge. She looked more erotic, more supple and more humiliated than ever before. Moreover, there floated from her, beside the aroma of flesh and sweat, the ever-present smell of sex tinged with the odour of sperm.

All eyes were now fixed on the two women - the omnipotent Gräfin about to avenge herself and the unmurmuring victim about to abandon herself.

I have, I think, recounted to you my tale of the terrible, ferocious wild cats that haunt the forests of Thuringia. They stand immobile when you encounter them between the trees, glaring, ready to tear out your eyes and rip you to shreds. All that lacked, in the comparison, was that the starched wings of Eliska's coif had none of those stiff flaring tufts of hair you see on the ears of the wild cats. Our lady of Zatoransky was about to lacerate her prey.

Eliska made a gesture with her whip hand, still flicking Sebastian's foreskin to and fro with the other, and several events took place. First, a number of naked or partially naked serving girls, who are nothing more than slaves, entered the dungeon by the side door. They were not, I noticed, the same as those who had serviced at the third session and the sweet lithe Ottla was unfortunately not among them. (I admit I was disappointed, Nephew, since I adored looking at her, especially while she was engaged in sex.) These were certainly not intended to be ornaments or spectators but destined to service Eliska's lovers. Each girl took up her place, as if this had been preordained, next to one of the men.

A young redhead with unbelievably white skin (a rarity here) and small hard breasts that had not yet been pierced and ringed sidled up to me. While she fumbled in the folds of my cloak, I made it clear that her determined little hands would be better placed in my own. She seemed dismayed since here she had the chance to demonstrate her sexual prowess and be promoted to serve in the bedchamber, as Ottla had been promoted. But she stood by me, hand in hand, to watch dutifully like a daughter.

Eliska dismissed the bailiffs to the head of the stairs, where they stood, arms crossed, awaiting orders and observing through the evil slits in their hoods - an unusual privilege. I also caught sight of Bojena's cropped head somewhere among the shadows of the huge dungeon and thought I discerned Brother Ignatius standing well behind Radka, who also awaited the Gräfin's commands.

The stage was thus set for the session. There was something impromptu about it; unplanned, with little privacy, somewhat unorthodox for Zatoransky; there were no silver bells, no special raiment or pretty masks, no ritual ceremony. Instead, there was merely a naked girl, trembling in chains, bowed before the smouldering eyes of her proprietor. I experienced a sharp stab of melancholic pity for Maryska, naked, docile and once again innocent and in perdition.

A further wave of the purple gloved hand set Sebastian in motion. He worked, as usual, with swift efficiency. My rough sketch attempts, Nephew, to allow you to appreciate how they tried to bend Maryska to their will and to a forced confession.

Maryska was led to a small platform. There she was again

plunged into oblivion as a strip of red velvet was tightened round the head and over the eyes. A chain was then encircled round the waist and hooked to a heavy series of iron links reaching to the beam above. This done, Sebastian abruptly thrust the girl backwards, causing her to lose her balance and hang, arched and curved like a longbow in tension. Slender chains were then hooked to the rings on the nipples, the three rings pierced through the sex-flesh and finally the neck ring. All were joined to the central ring above the belly. We watched the sex unfurl into extended triangles of dark-red flesh as it was tugged tight and upwards; the clitoris hood was uprooted and drawn out while the cones of the breasts elongated aloft until they were tautened to their utmost reach.

Sebastian completed the posture by manacling the wrists and ankles together below the slowly gyrating nude body that now formed a circle, the sinews and muscles fighting the curved stress. Meticulously, the man, obviously well accustomed to this type of torture, adjusted the minor chains to ensure that the most sensitive points were fully strained. Apart from her rapid panting, the opening and clenching of the hands and her teeth biting into the cusp of the lower lip, Maryska hardly reacted to the pain the man had induced into the body which was now readied for what was to follow.

In all I have had the misfortune to witness in this ominous, macabre castle, this bondage was the most strict and the most severe so far employed - except possibly the terrible impalement of three weeks ago. What is more disturbing is that countless females, I am told, are treated like this, merely to cleanse their bodies and souls. May God pardon these monsters, for I find it difficult to absolve them.

The man stood back to take stock of his work, curling his palm over the bulging head of his erection, spreading the sex liquids over the leather thongs down the shaft with evident lust. He seemed satisfied, to judge from the amount of sap that poured from his slit. He was in dire need of relief, as he gazed towards his Mistress.

"Is the whore wet?" she asked. Her man nodded repeatedly in dumb reply.

"Then fuck her! Fuck her with that knotted thing of yours. Get down deep into her prostituting entrails. Let us see her orgasm before you do, man! Get into her!"

Manifestly, the man required to spend urgently, for the erection appeared ready to burst the thongs that bound it. This performance, among so many other liberties the man was permitted to enjoy among the scores of females consigned to him, was a distinctive one, since it was being carried out before his Mistress and her lovers. And Sebastian was arrogant enough to know that he fucked as few men in Zatoransky fucked; if needed, he could use ten girls a night and leave them exhausted, but now I saw that he felt privileged to fuck before his Mistress prior to the session. Eliska understood her man.

"Fuck the whore with your leathers on!" she urged, as if incitement was necessary for a male whose sperm was boiling furiously within his sac. "Rape her cunt! Rip it! Fuck!"

And the man fucked the hanging girl as probably she had never been taken. He spread the tensed thighs before him, spread the chained lips further apart and bent his shaft to lie between the rigid fronds. Then he grasped the buttock flesh, sinking his nails into the skin, and thrust in until his hair was mixed with that of the girl.

Maryska heaved her whole body upwards, craning her head back as far as the throat strap allowed, and commenced to thrust against the man's loins as the knotted network round the girth of the prick ground into the wet vagina walls. The copulation, after a long moment of the girl's groans and grunts from the man, became frantic, Sebastian thumped into the cunt and remained within, as if Maryska had imprisoned him with her muscular grip. The man's thumb crushed the erect clitoris, circulating round the root and dragging the tip to its full reach. Then he commenced his most massive penetration, withdrawing the straining head to the edge of the stretched fronds, slapping it on to the pointed clitoris before submerging again into the uttermost reaches of the vagina tunnel. The rhythm accelerated with resounding slushing of the combined sex-juices as the sexes collided heavily, flesh on flesh, matted hair on matted hair, Sebastian's thonged balls slapping against the girl's wet undergrowth.

The man's head was arched backwards as he approached ecstasy, the buttocks clenched with the supreme effort to reach up into the farthest regions of the female's body. And then, as I watched, the extraordinary happened.

Eliska came over to the heaving, sweating couple and began to caress the girl's taut flesh, encouraging her man to fuck deeper.

"Get that thonged meat into her, man! Plough the whore's cunt!"

Sebastian, sweating profusely, redoubled his vicious plunging thrusts into the vagina, by now saturated and glutted with the juices surging from both organs. Eliska now let her hand, its jewelled rings of ruby and sapphire turned inwards, mould the body's tensed curves. The hand moved lasciviously, caressed, probed, as it did each time before it commenced a flagellation; it examined the various sinews, the flickering muscles in tension, the distended neck, the pectorals, deltoids and biceps stretched by the breasts and the downward tug of the arms, the hard abdomen muscles and the compact gluteal clench of the buttocks.

Eliska passed her fingers along the taut adductor muscles distended on the inside of the thighs, palpating their rigidity and following them up to the genital gash. Here she kneaded and twisted such flaccid flesh as the powerful elongation of the chains allowed to remain loose. Then, leaning over towards where Sebastian's penis was thudding into the cunt, she gripped the quivering clitoris.

"You like it, don't you, whore? Speak!"

Maryska's hoarse, convulsed reply filled the cellar. "Yes, yes, yes, fuck me!" she cried. "I need hot prick up my cunt! Deeper! Faster! My mouth wants it!"

The girls, hard at work on their Masters, froze in their fellatio, holding the ball-sacks and the erections immobile as they heard the cry. Eliska was equal to the situation. Realizing the state of the girl, she thrust her pelvis and crotch into Maryska's face.

"Suck, whore! Lick it! Get that whore's tongue of yours in. Suck the lips, suck the folds and the hair... Now the clit! Hold it like that - between the teeth!"

It was Maryska who orgasmed first with a cry of release. Then the man spent in a series of a dozen spasms of scalding sperm. It was too much for Eliska; she grabbed the breast chains, splaying her thighs out further and came over the girl's face, swearing at the whore's lust. Her orgasm rippled from spasm to spasm until she was fully spent, then she smoothed down her gown and regained her place on the rostrum.

"This lecherous harlot needs the severest correction possible. The body is still replete with the foulest of lusts which evidently have not been beaten out of her. I shall interrogate her where she hangs." Then she turned to Sebastian, whose declining penis was thick with stiffening semen and trailing liquids.

"Stand aside, man, and wipe the whore's foul spume off your prick. You have had your compensation. Now get back to the cellar and see to it that the lesbian down there is correctly whipped, front and back."

Sebastian, perfectly content with his public performance and the superb orgasm he had waited for so patiently, began to leave to resume his work on the crucified nun. It was again to the nun that Eliska referred when she added:

"If she is difficult, recalcitrant or wilful, as lesbians so often are, I have no objection to your treating her to an initial session of sex-torture; the nipples and clitoris could well do to have a twist of the tongs. And do not spare the crop over the rump! But mainly you will see to it that the lesbian bitch is fully broken in for use in all orifices and ready to carry out prolonged fellatio with energy and imagination Above all, man, make full use of your thong-strapped prick in her. I want her fully ready in time for the start of her formal flagellation sessions next week."

The Margravine paused as if mentally verifying her requirements.

During the pause, I realised that this was the first time I had heard my hostess issuing direct and detailed orders concerning a victim. She was painstaking and particularly fastidious regarding this young nun whose fate was being sealed.

"I think it would be wise,' she advised her whipmaster, "to put her to the whip each evening to toughen the flesh, which is far too tender at present. I wish it to be hardened and yet resilient. It will, as usual, be carefully explained to the slave through Radka how she should conduct herself while undergoing her preliminary stimulation under the quirt, while being chained in bondage, and while receiving the scourge. I want no stupid screaming or struggle. I demand absolute, naked submission. Is this clear?"

Sebastian bowed low. Radka had now, when she heard her name, appeared out of the gloomy background while Eliska listed her final recommendations.

"If, during her training," Eliska went on, "the female proves refractory or uncooperative, especially, since she is a lesbian, regarding fellatio and masturbation of the male, she must be flesh whipped immediately, suspended by the wrists. I leave the number of strokes and the use you make of her body entirely to you two. But on no account, as you know, do I want blood drawn or the flesh uselessly damaged."

The actors on the rostrum were enjoying listening to the orders which served to excite them further, while their serving-maids, kneeling before them, were hard at work, their mouths filled, awaiting the approaching discharge down the throat or over the face.

"I count on you, Radka, to ensure the slut is correctly initiated into the duty of cunnilingus as I require it. Clearly the slut has already had experience, but she requires detailed tuition, particularly on the tonguing and suction of the erect clitoris."

At this point a cry issued from one pair on the dais - I believe it was Ladislav and a young copper-haired girl - as the man spent over the expectant face.

Eliska paid no heed.

"Further," she pursued her train of thought, "she will need the usual instruction and disciplining to enable her, while servicing males, to swallow all promptly and with relish. I want no choking and no wanton wasting of semen, and Radka will explain that the slightest repudiation of sperm automatically leads to a chain-and-ratchet session on the leather shaft in the Red Cellar."

Again she paused for a moment.

"One last item, Radka. You will see to it that the mound is

kept perfectly shaved and, it goes without my having to stress it, that she will undergo all training and subsequent service stark naked, apart from her permanent bondage straps and, when ordered, cunt-belt, breast harnesses and blindfold. And, as usual, Radka, you will treat her welts every day so that she can be lashed viciously and regularly, according to our wishes. I think that is all. You may go now to your duties."

Eliska came across and slapped Maryska's taut belly.

"I shall call you here again when I am done with this whore. Meanwhile you can prepare the brazier, restraining chains and branding irons for midnight when she has confessed."

After this frightening set of orders, Sebastian left the dungeon to prepare for the branding and, if he found the time, to continue the breaking in of his lesbian to enable her to withstand the tortures to come. Radka, too, faded back into the shadows.

We watched the Margravine bend over Maryska's face.

"Now let us turn to this obdurate whore."

The interrogation commenced...

If I have time, I shall continue tomorrow. Give my greetings to Doctor Baldung, your good tutor. But say nothing of all this.

Huldrych

Letter the twenty-fourth

The interrogation was an interminable, dismal affair. I marvelled at the girl's tough peasant fortitude and her resolve to endure the traction of her chains and the Margravine's questioning. She proved, for once, unamenable, unmalleable and staunch. The more Eliska treated her as 'whore trash', 'sex fodder' and similar atrocities to vilify and revile her, the more stubborn she seemed to become.

Jerking the head backwards by the hair, Eliska hissed into her face menacingly in local dialect from which I could gather the gist of the interrogation.

"Listen carefully to me, wench. Only rarely do I have a guilty whore strung up naked in this manner. I do not wish to do this but your body will hang in pain until you disclose what is going on. Who are your associates? Who unlocked your chain and cell gate? Am I to believe you have allies within my castle? Impossible! But outside? Yes, outside! Speak!" Not a word came from the girl. Eliska resorted to threats.

"I'll have your sex thrashed until it's raw, and my men drip candle grease on your skin until every portion of your body is stiff with it - and then I'll have you whipped clean of every particle. I can have your nipples and your labia nailed to the great door of the castle. I can -" she hesitated, choking with vengeful anger - "I can play on your chains like a harp, strumpet, until your whole body sings out for mercy!" Her purple gloved hand strummed across the breast chains, tightening the nipples.

Maryska hung in silence. Eliska altered her voice to adopt tones of soft cajoling.

"It is sad to think that you desire to leave me, to escape from my palace, from my jewel-case of a dungeon. One only escapes from a prison and this is no prison. Let us say that you wanted to abscond, not escape, from my loving arms like a wilful child from its mother's care. I have had to have you scourged to rid your body and soul of its lusts and cure it of filthy illicit copulation. I have been kind, too. I have allowed you to be fucked and to orgasm freely. I have never imposed abstinence and you have profited from it, like the whore you are."

She stroked the girl's tear-stained cheek.

"Who is it who conspires to take your strong body away from me, from your Mistress and your Margravine?"

An atrocious silence ensued, broken only by Maryska's hoarse breathing. After what seemed to be a century, Eliska swung the body round until the muscular splayed thighs faced her. Glutinous lumps of sperm oozed from the distended oval as the Gräfin, losing her feigned equanimity, suddenly jabbed the jewelled haft of her whip into the orifice; the lunge rammed in deep until the glove was grinding the ruby and sapphire rings into the delicate flesh. Maryska leapt bodily in her chains; her mouth gaped wide with a ghastly groan. Her muscles quivered as if moles were at work beneath the skin.

"Oh, Mistress, sweet, gracious Mistress, spare me!" came the faraway voice. "I want to stay with you forever. I mean no harm."

Exasperated, the Gräfin churned the whip within the vagina.

"Then let us start again, whore. What is behind this scheme of yours?"

At this point, Milan came up to me, thrusting my little red-head roughly aside. His voice was little more than a murmur.

"My lord, this business is going to last a long moment and the obstinate whore does not seem ready to confess. Whatever happens, my lord, she will be condemned in due course, particularly if the Margravine feels she has lost face. To spare ourselves more of this, which is hardly voluptuous, I suggest we take a stroll through the cellars. If we are fortunate, there may be something there to interest you. The young lesbian nun, for example."

I would have far rather enjoyed a walk through the gardens but, knowing Maryska's whole sorry story, I was relieved to absent myself from a scene which daunted my soul.

Quietly, I followed my young hooded host out of the stifling heat and removed my horrible cowl, leaving Eliska with her prisoner.

After treading carefully by the light of a dim candle down the curved stairway of cool granite, we came to a heavy studded door, precisely adjacent to the aperture through which Radka a week ago had shown me Maryska being impaled in the Red Cellar.

Amazingly, we found the great door ajar; evidently Sebastian was occupied with his braziers, after his urgent summons to wait upon his Mistress above. For Milan, smiling with a look of connivance, this was a gift of pure chance. He is, Nephew, the sort of individual on whom chance always smiles, contrary to me!

This was, of course, the grim, so-called Red Cellar to which, for some occult reason, Eliska denies her lovers entry. The darker area surrounded a pool of light thrown by two miserable tallow candles set in sconces on columns. Beneath the chain and pulley that had suspended Maryska, stood the impaling penis bolted to its block. To the left reared a huge rough timber cross, similar to that in the dungeon. Upon it, stretched wide, her wrists and ankles attached with broad leather straps nailed into the wood, hung a naked girl.

The sex, head and armpits had been shaved, the orthodoxy of Zatoransky castle allowing a lesbian no hair. The female seemed to have fainted, for she hung inert, the head lolling backwards between the arms of the crucifix.

I have to confess, Nephew, that the nude was certainly one of the most erotic sights I had yet seen. The slender limbs, taut with the elongated sinews like ropes, belied all the rest of the body which was comparatively heavily fleshed; the upper thighs and the crushed buttocks, swelling on either side, were particularly rich, as was the belly. Despite the strain through the muscles joining the biceps to the breasts, the latter seemed disproportionately large with substantial tips rising out of capacious purple areolae, forming strong cones on the partly flattened masses. An astonishing sight.

It was the sex that attracted my attention. It had been scrupulously shaved, which confirmed to all that the girl was a condemned lesbian. Round the waist, buried deep in the lavish flesh just above the pronounced pelvic bones, ran a thin thong of red leather, strapped tightly, from which descended from each extremity a couple of slim braided strips of red leather.

Each strip bit cruelly into the twin lips on each side of the dark oval entry, to disappear between the thighs and so up to rejoin the belt above the compressed rump to the rear. In this way, the sex was prized open before us.

I thought the girl was Zdenka, but I was uncertain. She had been severely flagellated. I found it hard to understand how a girl of this age, even if a guilty nun, could have been consigned by Eliska to be scourged so brutally. But no doubt she had her reasons. It was patent that the girl had been taken to the limit of what her flesh could tolerate. She was, as they put it, being broken in.

We approached the nude. Milan, the expert, pointed out that, indeed, both the inner and outer labia were wrenched outwards, cleaving the cunt and held in place by a series of small barbs or spikes fixed into the braided thongs and which had buried their minute prongs into the inflamed leaves of sex-flesh. Above it, the girl's clitoris stood out of the protective hood, offering itself for attention.

The sight excited Milan. He laid the ball of his thumb over the pale tip of sensitive flesh, circling, crushing and embellishing it skilfully, at which the naked body suddenly jerked. The pink stub rose into a full, trembling erection as Milan continued to maul it, but only a sigh issued from the nude with a quickening of the breathing as the thorax contracted.

The stimulation, however, produced an unexpected result. As if it had been safeguarded by the inner clenching muscles of the vagina, a thick grey sludge surged out from the oval to drip and fall to the flagstones, while sex spume seeped down the inner flanks of the thighs, seeming to prove that the girl had also orgasmed.

"To judge by the quality, sir, I would say that our dear whipmaster has been up there," was Milan's sole comment. "Let us trust that the slut spent more than once."

"And her crime?" I ventured, noticing, at the same time, that his erection had raised the cloth of his cloak. "To be flogged, taken and made to orgasm in this terrible posture?"

"But surely you see, sir!" He pointed to the cleanly shaved crotch. "Another dirty, obscene, lesbian nun. Most certainly from St. Barbara's. And a handsome one at that. She is being broken in for sexual service as a slave. Surely you heard the gracious

Margravine's directions concerning her a moment ago. Hereafter she will be used ten times a night in the three entries. Personally, sir, as long as a girl has fine plump breasts that respond readily to the braided flogging crop, I do not care whether she is a whore, a serf or a lesbian. All I want, my lord - and forgive me for my crudity - is a pair of rich breasts to beat until the female is begging to be fucked, taken between the buttocks or opens up her lips for me. You lash their breasts sufficiently and they are yours, in any way you desire. Anything to spare the breasts rebounding under the crop. This one," he squeezed the girl's nipples and dragged them outwards, "will be no exception. If all goes well, my lord, and if Eliska permits it, I shall have endless nights with this slut in the great bedchamber with a riding crop. If I may confide in you, my most enjoyable moment is to have such a female to myself in the whipping chamber - the same as is used and will used be used later tonight for the branding - and to flagellate the breasts until she will give you anything." He paused a moment as if about to divulge a secret. "But the Margravine's demands must be satisfied above all. She, as you heard, has ordered that this female, once broken, serve in the bedchamber, and this, of course, is a supreme honour for the girl. The Margravine delights in a fresh new female, particularly a young lesbian who has been broken in to serve both men and women."

I nodded, for indeed this was the victim in question. I felt distraught on her account. Without a trace of shame, Milan brought out his pounding shaft before me and proceeded to anoint it with the copious secretions flowing from the slit.

"I will not deny my interest in the body, my lord," he remarked, smoothing the belly and running his finger round the whorl of the crucified girl's navel. "I think you are aware of my predilection for breasts like this. In a manner of speaking, I rather envy this dumb servant of ours sometimes. I would relish an hour or two down here with this slut. But Eliska is obstinate about this cellar, insisting it remain Sebastian's own. Naturally the man has to have his own enjoyments, as we have ours."

He then invited me to take stock of the chamber, eagerly describing the racks of whips, scourges and riding crops, the stout wooden leather-bound penises, leather masks and strange nail-studded cache-sexes. He spent a long moment admiring the whipping pillars, the stone benches with their bondage rings and the multitude of chains hanging from the beams. I did not, I assure you, Nephew, mention that I had seen the impaling monster on the block in action. He would have been consumed with envy.

I glanced surreptitiously at his erection. "You are obviously in great need of relief, my lord," I muttered, expressing genuine concern. "Why do you not make use of this lovely crucified body before we mount? The young lady, I am sure, would be honoured beyond words."

Milan smiled. "No, to use her now would never do. We must rejoin the group before the Margravine notices my absence."

As we left the chamber, ensuring the door was ajar as before, Milan said: "It would be appropriate, sir, if you were not to mention this visit." His plea was similar to that of a lad who envisages trouble.

I assured him of my ability to keep a secret and mused again at the power this terrible woman wielded even over her lovers. As we climbed the steps, leaving the crucified one to suffer her forthcoming buttock whipping and subsequent tuition, Milan mentioned the word '*cistici*', which they employ to mean 'cleansing'.

"If our province is to be cleansed, sir, then every living lesbian must be rooted out and put to the whip and, if recalcitrant, submit themselves to a certain degree of sex-torture and serve as sex slaves until this curse is eliminated. Lesbians deny us access to their bodies and therefore must be whipped to be made available for normal use."

I risked a comment. "I understand that the gracious Gräfin herself is not averse of enjoying such creatures."

Milan stared at me in astonishment. "Perhaps, but then the Margravine of Zatoransky is above our local laws and customs!"

With that, we donned the detestable cowls and stole quietly into the dungeon. Both Ladislav and Premsyl were making full use of the serving-girls kneeling before them, and Maryska had been released - no doubt by Sebastian, recalled momentarily to the dungeon. She was kneeling submissively before her resentful owner.

Thrusting his serving-maid aside, Ladislav came forward with parchments in his hand.

Pray for your weary uncle, Nephew.

Huldrych.

Letter the twenty-fifth

The Margravine's voice made me turn cold.

"Read the sentence!"

As a month ago, it was Ladislav who unrolled the parchment spelling out Maryska's doom. It began with the usual pompous preamble which irked me and which, I noted, did not make any reference to the Emperor - not that His Majesty would have wished to be included in such a scurrilous paper. Everyone gazed at the wretched Maryska while I, for my part, strove to understand the clauses. In case your legal mind is interested, Nephew, they went something like this:

Exordium:

In the name of the gracious and bountiful Eliska Helena, Margravine of Zatoransky and hereditary territories, we declare this illicit whore guilty of attempted escape from due justice and therefore condemn her body to further cleansing.

Expositio:

Item the first: At the stroke of midnight on this same day by the castle chapel bell, the whore shall, *ex curia* and at the hand of the Peitschmeister, be put to the scourge naked in the preparation cell to ready the buttock flesh;

Item the second: The whore shall be taken to the branding chamber, chained, and marked with the heated irons on both buttocks;

Item the third: Thereafter, the whore shall be conducted by the bailiffs into the town and there be chained beneath the sign of the phallus before our brothel which she profaned in perpetrating her initial crime, and there be exposed naked before the populace for vilification;

Item the fourth: Thereafter, the whore shall be conducted to the dungeon, suspended, and flagellated by the hand of her Mistress and proprietor, the gracious Margravine.

Hardly able to believe my ears, I looked over at Eliska to gauge her attitude. Her anger dissipated, she was absently admiring her sapphire rings and looking calmly down at Maryska motionless on her knees before her. Ladislav continued in a colourless voice:

Item the fifth: Thereafter, the whore shall be conducted back to the brothel where she shall thenceforward be offered for prostitution, chained by the neck;

Item the sixth: The Chief Bailiff shall issue orders to the Brothel Master to ensure the closest supervision of the whore at all times, permitting absence from the pallet or palliasse of work solely at feeding and ablution times;

Item the seventh: The Chief Bailiff or his assistant shall ensure that the whore is put to the whip naked in the brothel every Sunday, on Feast days and other rest days. The number of strokes is left to the discretion of the Bailiffs, on the basis of conduct and fornication reports from the Brothel Master or Mistress.

By order of the Margravine. May God cleanse her realm - Excudit.

There followed a series of other flourishes - among which, stipulations regarding the monk's prior sanctifying of the instruments and their purification after use, & cetera, after which Ladislav rolled up the parchments with their weighty seal.

Preening themselves like cockerels at the mention of their roles, the two bailiffs seized Maryska brutally and led her out. In a hubbub of conversation, the group went up for supper.

You must bear with me, for I have little time, as you can imagine, for writing or sketching.

Huldrych

Letter the twenty-sixth

The supper I mentioned in my last letter was a grand affair. We were treated to thick pea soup, roasted rabbit, a superb goose with dumplings and cabbage, then, best of all the desserts here, we had a sort of bread pudding with apples (which they store carefully in the attics on racks to preserve them from all the vermin).

During a walk in the night air in the garden, I was again accosted by an excited and nervous Brother Ignatius. Evidently trouble was afoot in the valley and Radka, he confided in a whisper, was at that moment with the Eliska's elusive lansquenet somewhere in the woods to the east of the castle.

Corruption of the bailiffs, he claimed, was making progress, but slow and expensive progress. For some reason, neither Radka nor Ignatius is suspected over the Maryska incident - possibly because the old nurse and he, the priest, are privy to too many secrets, in and out of confessional.

Following Eliska's loss of face before her lovers (who are too besotted with her to notice), her servants (too terrified to mutter a word except behind her back), and before me her guest (who, being on the eve of departure, hardly counts), it is on Maryska that she will now vent her rage.

She seemed oblivious to happenings outside the narrow circle of the castle and, as she is feared, no one brings rumours to her ears.

Broadly the news is this: the lansquenet, hiding out in an abandoned barn, is gathering together an ever-growing number of starving peasants, wandering soldiers and deserters, impoverished artisans and journeymen, beggars and even widows, whores and waifs. He firmly meant to wrench Maryska from the talons of the Gräfin. And avenge her.

The failure of the escape has complicated matters. Little could be done tonight, Ignatius admitted, which implied that Maryska could not be saved from the irons. Possibly the next day? But seizure before the populous brothel-inn was considered hazardous.

Brother Ignatius therefore, on behalf of all concerned, including the soldier himself, formally requested me now to intervene with Eliska. Above all to prevent Maryska's condemnation to the brothel from which there would be no chance of escape at all. If this failed, he was prepared to attack the castle itself.

I tried hard to dissuade Ignatius, and through him our lansquenet, from such a foolhardy scheme, which might well put Maryska in far more danger, lodged down there with the pitiless Sebastian, only too close to the moat. Moreover, I warned him that I myself as an Imperial envoy was under the protection of both Nuremberg and the Gräfin and if anything should befall me... I immediately reproached myself for my self-serving vanity, as Brother Ignatius left me to find Radka.

Thoroughly disturbed at the way matters seemed to be developing, I determined to speak to the Margravine at some appropriate moment the next day. Meanwhile, I sealed my despatches and wondered whether I had now covered every aspect of the region. The work has been hard but complete and really the sole harassment I have suffered are these sessions I am made to attend below. Otherwise, people have left me alone and so I cannot complain. I am far more preoccupied about Maryska and now about her lansquenet and the disturbances in the valleys below.

Just before midnight, as I was reading by the light of the modest candle they give me, Jakub knocked and requested me to attend the 'ceremony' below. I followed him more unwillingly than ever before.

I find sketches, however inadequate, quicker than writing - and less painful - but I shall do my best one way or the other.

Huldrych

Letter the twenty-seventh

The chamber I was led to was new to me; this labyrinthine castle is an ants' nest.

The smoke from Sebastian's brazier seemed to be perfumed with some sort of leaf or herb. The odour, which I had anticipated would be acrid, was far from unpleasant as it spiralled and found its way out of the only aperture high in the wall. The chamber was lit by several candles in sconces and holders and these made the many chains, hanging from the beams, glint in an ominous readiness as Maryska was led in, superbly naked.

Her lavishly oiled curves glistened as she stumbled forward; the buttocks had been specially smeared with a honey-coloured grease - no doubt a sure sign of dear old Radka's administration and which, to me, indicated that she was safely back in the castle after her dangerous nocturnal encounters in the woods.

Blind behind her purple velvet masking, Maryska passed close to the flickering brazier and sensed the threatening heat. For once she hesitated and tugged on her chains held firmly in Sebastian's grasp and spreading out to the neck, nipples and sex. Sebastian jerked on the bonds to bring the beautiful body to the centre of the chamber before a central pillar. She stood, magnificently naked, erect and submissive; I marvelled at this attitude, concluding that whatever thoughts of resistance may momentarily enter her paralysed mind, the body will not respond to them. Somehow, as Premsyl had so eloquently expounded, that mystifying combination of resignation and erotic willingness conspired to make her offer herself.

Sebastian, also oiled, exhibited his erection by smoothing its length with several slow caresses, excited at the prospect of what he was about to be called upon to do. He secured the body in what the voluble Radka later told me is the classical posture for all branding sessions, no matter which part of the body is to be marked: legs attached apart to floor rings, arms taut above the head, clitoris and neck chains hooked to the pillar and the labia drawn down and backwards to be chained tight to a further floor ring.

We were treated to a long moment of her gleaming flesh,

fully prepared, the glow of the coals stippling the skin with bars of crimson amid the pungent, aromatic, perfumed smoke. After stirring the irons in the brazier, Sebastian also enjoyed a few minutes of pleasure, sliding his hands down the superb, sleek loins before him, seeking out the most sensitive points until the girl was quivering, jerking, imploring with soft groans some relief, urging the man to take her there and then.

Although fully aware what was now about to be done to her, Maryska showed how gifted - or cursed - she is with this sexual lust of hers and which draws men to her.

The man slowly and deliberately extracted one of the irons from the incandescent coals, tapped it against the wall and then thrust the white-hot H down into the profusion of the right buttock-bulge.

Maryska screamed once - a hoarse shriek from the depth of her lungs. The body rose on tiptoe and hung, shuddering. A moment later, the second iron seared the left buttock. A cry like a white arrow through the darkness of the cellar pierced the walls as Maryska reared again and slumped. Each cheek was inscribed for all time with H for *Hure* - a strange custom, I found myself thinking (as if to distance myself from the scene), to use the German word for whore instead of the local one - but I am told, Nephew, that the practice comes, alas, from us.

In silence the group left the chamber, consigning the girl to Sebastian's further care. I watched him raking out his brazier and then unchaining the stunned woman. Eliska and her companions, suitably satisfied and excited, retired together, after bidding me a good night. For my part, I needed fresh air to clear my mind and so walked the terrace garden in the moonlight and under the impartial stars. I had hardly walked the battlements twice before Radka stole up to me. She was agitated.

"My noble and charitable lord -" she curtsied briefly, drawing her homespun cloak around her, while I wondered what was to follow this greeting "- I beg of you to follow me down to the girl's cell where I must go to treat her. We have to speak to her urgently, before it is too late. It is important and only you can convince her." Then she indicated a grating set low down in a hollow against the castle wall. "Come, my lord, when you see a light in that grid. Do not fail us."

Testy, tired and uncertain of what was afoot, I was brusque. "Cannot all this wait, woman? It's late. The evening has been trying. I have work to do. Can it not wait?"

"It cannot, sir, and beware!" She was gone like a spectre from a graveyard.

I sensed that Maryska's fate was at stake again and, despite my hesitations, I knew I would go down. While awaiting the signal, I wandered back to the great hall out of the chill of the night. Suddenly I saw Sebastian carrying Maryska's body over his arms, heading in the direction of the stairway to the cells. Where he had come from I could not tell - this place is full of mysteries, Nephew. Had she been taken up and then down again from Eliska's bedchamber? If so, why? The dumb man bore the girl almost with tenderness, two creatures condemned to the underworld. Why did no one ever revolt here?

Again in the garden, it was a long time before the signal came. I felt warmed by Radka's courage and defiance in this world where force prevails over law. Although it was Maryska who was suffering like an expiatory victim for the foiled escape, it was Radka who remained the valid instrument in guiding the obscure - but probably militant - forces outside the castle.

In the cell Radka was caring for Maryska, who lay prostrate on her slab. The old nurse was smearing ointments gently into the scorched buttocks, talking to the girl in soft tones.

"She will heal quickly. The marks are not too deep." She stroked the girl's hair. "Tell this good lord you decision, girl." Radka stripped off the blindfold and Maryska looked up at me, as Radka added: "Even if you often enjoy the whip and sex here, say what you want."

"I have changed my mind, my noble lord." Radka helped me to understand her words. "I do not want to be their slave. Never again. They've made me into an animal. But even an animal fights. They've stolen my mind, my body. All I wait for is the whip and the men, one after another. And the chains. I'm an animal tethered to its stake, to be fucked and flogged." The girl paused, exhausted, as if she had lost her force to talk. Radka urged her on. "But tell the noble lord what you have decided, even if you enjoy the whip."

"I want to escape. I want to find my lover again. I don't want to be condemned to the brothel. I want my soldier man," she shouted. "Where is he? Where's my man?"

"Now, now, child. All in good time." Radka clapped a hand over the mouth. "As long as you will fight we will help. Your man is close to the castle, near the gates. Waiting for you. So first this good lord will intercede for you with the Margravine. This is your wish, isn't it, girl? You want to escape, yes?"

The girl nodded. Although she did not seem to recognise me, her self-confidence had returned and I supposed she could be relied upon to remain resolute and not surrender like the last time. Unless they flogged her again into submission and confiscated anew her courage by demanding more nudity, more connivance, fiercer orgasms from her.

"Very well," I said, "I shall do what I can, to the best of my ability, but I guarantee nothing. I cannot extricate you from the humiliation you must suffer in the town nor from the final whipping, but I shall try to see that there shall be no brothel."

"I shall fight," the girl said, to which Radka cried: "Good! At last she's fighting back!" Maryska stretched out her hand to touch mine and a strange thrill passed through my old body - what a fascination the girl exerts! It only made me all the more resolved to free her from Purgatory and to return her to the world of human beings. My mind was made up.

Back in my chamber I had a thought that I should be ashamed of, Nephew: if Radka and the impoverished Ignatius had been bribed by the lansquenet, what was the price? But that is not my affair.

Pray for me, Nephew - even though hopefully I'll see you before this letter arrives. Yet, pray!

Huldrych

(The two following letters are in a highly deteriorated state owing to their being at the bottom of the bundle, tied with string, when found)

Late in the morning next day Hans was preparing Zenon for me when Brother Ignatius came up with his nag and asked if he could accompany me. This pleased me as I intended visiting some of the abbots and Mothers Superior who had helped me, to say goodbye.

During the ride in fine weather through the lanes, the old monk began by questioning me closely about Luther and in return talked about the Hussites in Prague with a remarkably open mind. Then, when Hans and the guards had dropped well behind, he came to the point.

"Radka met with the lansquenet captain again this morning. The marking and further sufferings imposed on his woman has infuriated him to a degree which we think is dangerous. He is set on revenge, my lord, and now has over fifty followers armed with pikes, scythes, pitchforks - and even have captured a couple of wheel-lock arquebuses."

I became increasingly worried as Ignatius went on. "If the girl is not released, he is bent on storming the castle to free her, whatever the cost. We are beginning to fear for our lives, sir, and for yours. Moreover the girl will most probably be thrown into the moat if the castle is invested. We of the castle who still have our senses about us beg you to speak to the Margravine as soon as possible to prevent a massacre."

I confirmed that I had agreed to do so already but could not undertake to succeed or save Maryska from the remainder of her sentence.

Brother Ignatius' reply startled me: "Oh, one more whipping will not harm her. But if she is thrown into the brothel, I guarantee that blood will flow - if not before."

During the rest of the ride after my courtesy visits, we caught sight of several armed groups of peasants in the woods, huddled round huts and byres, talking in undertones. The monk's presence comforted me; often villagers saluted him as if to them he was more than just a miserable pauperized priest. The atmosphere reminded me, as it would have reminded you, Nephew, of the sinister Black Forest days of 1525. My enquiries as to the seriousness brought no answer from Ignatius. He shrugged his shoulders and it is difficult to know precisely where his allegiance lies. With the castle but against Eliska? With the people and against the castle? With the lansquenet? Certainly with Radka!

It was late afternoon before we reached the bottom road leading into Zatoransky; the outskirts seemed deserted. A few minutes later I saw the reason.

In the miserable centre square of the town a large clamouring crowd had gathered in front of the inn or brothel. From our horses, we could see over the heads and distinguish the attraction. Maryska stood, exposed completely naked, her arms bound upwards over the phallic brothel sign above the lintel of the door. She tottered on tiptoe, her rump bulging as she twisted to escape the rabble's probing hands, blows from dirty fists, spittle and insults. Standing guard next to her, watching the scene with apathy, was Jakub.

"Publicly exposed," Ignatius said. "Her nudity only excites the rabble."

"Perhaps, but it is a grim warning to people and that is your Gräfin's object."

It must have been our sudden presence that finally decided Jakub the girl had been exposed enough. He roused himself, whipping back the crowd and the screaming whores and prepared Maryska for her return to the castle and the loving arms of her owner. As they ascended, Jakub on horseback led her by a chain while Bohumil, following on foot, held another chain passed between her thighs from the sex. She stumbled on the rough pathway frequently; Bohumil merely tugged her to her feet and lashed her forward.

Ignatius looked at me and shook his head in dismay as we followed the sad procession up the hill.

"That we should come to this," he lamented. "It is the bailiffs who stimulate the hatred visited on the girl. She becomes a popular expiation. The people hate her because she might have brought retribution upon them. And the Gräfin's retribution is terrible indeed."

I was impressed by the forthrightness of his views and said so as we passed under the portcullis. Ignatius' reply was radical: "Zatoransky and Bohemia would be better places in God's eyes were the Great Whore of Babylon at the bottom of that moat."

"Be prudent, Brother!" I warned him. "Be very prudent if we are to succeed"

(At this point a hiatus occurs in the MS, owing to torn pages)

... back in my chamber when six hours sounded and I was considering how best to obtain some measure of clemency for Maryska. I tried to imagine Eliska's reaction. Why should a man of my standing intervene on behalf of a common strumpet? And a strumpet the property of my hostess! What right had I to steal the bread out of the Gräfin's mouth by subtracting workable flesh from her profitable brothels?

As I was finishing my lists of grazing, fallow and sown ground of the Beremec area, noting its cruel over-exploitation, a clatter of hooves reached me from the courtyard, announcing Eliska's return from hunting with her companions, retainers and guards.

I knew from experience that she would now enjoy her customary perfumed bath in the great tub next to her chamber, where her lovers and serving girls walked in and out during the ceremony. I had frequently been invited to sit and talk amid the swirling clouds of steam as Eliska was soaped, washed, massaged and, stepping naked and strikingly beautiful from her tub, towelled, scented and robed for the evening.

I found this small talk exasperating but it was also, I noticed, when Eliska was at her most relaxed and when favours seemed to be distributed. (Also - and I admit it, Nephew - it was an opportunity of admiring Eliska at one's ease, watching the girls greasing her breasts and combing the pubic triangle.)

So it was by her tub that the question was broached, there

and then, while she was deep in her musk and jasmine scents. And she played into my hand, Nephew!

She asked me once again about the Twelve Articles promulgated by Sebastian Lotzer (she asked me to remind her of the name) during the Peasants' War in southern Germany three years ago. Then she enquired how modest nobles (like herself, no doubt) could possibly entertain restraints on feudal privilege, on enclosures of common land and tithes, or question serfdom! Despite her total repudiation of such enormities, the discussion was calm and interesting. Meanwhile, the delicious Ottla, quite naked, brushed her Mistress's hair.

"Dear Graf von Mechtingen, we are going to miss you," Eliska smiled, "with all your learning. You are such a noble, upstanding counsellor. Your niche in Paradise is assured. You are so deferential, so forgiving, so indulgent. I only trust you will speak well of me to those at court and to the Archduke." (I hardly dared to think what the dour august chancellors and chamberlains in Nuremberg and Salzburg would think if they had seen what I have seen!)

The juncture was propitious and I seized it. "Indeed, gracious lady, I shall speak of you. I shall stress your search for justice and order and your qualities of mercy and understanding."

My flattery was met by a burst of sardonic laughter from the lovers that ceased only when Eliska straightened and frowned. I wore a hurt expression and then said:

"If only, dear Gräfin, I could take back with me an example of your forbearance as well as your justice. For instance - it just came to my mind - this whore, now cleansed, might be returned to the world to live a better life."

There was a silence in which you could hear all the stars in heaven tinkle like bells.

"Which whore?" Eliska asked from her soap suds.

"The one who was exposed today and whose cleansing is completed."

"But why her?" She looked genuinely surprised.

"I know no other to serve as an example."

She did not appear to sense anything but a naive request in

my suggestion and if she did mistrust it, she kept her suspicion well concealed. Of course, I could well have confided in her fully and warned her of the problems that were brewing under her lovely nose.

"Ah, the slut that tried to abscond. Which testifies to a certain courage, quite out of place here but useful in the world outside. A quaint request, my dear lord, but I see your point. Moreover this is about the sole demand you have made of me in all our dealings and all our secret meetings. So, I agree. Such a small request!"

The sturdy Bojena was summoned to the tub: "Order Jakub to release the dark-haired whore tomorrow at dawn outside the gates before his Lordship leaves us."

The overseer hurried away as I reached for the wet fingers of my sparkling hostess to thank her. It was Ladislav who spoke.

"But, dearest love, have you forgotten? There is still tonight! And the wench was sentenced to the brothel!"

She answered Ladislav with a smile. "My dearest, there are so many other wenches for our brothels, although I admit this one is viciously sexed. And don't forget, Ladislav, we have to deal with the pretty nun and her unhealthy lesbian desires." Her gaze then settled on Ottla. "We have so many others dying to please us, don't we?" and here she passed her wet hand over the swelling curves of the girl's buttocks and thrust in between the thighs, as Ottla caught her breath and paled in the eye of the storm.

Then she turned to me.

"But there is tonight. My lord, you would not wish to deprive me of her delicious body and her of my whip which she does not dislike, would you?"

"By no means," I said.

That was the end of the matter. Eliska had taken my words at their face value and remained in the best of spirits. It is when people are happy that they are the most credulous, Nephew.

Tomorrow we leave!

Huldrych - what remains of him.

Letter the twenty-ninth

(Editing has remedied to some extent the poor condition of this MS)

As this was to be my final supper, the Margravine had ordered a splendid and flattering array of delicacies, including the wild boar they had hunted and marinated for this farewell dinner. We were served by three very lovely new girls, stark naked but for gloves and the ceremonial red neckband. The eldest nude bore over the curve of her magnificent rump the marks of a recent scourging with the crop; she seemed proud to exhibit the damage, being the only one to have been honoured with welts.

The discussion was more animated than usual, with many toasts to everyone from the Emperor Charles and the Archduke Ferdinand to Eliska and myself! I amused the table with my account (which you know, Nephew) of the Beautiful Virgin carved for Regensburg in 1519 by old Heydenreich, the architect of the cathedral, and which became the object of a massive, ecstatic cult, attracting thousands of pilgrims and immense sales of votaries and medallions.

It should be the same, I claimed, with the beautiful Margravine. Although in detestable taste, my compliment met with delight and laughter. Eliska a virgin! She and they all relished the witticism. (What of course, Nephew, I did not mention was Dürer's utter scorn of this ugly piece of idolatrous statuary and that the cult came to a sudden end in 1525 when catastrophe struck southern Germany and the statue did not respond!)

After more farewell speeches and good wishes, we listened to a charming concert on the lute and tabor which ushered in one of the mightiest thunderstorms I have experienced. The heavens cracked open after the end of the sultry day and the rain fell like silver ducats, the lightning painting the hall blue and white. This put an end to the music.

Eliska probably took the storm to be appropriately inaugural for her last session with Maryska. Inevitably we were invited down to the dungeon, despite my attempt to excuse myself. I was taken by the arm so that I could not escape.

(Although the author's sketches have survived, the text has suffered badly here from wear and mildew. The account takes up as follows)

... not only were Eliska's companions favoured with special attentions but they seemed determined to enjoy the session fully. Each man was attended by a naked girl, the same ones as had served at table. I received a lithe young woman with fine breasts (Milan had already noted them), a deeply sunk navel and carefully combed sex-hair. She smelt of something like almonds. There were sharp little darts at the side of the eyes and dimples in the cheeks. For the first time your old uncle felt quite attracted! And she was intent on pleasuring me, just as my companions were being serviced.

Softly I asked her her name.

"Jana, and it please you, sir."

I told her I would prefer if she were to caress herself, which, without demur, she did and began to enjoy it, spreading herself open and wetting her middle finger. Her stub of a clitoris rose abruptly out of its sheath while the girl looked down and then smiled at me.

Sebastian brought Maryska in. She was oiled and chained as usual and again as usual, to judge from the state of her nipples, seemed fully excited sexually and had probably received the quirt to stimulate the loins during her preparation while we had been at supper. The thunder, clearly audible down in the depths, greeted her entry.

She was made to kneel on a stool while the breasts were put into harness, Eliska supervising the strappings. Sebastian attached a sturdy length of chain and hook from the harness to the beam above, using a ladder to allow him to complete the positioning of the bondaged nude for flagellation.

Then I noticed that, while the man had been cording the wrists to the neck-strap, Eliska had stripped, divesting herself as on previous occasions of everything apart from her ruff and starched coif, long scarlet gloves adorned with her jewelled rings, and the shining spurred boots. She ran the thongs of a fairly long whip through her fingers and waited.

Suddenly the man drew away the stool from beneath Maryska. With a groan, the body swung free, suspended by the harness - a choice posture, according to Eliska and Milan, for a robust peasant girl with strong breasts and muscles. The ankles were then attached to a floor-ring which proved that this was the precise location where such whipping was routinely done. The body presented a smooth column of taut flesh, oiled to perfection, almost immobile except for the rapid respiration of the thorax as Maryska lunged upwards as if she could assuage the traction on the breasts. The nipples and areolae were swollen to twice or three times their usual volume.

To complete the bondage and make the victim contend with a certain degree of sex-torture to accompany the scourge, Sebastian dutifully and deftly...

(A torn page creates a hiatus at this point. The text then continues:)

... the muscles and tendons flickered under the stretched skin as she was whipped. Eliska somehow seemed to sense the girl's surge of newborn courage and even of assurance, accordingly she lashed the body with vengeance. The strokes, though mainly across the hips and buttocks, did mount the body, avoiding only the kidneys and ensuring no blood was drawn, and in so doing, snapped now and then at the chains, sending a shoot of pain into the girl's most acutely delicate parts.

It was a whipping worthy of Eliska, carried out with skill and savage lust, as she applied the thong-tips to the rib cage, belly and the straining breasts. Maryska bore the punishment without more than long groans and an occasional sudden scream as the nipples were slashed or the fang of the leathers sliced into the elongated membranes of the sex-labia and into the cunt slit itself.

My companions all enjoyed lengthy and repeated ejaculations in the mouths of their acquiescent and respectful serving slaves and suddenly it was over.

Eliska threw away her whip and came up to her victim, and grasped Maryska's hips with her scarlet, gloved hands. She kissed the girl's taut breasts lightly and then slipped her hand in between the labia of the soaking sex. We watched the extraordinary take place. Maryska began to writhe and jerk her whole body, calling out to Eliska to frig her, to fuck her, to flog her... to make her come in her hand, over the gloved fingers that had done her body so much harm.

In the midst of her screaming and oaths and mad cries, Maryska orgasmed beyond any degree of mental or physical control. Everyone watched the sight as Eliska rubbed her groin against the girl's thigh, clasping the suspended human tube of panting flesh round the beaten rump.

"I am going to miss you, my little sex-whore, my flagellated, tortured beauty..."

And then she came as the thunder above appropriately greeted her enormous spending with a roll like the drums at the battle of Pavia, like the end of the world... And through the dungeon's narrow gridded window slits, a bright blue flash lit up the sweat-drenched bodies of the two women, Eliska madly clawing the swinging figure as it was about to escape her, to dissolve, to become insubstantial lightning.

The storm that had heralded the onset of the session subsided like the tensions in the dungeon, leaving the place as if cobwebbed with thin threads of silence.

Maryska was slipping away from them. She was defying them. She was almost free.

I left them all to what was left, such as the guttering tallow candles, the plaintive cries of the nightjars and owls and the imperceptible sound of swords being sharpened beyond the rotting walls of the castle, deep in the evergreen woods.

I bedded down in my feathers for the last time under the vaulted ceiling with its golden stars glinting patiently in the azure spandrels. But as I fell asleep, a chilled small body snuggled in beside me. "Take me with you, sir, like you take Tereza," whispered the tiny voice. "I make love very well, I am very passionate, sir. Touch me!" Dreams are troublesome, are they not? Treacherous things.

Tomorrow is almost here! I cannot believe it.

Huldrych

Letter the thirtieth

I do not know, Nephew, what disappointments you at your young age have had to contend with, but I have had many. What happened to us that morning, the very day of our long-awaited departure, will remain as one of my most bitter frustrations.

Despite the bewildering happenings I was obliged to watch in the cellars and my fatigue, I rose early and walked out on the rain-soaked terrace, watching the larks in the blue sky and the swifts skimming the castle turrets. My baggage, books and papers had already been collected by Hans. I could see him strapping the bundles to the pack horse while Tereza washed and groomed Zenon.

I was surprised to see Jakub coming towards me across the wet paving. Although, as usual, his features were concealed under his hood, I sensed he was in haste and ill at ease. He greeted me civilly enough before delivering his curt message,

"My Gracious lady requires you to attend on her in the Great Bedchamber, sir. At once."

If this was her manner of bidding farewell to a guest of my standing, I would take umbrage. I would lodge an official complaint. Was I not an Imperial envoy to a paltry dependent province? Moreover, to be summoned to her bedside (of all places!) where heaven knows what ghastly things had taken place, vexed my pride profoundly.

Yet I was obliged to follow the menial into the inner sanctum. Anyway, it was the last day. Or so I thought, Nephew.

On entering the splendid room, where the light of dawn had not yet been allowed to penetrate, the candles still guttering, I received a shock of the same order as on so many occasions in the past. It even made me forget to bow to the noble presence.

Noble was hardly the term for my hostess under the circumstances, As Jakub drew back the tapestry shielding the entry, two distinct scenes met my astonished eyes. I halted in the centre of the chamber and stood as if rigor mortis had seized me.

Eliska was nude, glistening with perspiration and no doubt other liquids. Her slender body was half-turned amid the chaos of the royal bed, her lips forming a perfect 0 round Premsyl's cock, her cheeks hollowed, the chin running with curd, as she slid up and down the blue-veined erection, gulping the length deep into her gullet. With one hand she held the testicles tight at the root, with the other she controlled the rhythm of the suction. She was oblivious of anything else other than the pleasure she was giving and receiving.

I stood there totally ignored.

Of course, I had seen this before when old Radka had cunningly inveigled me down that night to watch from the passage. But here I was within the confines of the great lady's room itself, only four paces from her lascivious abandon. Ladislav was busy over her split thighs, twisting her rich clitoris, flicking it with his tongue, his beard dripping with her discharges as she serviced Premsyl.

The trio worked like a well-drilled team. Early morning sex, after repose, as Milan had told me, can be stimulating and bracing...

At a loss as to what to do and thinking of Milan, I looked round for him. Turning my gaze from the thumping and slushings on the bed where fortunately orgasms seemed to be approaching, a second spectacle unfolded. It shook me still further.

In the shadows to the left of the entry, Milan was dealing with two naked slaves. He was flushed like the magenta-coloured velvet riding boots he wore, sweat trickling down his handsome chest, admiring the bodies and caressing his huge prick luxuriously. In the other hand he held his favourite quirt of black leather. Either he had just completed a beating or was pausing to refresh himself.

Before him, chained to the uttermost reach of their limbs, his two victims were curved forward and outward from hooks in the panelling behind. The shackled wrists and ankles strained to the rear, both victims impaled on long shafts bolted at an angle on the wall, the extremities penetrating deep into the anuses. Both bodies had been well scourged. One of the slaves was a very beautiful young woman, to judge by her body, for her head was entirely hooded up in worn leather, leaving only the mouthpiece open to breathe through - and doubtless to carry out the sexual services mouths only exist for here.

Somehow, she reminded me of an earlier night in this same chamber. And indeed I realized the exquisite sufferer was none other than Zdenka, the gentle nun with the shaven pate, caught up in the Zatoransky maelstrom, and whom I had seen at work between Eliska's thighs.

The tight bowstring of muscle and flesh gleamed in the wavering candlelight, she had been oiled or drenched with water, which Radka had told me is customary here to enhance the effect of flagellation - why, I do not know, but apparently it does so.

The girl now carried numerous rings, including an extra one through the septum of het nose, just visible through the opening before the mouth slot. Piercing and ringing, Nephew, is done so rapidly here, allowing scant time for healing. Zdenka, for it had to be her, had been well prepared for punishment. I guessed the girl had been impaled there for much of the night and she had been well whipped, probably several times

The figure next to her gave me a further jolt, For the first time I was brought face to face with a male slave. I thought males were consigned to the town authorities, but evidently exceptions are made.

A handsome youth he was indeed.

The young man, unhooded, with tonsured crown but otherwise shaved of all body hair, was, I must avow, one of the most perfect male physiques I have ever seen. From the lean curve of the hips the cock stood up in strenuous erection, a thin thread of lubrication extending from the slit. The constriction caused the muscles to ripple and jerk in full tension, for he was more inexorably bound even than the female. The way the shaved groin and genitals bulged from the loins was extraordinary!

The cock in its stark reach upwards matched in dimension any of my hosts' or the bailiffs' or even Sebastian's. It was superb. Eliska obviously selected her male sex slaves meticulously.

Milan suddenly saw me and smiled as he came over, fondling his penis and flaunting his silver-hafted whip.

"Ah, Graf von Mechtingen, there you are, bright and early. I'm afraid we've had quite a night of it! Eliska has some bad news for you. But let her finish. It would be best if she were to break it to you herself." He turned towards the pair of impaled slaves in bondage. "Could you imagine a more sexually handsome couple? Fine breasts on the whore and a splendid piston of raw meat on the fornicator, don't you agree?"

I felt it best to agree. "Isn't she the nun?" I asked, for something to say.

"Correct, my lord. A lesbian nun called Zdenka who can't resist another nun's cunt. And the young scoundrel with the elegant cock is, or rather was, a monk from our main priory. Apparently a little too interested in sex. Sent up, at Eliska's command, to be dealt with here rather than in the priory cellars. And - would you believe it? - caught fucking while in our holding cells with the little nun who is little more than a prostitute. I can't understand how the damn bailiffs let them get together. Anyway, they have been condemned. It was shame you were not present to attend the first whippings."

He paused to handle the girl's magnificent breasts. "They are to be punished in full ceremony in a day or two. Tonight was just a trot before the gallop. Incidentally, my lord, we have decided to incarcerate them together, although she a lesbian, so that they can repeat their act before us. We've set up a special cell for them. You should go down sometime to inspect the installation. They are kept bound and gagged on a wide slab of stone, side by side, unable to touch each other, the arms and neck yoked securely to the stone with a hinged iron bar. The spread ankles likewise. An entertaining sight."

Again he mauled Zdenka's nipples. "Hm, extremely fine and highly responsive to this." He lifted his quirt. "She seems to enjoy it more than I expected."

As if to prove his point, he brought the leather down into the hanging breast flesh. The girl heaved and groaned. "Yes, she's grown very fond of the whip. A born slave and now fucks when told to with added energy when flogged."

He turned to the youth, seizing the pulsing erection in a firm grasp.

"This licentious Capucin enjoys a good whipping too." The remark was accompanied by a sharp slash across the distended testicles. "He has become inured to flagellation down there at the monastery. Flogged daily by the Brothers and, what interests me, stark naked and in erection. Ah, we have competition in the monasteries, sir! But here we keep him stiff whenever he's to be worked upon."

He gazed at the twin nudes with delight. "Quite a windfall for us, sir! A couple of what are now illicit fornicators, not just a mere priory masturbator and a lesbian nun.

"They certainly are a handsome pair," I murmured, appalled at the man's lust.

"Eliska made they fuck together a little while back. Chained to the ceiling," Milan informed me. "Quite a performance. We flogged them until they came. But they need considerable training, of course, under the scourge."

I found myself wondering whether Zdenka really enjoyed the young Capucin's cock ring scraping her delicate inner membranes. Obviously she had no choice, and probably it was more acceptable than the hard circle of bristles Jakub and Sebastian wore round their cocks when fucking lesbians - something I learnt from Radka.

I was impatient to hear the bad news announced by Milan, hoping nothing had gone amiss. My reports had not left on time? Hans had got drunk on local beer with the guards? Maryska? Maryska, who in one of those erotic trances she entered when being whipped, had she changed her mind, deciding to remain with her floggers?

Or perhaps Eliska had heard the rumblings of revolt at last in the woods to the south? Distressed by what was going on before me, I began to become nervous.

Finally, after pantings and obscene, raucous spendings on the massive four-poster, my presence was acknowledged.

Wiping her flushed face clean of a trail of sperm with a cambric kerchief, Eliska lay back on the goosedown pillows, replete. She only half apologized, looking me in the eyes.

"My dear lord, how kind of you to disturb yourself. My colleagues are such eager lovers, as you know, and you are accustomed to their desires by now. And then we have had to deal with those two miscreants over there," she added, her eyes narrowing with erotic satisfaction. "So much to handle, you know. The Bishop's entrusted both these bodies to my care, you see. They have to be flogged and tortured properly, When I have the time."

The mention of the Bishop must have reminded her why she had summoned me at such a private hour.

"Yes, the Bishop." Her expression became grave as she drew up the silken sheets over her slender nakedness. "I'm afraid I have disappointing news for you, my lord. His Grace, you see, is not in a position to endorse the Regensburg papers for your departure. They have to be authorized by Prague. It will take a day or so."

I thought she was about to say a week or two which would have driven me to leave without diplomatic protection. A dangerous prospect.

"I have to ensure your safety, my noble lord," she went on. "I would not want your, I mean our, Emperor to be deprived of your august service by seeing you cut down by robbers and scoundrels. There are, I think, certain disturbances brewing, even, alas, in my own lands."

So she knew, Nephew!

I was in her hands. I cursed my indolence in not ensuring our papers were in order earlier. I showed my annoyance plainly. It was the frustration rather than the delay itself that disconcerted me. And what were a few more days in purgatory?

"Then I must send a despatch by rider to Nuremberg," I said uselessly, "to notify my superiors." Of course, I knew no high functionary at Court would worry one jot. Time at Court was infinitely extensible, as long as I finally returned. I supposed too that I myself was expendable, in a sense. But I hoped not.

"As you wish. My own personal messenger, Jiri, can oblige," Eliska replied. "At your expense, of course." Her reply was honest enough.

It was then that I noticed Ladislav's restlessness as he leaned over to whisper in his Mistress's ear.

"Oh, yes, my sweet lord," Eliska added. "My dearest Ladislav is by no means happy about my decision to release the common whore - I forget her name - on whose behalf, for reasons that defeat me, you have interceded. He wants her to be put into the brothel and made available for regular whipping and torture, which she appears to enjoy. I'm afraid he feels attracted to the slut."

Ladislav gave me a look of sheer animosity as if I was responsible for extracting from his lustful clutches a submissive flesh slave whom he still desired. Although there were scores of other good-looking, sexually willing females available for him to use and torture in the dungeons, he seemed attracted to Maryska. He felt thwarted. I didn't blame him.

I felt more uneasy than ever. Was this Ladislav about to jeopardize my plans? Surely the noble lady would not go back on her word given to a senior servant of His Imperial Majesty? Even if what was at stake was a whore fit only for fucking and flogging...

As I frowned, Eliska put me at ease.

"On no account, Graf von Mechtingen," she purred, "will I fail to honour my word to you. The whore will be thrown out of my gates the very moment of your departure. That I promise. What happens to her thereafter, I'll be hanged if I care."

There lurked in that phrase a certain irony. Why, I could not puzzle out but it had an ominous ring somehow...

"By way of compensation," my hostess went on, "and while you await your papers, I'm sure you will not object to my giving your" - she emphasized the word - "slag of a protégée to Ladislav to amuse himself in one more session? We'll make it a splendid occasion, a feast - and throw in those two over there as dessert. Like that, all three of my men will be content. It will help Ladislav, my obstreperous Ladislav, to digest a loss!"

It was a compromise. What could I do but agree? My hands were tied, if I may use a phrase apt to the occasion. Ladislav could be dangerous to my plans. The best policy was to concur, hoping Maryska, already exhausted from her recent floggings, would forgive me. Perhaps she might even enjoy it, as she seemed to enjoy previous sessions...

"Very well," Eliska concluded. "So be it. The three together, on Monday night."

I was satisfied with the negotiated agreement. After all, my papers were still to come.

"I naturally insist on your presence, my lord," Eliska smiled. "You are probably beginning to enjoy our little sessions to ensure my yearnings for justice. Now, if you will excuse us, and as there is no hurry over your temporarily postponed departure, we shall continue dealing with these two worthless creatures. As you see, the fornicator's erection is demanding further attention and that slag of a nun, that insatiable whore, is in dire need to have her stupid breasts throttled and whipped. As well as lower down between the thighs. Are the instruments ready, Milan dearest?"

I bowed myself out of the presence.

It had been a gamble. I felt relieved and pleased at having saved Maryska from the brothels, if from nothing else. I decided to use the days of waiting in polishing up my final report and in riding out on Zenon among the oak forests, But not too far. Whatever Eliska thought, the tumult of revolt was growing and outlaws paid little heed to rank. Even Imperial rank.

As I descended the broad staircase, I heard a piercing scream from the bedchamber. Male or female? In any event Milan had recommenced his interrupted labours on the naked bodies.

It had been a weird start to an inauspicious day.

Naturally, Nephew, I did not pursue the idle threat to contact Nuremberg. It would have cost me too many of my Venetian ducats and Eliska gave nothing away. Except, incredibly, one naked female prisoner. And there I still had to see the liberation with my own eyes.

Meanwhile, neither Hans or Tereza grumbled over the delayed departure. They duly unstrapped the baggage and presumably spent most of the time in bed, far preferable to losing money playing cards, And contrary to my fears, the following days proved rather pleasant. No visits to grim nunneries or fallow land. No interruptions from the bailiffs. No invitations - yet - to the cellars and the rancid smell of whipped bodies. Yet Radka and Brother Ignatius worried themselves sick over the delay in freeing Maryska.

"The girl's lansquenet is fuming, my lord," the old dame

warned me. "Trouble's coming, sure enough, if she's not restored to him.

Two days later I was quietly eating my supper of beef and dumplings when Bohumil knocked. He was the harbinger of two pieces of news. I say 'pieces' because the first item was a scroll of parchment that had evidently passed through many hands. It announced in florid phrases that I, my two servants, and an armed guard, were permitted to cross the land unheeded and unchallenged to the border octroi. It was valid from the morrow. I was delighted and withdrew some - but certainly not all - of my suspicions of the Bishop.

The second 'piece' was less welcome: the loathsome burlap hood I had handed back several days ago was proffered again. I was to be conducted to the Red Cellar by Bohumil after the sixth canonical hour had sounded. A late collation would be served there.

It looked like being a lengthy affair. I stored away my precious parchment, visa and seal under my pillow.

The trudge down the eerie steps among the guttering candles almost broke my spirit. It was only the thought of Maryska's trim body and her liberation that buoyed me up.

The long chamber was almost inviting. Flowers adorned it and the perfumes were more than pleasant, despite the array of appliances of torture. The drapings were deep scarlet.

My hosts made their entry ceremoniously. Eliska was no longer wimpled; the dark hair was drawn back strictly to a black bow and, to mystify her face, a short purple veil of Bruges lace hid her eyes. She was sheathed in tight black leather, probably dyed chamois skins, that left her breasts bare, the tips painted violet, the triangle of her sex brushed to the full to reveal her rolled labia. Her spurs jangled on the supple calfskin boots. Superb.

For their part, her lovers only wore boots and strapping, leaving the pectorals to ripple under the chest hair. The cocks were cradled in thongs to hold the scrotum and lift the great shafts into frightening protrusion. Eliska was a woman who worshipped a hard strapped cock, and I'd seen Maryska , too, revel in the rasping of leather knots.

A host of serving girls followed them in, each delightfully naked and powdered, pattering about attending to the wine and sweetmeats to be offered later. For the moment, while awaiting the condemned, my hosts offered their cocks for a rapid suck or frigging.

At the usual tinkle of the silver bell that could summon up the ghouls of hell, Sebastian dragged in the three victims, lashing them forward with his whip. Like galley slaves, the trio hobbled to the centre. They were completely naked and oiled, their wrists shackled to the back of the neck straps. Zdenka led, trembling and blanched, her nipples erect from a stimulation obviously just received. Her breasts seemed enormous, almost as copious as Maryska's, who followed her.

Maryska looked magnificent. Even the branded letters on her rump, burnt deep into the gluteal mounds, looked attractive. She was, of course, the senior sex slave of the three and knew it. But she also knew she was to whipped severely. Perhaps she looked forward to it and to displaying her sublime nudity and sexuality. She certainly looked erotic.

Behind her trod the the young monk, his fine circumcised prick in rigid erection, an iron ring swinging from the underneath of the curtailed prepuce. His narrow hips and finely shaped, clenched buttocks, together with his hairless, shaved body, gave him a look of pure sexuality, as if born to be a sex slave and put to the whip for pleasure.

While the two novices knelt bolt upright, Maryska swayed to show off her perfect curves that were inured to being displayed. She at least knew what her torturers wanted of her. She had been flushed out, oiled, and her rings burnished by the ever-present Radka who sought to show her at her best for this, the last flagellation. She looked neither compliant nor proud; she was already in a sort of ecstasy. She seemed to adore the presentation.

Eliska's voice was as smooth as silk. "You have been brought before us to give us pleasure as well as to be cleansed in soul and body. What we are about to inflict on your guilty flesh will help you to requite your carnal sins and obey our laws. Prepare them!"

I was again nauseated by the sanctimonious hypocrisy.

Zdenka was prepared first. The bald quivering nude was hauled to the great wooden horse, a monster half-covered with leather; soiled with the sweat and discharges of so many unfortunates before her. It was perfectly designed for female flagellation.

Sebastian hooked the wrist rings to the chain above the girl and wound her up until she was swinging over the hump of the horse. Then he lowered her on to something I had not noticed until that second. Jamming the ratchet and chain, he raised two hinged shafts in the form of human cocks, each embossed with gnarling studs hammered into the leather.

He adjusted the angle of the opposing artefacts and let the victim sink down on to the greased stakes. Zdenka's cry was the cry of the neophyte as she was doubly impaled. As the buttocks flattened, the ankles were chained under the belly of the horse.

Sebastian whipped the young monk to a rugged flogging post. He stood calmly, facing the stake, made to stand on a block no thicker than a church bible, if I may be permitted the comparison. The whipmaster slipped the prepuce ring over a crude iron hook and removed the step, leaving the man teetering on tiptoe, straining to alleviate the abrupt tug on his penis. Arms bound behind the neck, the youth arched back, tethered by his cock. After seeing this, I hoped they would be lenient with Maryska on her last night.

The contrary was the case. She was bound atrociously for Ladislav's pleasure.

The legs were chained far apart to the floor rings, the shackled wrists drawn up behind her back, making her crane forwards from the hips. Her superb breasts swung voluptuously beneath the horizontal thorax. Ladislav ordered Sebastian to pull back the head and secure it to the tensed arms with a chain passed across the mouth. Typically, Maryska did not seem reluctant to being prepared in this manner. She hardly groaned.

Suddenly the tintinnabulation announced supper, leaving the three bodies fully prepared for later. The meal, at least for me, was more than welcome. There were my preferred dishes. salads, ham, tongue and anchovies in smetana, followed by smoked trout, cold roast pheasant and a wine my hosts call 'Whore's Blood'. That was all the more delicious being offered to me by the bewitching Ottla in Bohemian cut glass flutes.

Ladislav studiously avoided me for reasons now obvious. The others chatted about hunting, raising cygnets and the best height for hop trellises. No one afforded a mustard seed's worth of attention to the naked victims. The only one to moan was Zdenka, fully plugged up and distended. I wondered why they had not gagged her third orifice. I think they relished the gasps and sighs of the newcomer, the petrified little lesbian...

The supper finished, it was for Zdenka to suffer first at Milan's hand, the young monk being given to Premsyl who plainly had devised the position imposed for whipping.

Zdenka showed courage as Milan thrashed her, but not when it came to the needles.

To my surprise, it was the beautiful Ottla who presented the tray of silver bodkins to Milan. It was fright rather than pain that swept through the horsed girl as she was pierced many times. She looked very beautiful as she was tortured. That I must admit, Nephew.

Now Milan jabbed his whip haft into the girl's clitoris, between the needles, and brought her to her climax at once. The shrieks, if I understood them, were highly inappropriate for a nun, as she dived headlong into the abyss of her orgasm. She was learning fast...

The young monk took Premsyl's six-thonged whip heroically. The pale flesh, so common among prelates, reddened immediately and it was clear he was used to being beaten. Then Premsyl began sodomizing the man. It was the first time I had witnessed this act. At least between males.

Whatever Premsyl left inside the youth, it was matched by an explosion from the hooked cock. The thick grey sperm spurted out in a jagged series of jets, slapping the torture stake, before slithering down the timber. It was a copious discharge and Eliska approved.

I was glad I would not be around to witness what Eliska had

in further store for the youth in the weeks to come. And then? Back to the monastery? Chained in a secret room in the brothel to satisfy the wealthier widows of Zatoransky? Or the slimy moat? Enough for tonight, Nephew, I need strength to recount Ladislav's revenge on Maryska. May God protect you from such monsters.

Letter the thirty-first

"You see," Milan whispered to me as we watched Ladislav prepare, "the whore's prong has swollen to three times the size it was when she was arrested. The mashing it has received from the bailiffs and our friend Sebastian, and the regular elongation with the sex tongs, leave alone her own continuous clandestine frigging, have enlarged it to the dimension of a thumb." He held up his own gloved digit to compare it with Maryska's protuberance. "She's able to grasp and frig the thing between her fingers. It's like a small cock. I made her do it one night. Quite remarkable, my lord! A gifted slave."

After a pause, Ladislav began to take his revenge. And in sheer spite.

In point of fact, as I am becoming something of an expert, Nephew, what the man did to Maryska was classical enough. But brutal to a degree.

He flogged the branded buttocks, adding to what Eliska had inflicted the night she had hung the beauty by the breasts for the supposedly final flogging. He lashed into the bent body with a vehemence that shocked me, using the same crop he used when out hunting. A horse can take such occasional incentives, but Maryska's rump was already very tender.

Although the victim reacted bravely, Eliska had to caution her lover.

"Whatever your sentiments, Ladislav, my angel," she murmured, enjoying the expert flagellation as much as he, "I don't want spatterings of whore blood on the floor of my residence. Whip the bitch to your sweet heart's content but don't slit her open. Get to the breasts!" she urged. "They're there for your enjoyment. So use them and slake your anger."

Indeed he did, despite what previous torture had done. With savage horizontal strokes, Ladislav gave the breasts a whipping he hoped the absconding whore would never forget. Each lash sent the bulges slapping against the ribs and upwards to the clavicles. For all the world, Nephew, the breasts resembled heavy burnished bells of red flesh tolling, the nipple rings swinging like clappers.

In his fury, Ladislav spared the girl nothing. Soon she was moaning, unintelligible sounds issuing from her chained mouth. I thought the mammary capillaries and ducts were about to burst or at least spurt from the swollen teats, It was one of the most ruthless whippings I had yet seen, then suddenly the flogger stayed his hand, discarding his whip on the flagstones.

His taking of Maryska became violent. After twisting the scorched cheeks, he wrenched them apart and penetrated. After a long reaming of the anus, during which the dark inner membranes extruded with the withdrawal of the strapped cock, he forced the girl to flex downwards to the extent her arms allowed. He pulled out callously, leaving the anus gaping, paralysed by the fierce sodomy, only to ram into the wet vagina, slapping the buttocks with his studded gloves.

Maryska was equal to the challenge. She lifted her tear-stained face as far as the chain permitted, spitting out obscenities, yelling her craving, and came. She seemed to launch out into space among the stars, disintegrating under Ladislav's cock thrust. The orgasm continued through at least six spasms.

As if to stop up her crazed jubilant gullet, the man tore away the bit across the mouth and went in, thudding against the back of the throat.

It was then, mercifully, that he emptied into her. And even there he tried to choke her with his cock and its thick clots of sperm. Maryska defied him, swallowing the full load of the discharge with a sort of relish, pleasure written on her face.

"Whore!" the man cried through his clenched teeth. "Bitch of a cunt whore!"

To see Maryska orgasm so victoriously was one thing, but to see her escape the brothel was quite another. He was doubly thwarted. I thought he resembled a spoilt child, deprived of a precious toy.

"Ladislav, my love," Eliska soothed from her throne, "we have plenty like her. Calm your passion, darling. Look," she extended a scarlet, gloved finger towards Ottla, "you can use this one from now on and flog her until her body craves only for you, until she can't live without the kiss of your riding crop. I give her to you."

I saw the blood drain from the sweet countenance of this most sensuous of all the serving girls. Poor, exquisite, ambitious Ottla! For my part, the prospect of seeing Ottla bound naked to the torture wheel, her limbs strapped to the rim, the loins arched over the great hub, waiting for the whip and irons, was unbearable. But who am I to defend such delicate, white angels? I have sufficient problems wresting the sensuous carcass of the lansquenet's mistress from hell.

Eliska rose and faced me. "The girl is yours, my lord," she announced. "She will remain chained tonight in her holding cell and be thrown out of the castle tomorrow. I want no more of her and her pestilential orgasms." The noble lady paused a second. "I should have flogged her to death long ago or driven her to suicide in the brothels. But take her!"

The whole company swept out of the cellar in her wake, leaving me with Sebastian, who unbound the two other slaves and whipped them back in the direction of their cells or rather cell, since they were to be chained next to each other. I was left alone, face to face with Maryska.

"Tomorrow," I said, touching her sweating shoulder, "you will be free."

The girl's head lifted slowly, mauve circles of fatigue under her expressionless eyes. In her soft dialect she said: "That flogger whips hard and well. He excites me. He makes me come. But you are right, it's my dear soldier of fortune I want... He makes me come with a kiss."

In my chamber, the lancet stood wide open on the warm, calm night sprinkled with stars, gleaming over this castle of terror. The moon was almost full and the air alive with wise owls and knowledgable nightingales telling me I had done well. But they also warned me to watch my step.

I felt for my precious documents under the goose-down pillow. They were still there, crisp and real, bound with the episcopal ribbon.

I dozed off, wishing the soldier and his mistress the good fortune they merited. What I had done was not much but well worth it, even if beyond the mandate of my mission. All that remained was to see that Eliska stood by her word.

And if not?

My weary salutational Nephew,

Huldrych

Letter the thirty-second

(This letter has come down to us in perfect condition, possibly owing to its having been added to the batch later)

Eliska and her companions stood on the castle steps as dawn broke. I confess it was a moment that raised a lump in my throat - although I have never been more delighted to leave a place (except perhaps the battlefield of Marignano near Milan where, as I told you once, Nephew, the French nearly annihilated me as well as our army in 1515). It was very chilly and, as Hans secured our baggage to the pack-horse, we three stood there to say goodbye with mixed feelings. The courtyard filled up with people, mainly the female servants, many of whom were weeping to see Tereza, the fortunate Tereza, leave.

Bojena was there also and Jana and Ottla and, of course, Radka, grieving with a dirty kerchief to her old nose. The aged Ignatius mumbled a blessing over us, just as he mumbled in the chapel or when sanctifying the instruments of flagellation in the dungeon - the same old priest who had risked so much.

I put my lips to Eliska's fingers and our eyes met, sealing so, so many secrets. She smiled once and then we moved off with the two guards we had been given as escort as far as the border where we would enter the Palatinate.

It was Tereza, sitting behind Hans on the horse they were sharing, her arms tight round his leather jacket, who noticed it first.

"Look," she cried, "it's Maryska!"

And indeed, there were the bailiffs carrying Maryska out bodily from the door of the guardhouse. She was stark naked, still pierced with her flesh rings but without her manacles. She looked very beautiful. Once beyond the drawbridge and portcullis, the masked men deposited her in the wet grass at the side of the road. A bargain, I said to myself, is a bargain.

We rode slowly to the gatehouse and this time it was I who saw him first.

Out of the broom and lilac bushes, a figure hurried towards the prostrate naked body. Immediately I recognized the silhouette, profile and beard. The lansquenet officer, her soldier, knelt down over the girl. He stared at her body for a moment and then gently raised her.

Maryska struggled to her feet before recognizing her man, then clung to him as that vine clings to the castle wall. The man passed his cloak over her bare shoulders that glistened not now with oil but with fresh dew, led her towards his piebald stallion grazing a little way down the slope and helped her to mount.

As my little troop drew level with them, they both looked at me from afar. It was I who raised my hand in casual greeting as if they were chance travellers encountered on the way. Then they were gone, cantering east as the sun rose over the distant hills.

Only once did I look back to glance for the last time at the ugly hulk of Zatoransky Castle - perhaps partly in the hope of catching sight of Radka's bent figure somewhere. But already the great drawbridge had creaked upwards, sealing up its secrets. No one was to be seen, only the pennons fluttering on the towers with their solitary E for Eliska.

Crossing the heartland of the province through the lanes soaked from last night's storm, I listened to the guards talking together and Tereza chirping like a jay, and felt I had drowned in the vicissitudes of a history that had nothing to do with me. Nothing. Except a mission carried out under special orders.

We crossed the borderline and the octroi last night and I seem unexpectedly to emerge from a pernicious dream, the sort I do not wish to dream again.

Huldrych.

Imperial Court, Nuremberg.
Letter the thirty-third

My dearest Nephew:

So, finally, we have arrived, tired but without incident. I bought a young gelding for Tereza once in the Oberpfalz, so from Tiefenbach onwards we had the four horses. Tereza rides competently but then, of course, she has a pair of well-hardened buttocks!

Speaking of her, I want to make arrangements as soon as possible here for her to marry my faithful Hans; it will make them happy and avoid offending propriety in this now partly Lutheran city. They are truly in love. Nevertheless I intend to keep Hans on as my servant and have told them so; hence she must become accustomed to his absences or travel with him, which I would not object to. They are lodged with the domestics at the Bishop's residence for the moment. It is a pity that Radka and Ignatius - and, for that matter, the lansquenet, whose name I never learnt and his Maryska, will not be here for the marriage.

I am becoming sentimental or nostalgic!

I have met with the authorities - now both Catholic and Lutheran - and have presented my confidential report with which they seem highly pleased.

By the way, near Unterkoblitz an Imperial messenger overtook us and shared some disturbing tidings with me. He had traversed the region we had left and witnessed grave disturbances there, precisely around Zatoransky of all places. It seems that a local revolt has taken place with much bloodshed but more than this I do not know.

I shall journey next month along the Danube to Tübingen to see you and, having read your letters awaiting me here, we can discuss the religious matters you raise - which preoccupy me also, Nephew.

You do not mention my private and rather risky letters I sent you. Please make sure, as I have asked before, to destroy them all. It would be delicate for me if they were to fall into the wrong hands, you understand. I do not, of course, regret writing them because that I felt you should know these things. But get rid of them.

Your mother Margretlin is here and sends her love and greetings.

As I do.

Ever in God, your loving uncle,

Huldrych von Mechtingen.

Would you care to travel with me to Münster this summer? I have work to do there.

Afterword

The noble writer's account of his mission ends here.

Leaving aside its indecencies, the account merits certain comments.

First, it appears from other despatches found in Bamberg that this was only one of several missions von Mechtingen carried out in Bohemia, Lusatia and Moravia as well as in the Low Countries on behalf of his Imperial masters.

Secondly, what von Mechtingen's letters do not disclose, for obvious reasons, is the real nature of his mission, although a hint is given in his thirteenth letter. After the death on 29 August 1528 at the fateful battle of Mohacz of Louis II, the childless monarch of Bohemia and Hungary, the crown was 'offered' to the Emperor's brother, the Archduke Ferdinand, by reason of his marriage to Louis' sister, Anne of Hungary. To achieve this election and vote of loyalty to the Habsburgs and the Empire, great amounts of work and ducats were expended. Even after his coronation in February 1527, Ferdinand continued to send his most trusted servants on secret missions of negotiation to consolidate the allegiance of the Princes and local rulers. This visit of von Mechtingen to the principled but volatile and ruthless Margravine of Zatoransky constituted one such mission.

While it is inconceivable that he would have carried with him the monies involved in the election bribery, it is clear that the Margravine awaited her recompense which was slow in materializing. Von Mechtingen's long-suffering, tolerant condoning of his callous hosts' behaviour can thus be explained, as well as the image he gives of himself as an urbane, indulgent but conscientious assessor. Shrewdly he allows nothing to emerge from his long and no doubt delicate secret negotiations in Zatoransky, astutely masking these with lurid details of the scandalous life of the community. Not that the tales are untrue; they are simply not the whole story. As an Imperial envoy, he proves himself worthy of his great masters.

A third item of some interest is reported by a certain Freiherr Rochus Frey, another Imperial envoy who in the summer of that year 1528 passed through the region on his way from Prague to

Salzburg. From this it appears that in the early days of July a violent uprising had broken out in the area. It was not connected, for once, with the Taborites, the Hussites or any recognizable religious group; nor was it confined to the poor peasantry but involved artisans, small landowners, poor clergy and even individuals from a certain castle near Zatoransky. The revolt was well planned, thorough, unexpected and bloody.

Six churches, two nunneries and a monastery were burnt to the ground, the episcopal residence looted and, while - ironically - the inmates were at High Mass, the castle itself was stormed, the drawbridge having been lowered by persons unknown.

The report submitted to the Imperial capital at Salzburg tells of an unprecedented carnage as the castle was sacked and torched. Among the ruins were found the bodies of two noblemen (according to local records, a certain Premsyl, Count Pauska and a Lord Milan of Rozenvice); a couple of bailiffs who had put up a staunch defence, numerous Landsknechte, pikemen, male servants, smithies and an executioner by the name of Sebasal or Sebastian, found in a sort of torture cellar, stabbed through with a pitchfork.

Further, the unclothed body of the ruling Gräfin, Eliska Helena of Zatoransky, was found in the moat where it had been thrown, weighted round the neck, from her bedchamber casement. A young girl found in her bed was saved and freed as were numerous other females throughout the castle.

Subsequently, the report states, the principal brothel in the town was put to the torch, the inn keeper and his wife being hanged from the lintel of the doorway.

No mention is made of names such as Mistress Radka Zidka, Brother Ignatius, Bojena, Ottla or others.

Little other information has come down to us. The document does, however, disclose that the marauding mob was led by a bearded officer of the Sixth Imperial Lansquenets who acted in a frenzied manner. Next to him, in leather breeches and jerkin, a beautiful young woman was seen dismounting from a grey stallion to set fire with a torch of burning pitch to straw In the underground dungeon and cells of the castle.

The uprising was gradually pacified but it was not possible to trace either the officer or the woman in question.

Finally, it can be confirmed that the late Gräfin was summarily buried next to the ruined gatehouse among the broom. Mysteriously a loving epitaph was found on the grave, said to have been placed there by a Vladislas or Ladislav, a middle-aged man in peasant homespun. This indeed may be our man, having escaped the massacre and still sought by the authorities. But there is no proof. The grave was also visited by a certain Beguine from the Rhineland but this is not substantiated either in any document that has come to hand. The grave apparently was later badly desecrated.

While we have no ready record regarding the Zatoransky succession (which was referred to the Diet for settlement), on the other hand a source in the prosperous city of Munster reported that a certain Huldrych Schonheimer; a retired diplomatic secretary in the Imperial court, embraced the Lutheran faith and, accompanied by his newly-ordained nephew and a married sister from Eisleben, laboured to question the massive structures of the medieval church and justify the fragile faith just emerging.

Nothing more is known.

We hope to develop our Bonus pages into a magazine, possibly by the time we publish our March title, ANGEL OF LUST - and that is something to watch out for anyway, as it is by Lia Anderssen, author of 'Bikers' Girl', 'Biker's Girl on the Run', 'The Hunted Aristocrat' and 'Bush Slave'

There is another scoop before that - in February we have HACI-ENDA, and that is by Allan Aldiss of the Barbary series. Here is how it starts:

Carlos Ortiz lay swinging in the big hammock that was slung across the wide porch at the back of the large and luxurious hacienda ranch house in Costa Negra, a small little known country in Latin America.

He lay sideways across it in the usual Latin American way, his muscular body stretched out comfortably.

He wore only a sarong in the warm tropical afternoon sun - a sarong which he had untied, displaying his hard, tanned figure - as well as baring it for the attentions of the two young girls that the hammock also held.

The girls were sisters, indentured servants, virtually a replacement for slavery, which had been abolished in the middle of the last century. They were coffee coloured, half Indian, with a dash of Negro and white blood. They snuggled up to their Master, one on either side - pretty young creatures with pert little breasts. Round their necks iron collars had been riveted from which hung discs giving the name of the estate, El Paraiso, and the numbers under which they were listed in the hacienda's official register.

By Costa Negra law, going back to the days of slavery, livestock was divided into cattle, pigs, horses, and slaves, the latter now replaced by indentured servants. The female indentured servant section of the register was further sub-divided into several distinct types of women...

... the girls were greatly relieved to hear wheels on the gravel approach to the other side of the house. Diverted by this fortunate event, Carlos jumped out of the hammock and went to the window that looked out onto the drive.

It was his great friend and secret lover, Senora Inez Mendoza, whose husband owned the neighbouring hacienda. Inez, he knew, enjoyed girls as well as men, and he saw that she was driving her little dog cart which was being drawn by a perfectly matched pair of slightly coffee coloured girls harnessed one behind the other.

Most of the tracks and paths that wound around the estates in the area were too narrow for a horse drawn carriage, or a car or truck, and it was therefore usual to use indentured servants to pull their masters and mistresses around their estates in dog carts. These resembled Chinese rickshaws with shafts between which a woman could be chained, with if necessary another in front of her to to provide more pulling power.

The two sweating girls were naked, except for a small leather belly flap, that hung down in front over their intimacies from a wide leather girth strap that was buckled tightly round their waists. The front of the belly flap was prettily decorated with the brand mark of the Mendoza hacienda...

WHEN 'BONUS PAGES' do become 'Bonus Magazine', there will be some new features. One will be readers letters, where we will forward replies if we know the address (not to be published), and another will be a short story competition, £50 plus publicatiuon for the winner. Start writing now!

There will also be 'A VICTORIAN SCRAPBOOK - Vignettes from a sterner age'. This will be contributed by Stephen Rawlings, author of our best seller 'Jane and her Master'. We start here, in a small way, and will build up month by month:

DOMESTIC DISCIPLINE IN VICTORIAN TIMES.

The Victorians and, indeed, their predecessors, believed firmly in the adage 'spare the rod and spoil the child', and did not hesitate to include their womenfolk under the heading of children, subject to stern correction by husbands and fathers. The strap, the cane and the birch were employed enthusiastically on bare female buttocks of all ages and classes, one of the great levellers in a very divided society.

The young Victoria was not exempt. She had a stern German governess, one Leben, later created Baroness Leben by her grateful pupil, who kept her by her side until Albert exerted his familial rights and had her sent away from court. The young aristocrats who shared Victoria's schoolroom regularly lifted their skirts and deployed their bare young bums for Leben's rod, although it is said that Victoria herself, out of respect for her Royal destiny, was only caned on the hand.

Discipline in schools and classrooms throughout the land was firm, not to say strict, but there were few complaints, or arguments for its abolition, except where particular cases of extreme abuse, usually involving orphans and wards, were concerned.

One of the many interesting characters from Victoria's reign was Lord Melbourne, the young Queen's first Prime Minister and adviser. He was a great advocate of the rod, and there are, apparently, many letters extant to his mistress, Lady Branden, urging her not to spare it for her girls, saying it's the best thing in the world for them, and much else. He also wrote a series of letters in the MORNING CHRONICLE relating to the whipping of teenage girls in school, and how the birch only 'scratches' them a little and on a part that quickly heals.

"We live in strange times if a girl of thirteen cannot be whipped at a boarding school, without it becoming a subject for discussion in the newspapers. If I had a girl to educate, I would find out where that school was and send her there immediately. It's a smart whipping that cures, and a few scratches after two days. Nothing heals so rapidly as the part to which the birch is usually applied."

Melbourne had a young ward who he thrashed from time to time, also:

"A few twigs of a birch applied to the naked skin of a young lady produce, with very little effort, a considerable sensation. The little girl I never whipped but three times for disobedience, and she never disobeyed me any more."

The 'little girl' was Melbourne's ward, Susan Churchill, who was occasionally chastised by her guardian. Later she wrote to him, telling him she was following the same practice with her own daughter. Nor did she bear him any ill will for whipping her:

"I remember the occasion," she wrote, "then being thrown in a corner of a couch that was there. You used to leave the room and I remember you coming back and saying 'well, cocky, does it smart still?' at which, of course, I could not help laughing, instead of crying."

AND NOW FOR SOMETHING QUITE DIFFERENT!!

We received an exceptional manuscript several years ago. The package was posted in Hong Kong but gave no address for the Author. We would love to publish his book, but we have given up on finding him.

So here is what we have, the first six chapters, and what a treat they are! We shall be more than happy to pay for it if we can locate him, and to publish it all as a proper book if we ever get it.

TART OF DARKNESS.

1

In 1921 Somerset Maugham described Penang, Malaysia, as 'A pleasant little town, but the stranger finds little to do there, and time hangs heavy on his hands.' In more than seventy-five years nothing has changed, and time still passes slowly in Penang. It's quite a contrast from my home in Bangkok. For the man who likes pussy and beer Bangkok is as close to Heaven as you're likely to get. Leaving my house, you pass three brothels and a dozen bars before you come across any place that sells milk, bread, or eggs. Penang, on the other hand, is a city where the laws are Islamic, the food Indian, and the manners Chinese. They hang you there for winking at teenage girls in the mall.

Unfortunately, the powers-that-be require all foreigners to leave Paradise every three months and renew their visas. Penang is the closest Purgatory that boasts a Thai consulate, so four times a year I fly down to check in at the New Cathay Hotel on Leith Street, there to meet a stocky Tamil names Mr Metha who takes my passport and a small gratuity to fight the bureaucracy at the Thai consulate on my behalf.

I spend the required three days in a stupor of boredom, locked into my barren cell on the third floor, smoking clove-scented Marlboros made by license in Sri Lanka and thinking of the tiny, nearly hairless and oh-so-accommodating snatches back in Bangkok. However, on my last trip, made in the gloom and drizzle on the monsoon season, shit happened.

I got out of the cab in front of the ornate double doors of the New Cathay, guarded by a couple of crumbling hundred year old wooden dragons, and carried my bags through the rain into the lobby. You always carry your bags in the New Cathay, because nobody on the staff is any younger than the wooden dragons outside, and in the rooms you'll find no mint on your pillow. Nor will you find towels, toilet paper, soap, or a phone. Your room will always be an airless little box with a creaky ceiling fan and a broad population of insect life. There will be a sink in one corner that smells like pass, and every room in the place gives you the feeling that over the years about a hundred people must have killed themselves here.

There was a young couple checking in at the desk when I arrived. He was pure Eurotrash: heavy guttural accent that made him sound like he was choking every time he spoke, spiky hair, pegged and greasy black jeans, torn T-shirt, and Nihilist Deutschrock coming over loud and clear from his walkman headphones. His companion was Thai, trim and neat with fine tits and a big round butt peeking out from the frayed edges of her cut-off Levis. She had long shiny black hair that fell past the word 'Airborne' tattooed on her shoulder, and her attitude as she leaned against the counter, one hip shot out and examining her nails, was one of 'I'm a prostitute of the lowest order, and I don't give a damn who knows it.'

It's not uncommon for guys who can afford it to bring their Mia Chao, or 'rented wives' to Penang on visa runs. Makes the time go faster, I guess. The punk's companion looked to be about twenty years old, way over the hill by the standards of her profession. By now she should have made enough money on her back and on her knees to buy a little shop somewhere, or a bar, or at least some land and a water buffalo. The fact that she was still working meant that she liked her job.

The clerk slid the key to room twenty-two across the chipped teak wood of the old counter to the punk, and he led the way upstairs with his woman carrying both their bags. When I checked in I got the key to room twenty-four, right next door.

By nine o'clock that evening the lobby of the New Cathay looked like a casting call for Casablanca. Chinese gangsters in Armani suits say nervously next to Round-the-World Backpackers in Nepalese bloomers. Ageing European pensioners in shirts with missing buttons sat eating their dinner out of tin cans next to long-haired Americans on fake Irish passports who hadn't seen home since they went AWOL in '69.

My neighbours were at the end of a patched green vinyl sofa under the shrine to the House Gods. The punk was sitting on the one available cushion next to an Israeli with a Canadian passport and a briefcase full of brochures advertising light armoured vehicles. The girl was squatting, third world fashion as she had grown up doing back on the farm in Paddyland, at his feet. She looked sulky and he looked smug.

Metha came rolling in, and began a complicated ritual of illegal and supposedly secret negotiations with each client. While we waited our turn we all pretended interest in newspapers in ten languages and as many days old, politely ignoring each other's dealings.

The Tamil came over and greeted me with a voice that was oddly soft coming out of his bulk, but before we could do our business the punk got up and pulled Metha away from me. "I've been waiting fifteen minutes, old mahn!" he growled at the saffron-scented broker. "You giff to me serwiss or I go somebody else!" Metha gave me a look that said 'Do you mind?'

Knowing that time in Penang is a valueless commodity, I returned his look with a shrug and went back to looking at the cartoons in the South China Morning Post. Metha took the punk's papers and photos and a bribe that was three times the going rate for a visa, then came back and offered to buy me a beer, since I was his last customer for the evening. As we walked back to the tiny bar I saw the punk pull his moll up to her feet and drag her upstairs.

A man who'll buy you a beer is a rare thing in a Muslim nation, and Metha and I spent a few hours watching Mr Ed re-runs dubbed into Malay on the bar TV, then I excused myself and went upstairs. In my room I took a book to bed and crawled under the mosquito net. In ten minutes I was asleep.

Sometime after midnight I was awakened by a tremendous crash from the room next door. A piece of furniture had evidently been thrown, and there were voices too. I couldn't make out what the deeper voice was shouting, but the girl's high-pitched whine cut right through the thin plaster wall. She was calling her man a cheap, ignorant, dirty, giant lizard. His grasp of Thai must have been very slight, because a giant lizard is the worst thing you can call anybody in that language, and of the seven pronouns which mean 'you' in Thai, she was implying the one reserved for animals and the bastard offspring of slaves.

If she had called a Thai man that name, her life would have been in danger. As it was, the punk understood at least her tone of voice, because I heard a scream and then a steady whimpering punctuated by slow, steady smacks that let me know someone's ass was getting a good spanking. I would lay even money it was the big juicy brown ass I saw peeking out from under those ratty shorts in the lobby.

Finally the smacking increased its tempo as the girl's whimpers turned to wailing, until there was a sudden hush and then their door slammed open and I heard the unmistakable sound of a slight body flying across the hall, to hit the opposite wall and collapse in a heap on the floor.

The door to room twenty-two slammed shut with a bang,

and in the ensuing silence I listened to the girl's moaning in the hall. After a minute I heard her scratching at his door, mumbling apologies in English, Thai and something that sounded vaguely Slavic.

No response from the Storm Trooper, but the sweet aroma of Cannabis slipped under my baseboards. Finally, one word, pronounced loud and clear, came from him. It was probably the Slobovian for 'female giant lizard', and after he said it, all was silence.

I was too shaken to go back to sleep, and I got up. While I was trying to light a cigarette I heard water splashing at the end of the hall, and realised that she had gone to the communal toilet. Male guests usually pissed in the sinks at night, but women could often be heard douching at odd hours.

I heard her come back and try the door to room twenty-two. I heard it rattle; it was locked. I heard her pound, then kick and shout with pain, but there was no response from the Storm Trooper. Probably passed out. There was a moment of whimpering and cursing, then about thirty seconds of silent consideration, then I heard her knock again.

This time at my door.

I make it a rule not to open my door in crummy hotels in Third World Countries after midnight, but the knocking went on and on, soft and insistent. "Who is it?" I said through the cheap plywood of the door. No response. I tried Thai: "Khrai ma?" This time she answered, also in Thai.

"Please, Noble Lord," she whimpered. "I am alone, and afraid." She was using all high-class pronouns with me. "My man kicked me out, Lord, and I have no clothes, only my sarong, I was bathing. Soon the police will come and I know what will happen to me then. Please help me, Lord. I beg you."

The mention of the police scared the shit out of this Noble Lord, but I could imagine what would happen to a foreign prostitute found causing a disturbance in a Malaysian hallway wearing only a damp rectangle of upcountry cotton - a sarong is nothing but a piece of cloth, similar to a large towel. She'd be taken to the old stone prison downtown and kept busy entertaining senior officers until she was worn out. Then they'd put her in the women's cells where she'd be raped with broomsticks and mop handles and the guards would watch and laugh because she was the wrong race and religion. In a year or two she'd be deported back home in a condition fit only for giving blow jobs to rickshaw pullers for enough pennies to buy a day's worth of heroin.

"Ro diaow, Nong!" I said, telling her in three words to wait a moment and that I accepted her socially on the level of a little sister. I grabbed a T-shirt and a pair of shorts from my bag and opened the door to hand them out to her.

But when the door swung open she pushed her way into the room so quickly I was left handing my clothes into an empty hallway. I turned, closing the door as I did so, and watched her in the light from the street lamp outside the room's single narrow window. She was naked, except for the tin and faded sarong, a pair of gold ear-rings and the tattoo.

Her breasts were neat but large for an Asian, indicating that her people came from the Laotion side of the parched drought planes of Northern Thailand rather than the Burmese side. She turned around until she faced the connecting wall, the one with the punk on the other side.

She was in profile to me, lit from behind, self-consciously holding one hand over her barely concealed breasts and the other over her pubes. "Hia!" she spat at the wall, calling the punk a lizard again. Her face glistened with tears, and after hurling that one word at the wall she seemed to lose all strength. She tumbled forward onto my bed, dragging the mosquito net with her, to land in a heap of sheets and soft flesh.

It was a fall performed by all the most popular female ingenues on Thai television dramas, and bar-girls practice it as well. Her arms wrapped around a pillow and her hair fanned over it to fall off the other side of the bed. The sarong had slipped its knot and was only loosely covering her from armpits to the small of her back. Her legs were opened slightly as she lay sobbing on her belly, and I could see her buttocks were rounded and full, and they shook and shivered with her weeping. Under her natural tan, they were glowing pink from the beating I'd listened to through the wall, and beneath them, peeping out at me, was the tiny split bun of her vulva, its bright pink lips merging into the dark crack of her ass.

Her skin was smooth and unblemished, except for the tattoo and a bruise on her shoulder where she'd hit the wall. I sat next to her, fairly impressed with the professionalism of her acting, pulled the sarong off her back and threw it with a wet plop into the farthest corner of the room.

"Look at me, Little Sister," I said.

She slowly rolled over, showing me her naked body.

Asian modesty dictated that she must not show her emotions to a stranger, so she covered her face with her hands as she wept, and I gazed down at two perfect globes of warm flesh, each tipped by a dark brown nipple the size of a raisin on a half-dollar. Her sparse pubic hair was a straight thin line pointing the way to her cunt. I yawned and began tweaking a nipple to show her I wasn't being taken in by the dramatics, and asked her what she needed.

She let her hands fall from her face to lie limp on either side of her head. She looked up at me through her crocodile's tears and pleaded "Let me stay, Elder Brother. He won't wake up until lunch time tomorrow, the door is locked and I have no clothes." Her eyes were half shut but glowing and I could smell alcohol on her breath. Her body, as she sprawled across the billows of the mosquito net and patched cotton sheets, had the languid floppiness of someone pleasantly drunk.

I've always had a soft spot for strays: kittens, puppies, chicks blown out of the nest. In this case, I was developing quite a hard spot. "Okay," I said, giving her nipple a stiff twist which produced a gasp and gave me her complete attention. "Little Sister can stay until morning, but then she has to go." She mumbled her thanks, putting her hands together in front of her forehead and touching her palms to my thigh three times in the traditional form of respect left over from the days when mandarins spared bound slaves from the headsman.

I let her complete the obeisance, then gabbed her by the scruff of the neck and held her head over my lap. She understood immediately, pulled open the fly of my boxers and swept out my organ with the skilled hand of a professional. I felt a few hot tears fall on my prick. Three quick slides of a velvet palm up and down its length and pop! it went right into her mouth.

She slid her small head up and down my shaft while her hair caressed my thighs. Little moans of satisfaction escaped us both, but the thought of Haga the Horrible, maybe sleeping, maybe just sulking on the other side of the wall, kept me at a happy floating buzz that produced no shouts or screaming.

She looked up at me with a big grin. "Malee thinks you're a very good man. Good for Malee. Malee will be good for you, too. Promise!"

That's how I learned her name.

I lay down full length on the bed and Malee got onto her knees, head down at my cock and ass hovering just in reach of my right hand. Even in the dim light coming from the street I could see the pink flesh, still raw from her recent beating. She saw me staring at it and said with noticeable pride "Noble Lord likes Malee ass, yes? All men like Malee's ass." I imagined that quite a few men had indeed paid attention to that ass, in fact my mind was at that moment full of scenarios involving Malee's ass and how she should be chastised for her immodest pride in it.

My cock was standing up like a flagpole and she took it in her mouth again and began to run her tongue up and down it, from hairy base to purple point, moaning as she did so. With both hands I kneaded her yielding buttocks and roughly dug a finger into her slit. She said "Ooooh, that feels good, Noble Lord, very good."

She looked up at me and I thought I saw the first glimmer of sincerity in her eyes as she faltered in broken English "You no hat. I like. More clean."

The term 'no hat' is how bar girls refer to a circumcised penis. She popped the tip of my hatless prick into her hot moist mouth one more time, revolving her head back and forth so that her slick lips circled my knob, just under the corona, round and round. I had two fingers inside her pussy now, and it was like a live thing, gripping and releasing my digits, drawing them deeper with tiny muscle contractions. I reached up with the other hand, and wetting my index finger with saliva, inserted it up to the second knuckle into the tiny puckered brown eye of her anus.

Malee seemed to like it.

"Ooooh," she moaned around my cock, her hot breath stirring my pubic hair. "Malee likes you, Noble Lord, Malee likes you very much." She went back to caressing my tool with her small, warm, experienced hands. She gave the very tip, just at its eye, a quick lizard-lick. She looked like a little girl with an ice cream she means to eat slowly and savour.

"When I was small," she said quietly and in her up-country accent. "I was a very naughty child. My Papa had to spank my legs with a stick all the time." She looked up at me over my belly, her ass swaying in the air and the fingers of both my hands playing about in there, and switched back to her bar-English. "Malee very bad girl now, you know? Do very bad things with man, many man, always foreign man. Now I'm bad, every day, every night, and I have nobody can spank me."

She was looking at my prick now, as if she was addressing it and it was the most beautiful thing she'd ever seen. "I need my Papa spank me now, but my Papa won't even talk me now."

The note of pleading in her voice told me all I needed to know. I took my finger out of her ass with a faint 'pop!' and the others out of her cunt with a wet 'slu-u-u-rp' and sat up. She let go of my cock but didn't change her position, on her knees with her head down.

I stood by the bed and looked down on her.

The rain started again outside, thundering against the shutters of the New Cathay Hotel and blurring the dim light from the street lamp outside as rivulets ran down the dusty pains of my window. In the fairy light I could see her, slender and toffee brown, her breasts hanging down and swaying slightly, their erect nipples brushing the rough gray mosquito net that was still spread on the bed, her big round ass pointing to the ceiling.

I put a hand on her back to hold her that way, though I knew it wouldn't be necessary. She closed her eyes and bit the sheet. Her hands reached out in front of her and grasped the wicker foot board where probably a hundred other pairs of slender brown fists had grasped on thousands of other nights in that room. I considered pulling my neck-tie and belt out of my bag and securing her that way, but decided I might like to keep her mobile.

I have her a solid THWACK on one cheek, just finding my

elevation and distance, and she gasped and then moaned deep in her throat. I was glad for the noise of the rain; even though I was pretty certain the punk next door was asleep I didn't want the Sikh night watchman who always slept in the lobby to come up checking on the noise.

I put one finger into her cunt to turn her for a better angle, and she leaned back against my hand, driving the finger deep inside her where it was tight and hot. I gave her a few more licks, harder and harder, until the pink skin she'd carried into my room of her ass was glowing a fiery red and she was sobbing freely into the mattress.

My cock was swinging back and forth with every stroke, and when it became uncomfortable I pulled out my finger and grabbed her hips. She spread her knees and arched her back to receive me, lifting one foot off the bed and putting it up on the wall to brace herself. She reached back to her pussy with one hand and spread her pink nether lips as wide as possible.

The blunt head of my shaft was wedged against her dripping cooze, and I was just about to drive it home when common sense took over.

I doubt if even Somerset Maugham ever thought to bring condoms to Malaysia. That would be like taking shrimp forks into the Sahara. Fucking Malee without a condom was definitely not a good idea. As I paused she moaned and looked back at me over her shoulder, strands of her long hair plastered across he face with sweat, and said in her fractured English learned from a thousand faceless foreigners "Fuck me! Please, darling, I want you fuck me now wi'you big cock!"

I was on the horns of a dilemma. While it would be easy enough to examine her cunt for any simplexes or warts, gonorrhoea hurts like hell, syphilis makes you crazy before it kills you, and AIDS takes its own sweet time, every moment of it painful.

I ad-libbed.

"Let me fuck those big juicy titties, baby!" I said, and, as I imagine a good proportion of those previous freelance English teachers had, grabbed the foot that was braced against the wall and gave her a flip onto her back.. She landed like an expert, legs spread wide and clutching her knockers with both hands to form an extra deep cleavage for me to dip into. My balls were aching and I could feel things twitching inside all the way back to me prostate; my own asshole was clenched and my butt bunched for the big thrust, and I stood on my knees over her rubbing my dick up and down her body, from navel to chin.

I climbed over her as the ancient bed creaked with the strain. Her eyes were half closed, but I could see the blades of the revolving ceiling fan in their dark irises as I poked my throbbing purple mushroom into her open and waiting mouth.

This time she sucked it like a babe at the bottle, and despite the awkward angle managed to take almost the whole length of it into her. I planted my ass on her chest and grabbed a handful of hair to immobilise her, rubbing my balls on her soft boobs and jamming my prick way down her throat. I let her suck for a minute, her cheeks bulging and her nostrils flaring for air, before I pulled it out and backed up a bit to slide the spit-slickened length of it between her titties. She squeezed them together around me, a sensation at once soft and firm.

"Noble Lord," she moaned, "please, I want to play with my pussy."

Believe it or not, this is a compliment, coming from a prostitute. Normally, these girls don't allow themselves to have real orgasms with a client. That kind of behaviour is considered unprofessional. They save their own desires until they're back in the dormitory-style apartments they share with several girlfriends, and in the long hot empty afternoons they laze in bed together, rubbing and licking each other's pussies for hours on end, burning off the sexual tensions raised by nights spent dancing naked or feigning passion in front of legions of men. If a bar girl wants to masturbate when she's with you, it means that you excite her as much as her girlfriend does.

I considered it for a moment, and then decided to let Malee have her pleasure.

I grabbed her two nipples, pulling them together until they were stretched and undoubtedly pained, keeping her boobs in a warm cocoon around my prick. I lifted first one knee and then the other off the mattress, allowing her to put her arms by her sides, where I pinned them securely with my legs. Immediately both of her hands dove for her own crotch. I rocked up and down for several minutes, enjoying the sight of the bulb of my prick poking in and out of view between those luscious titties, twisting and pulling her nipples mercilessly.

Occasionally I would turn around to watch her pleasure herself. She had three fingers buried in her slit, and the other hand was busy being just as rough on her little clitty as I was being on her nips. Her eyes had closed completely, now, her mouth open in a fixed and silent 'Oh!' and her head thrashed back and forth on the bunched mosquito netting.

I held myself in check as long as I could, until I saw her arch her neck and grit her teeth with her own orgasm. Then I let go, bucking and lunging on top of her chest like a bare-back rider at the rodeo, a flood of hot jizz spurting out onto her face, neck and hair. I hadn't had a woman for almost forty-eight hours, and my ducts were full of spunk. As she lay gasping under me I held my cock over her glistening face and squeezed the last few drops out to dribble onto her cheeks and closed eyelids, then pulled her slack jaw open and stuffed myself inside the warm wetness of her mouth.

She began to suck reflexively, and I watched her face, relaxed and at peace now, smeared with cream over its wide flat cheekbones, pug nose and full lips. We stayed that way until my knees grew uncomfortable, then I pulled my dick out of her mouth and backed off the bed. I told Malee to stay exactly as she was while I paced the length of the room to work the stiffness out of my knees.

She obeyed me satisfactorily, staying where she was while I washed my dick in the sink. She had one hand still deep in her cunt, the other cupping a breast, her slick and slimy face glistening in the feeble light.

When I was clean I went back and sat beside her. I looked at her for a moment, watching the beads of sweat rolling off her body. I decided that she'd played with herself long enough for now, and pulled her hand roughly away from her pussy. Her arm was limp and I held her sticky glistening fingers up to her mouth.

"Lick, Malee," I said.

She did as she was told, licking and sucking the juices off each finger. With one of my own fingers I wiped the cum from her eyelids and she opened them. She smiled at me and strands of jizz stretched between her lips. I stuck a gooey finger that I'd cleaned her eyes with into that perfect mouth and see giggled as she licked it clean. I ran the finger over her chin, forehead and cheeks, gathering rivulets of still hot and smelly sperm and feeding them to her.

When the stuff started to dry to stickiness, I took her down the hall to the bathroom for a wash. I insisted on watching, and even though we hadn't fucked, I made her douche thoroughly, enjoying her yelps and squeals when she tossed dipperfulls of chilly water up her snatch.

Then we went back to my room, and as we passed the door to number twenty-two I could hear the congested snoring of the punk on the other side. In my room I smoked a cigarette while Malee rehung the mosquito net, working naked in the cool blue light, her tits swinging gently, from time to time within reach of my hands.

Whenever I touched her she stopped what she was doing and stood still, letting me do anything I cared to, and when I let go of a tit or pulled my finger out of somewhere, she would smile and go back to making the bed, always smiling, always calm and gentle and soft.

We fell asleep spoon fashion, under the slowly revolving ceiling fan, with my cock nestled within the crack of her ass. Outside the rain fell onto the tiled gables of the New Cathay Hotel, ran from its eaves, and overflowed the garbage filled gutters of Leith Street.

2

Early the next morning I woke to find Malee kneeling next to the bed, her hands once again held in prayer fashion in front of her forehead. I didn't know how long she'd been on her knees on the rough old boards, hands raised and eyes downcast, waiting for me to wake up. I did know that her posture meant she was going to ask for a favour.

I stretched lazily and yawned. "Good morning, Malee," I said in English.

She raised her gaze from the floor when I addressed her, and gave me a warm smile. "Noble Lord, I am glad to see you have slept well."

The high class language, pronounced in her backwoods hillbilly accent, made me chuckle as I sat up. When I id, my morning hard-on was right in Malee's face, and she leaned forward to put her mouth on it, but I stopped her.

"Not yet, Malee," I said, and stood up. It was just a piss-hard, and I didn't want to use Malee again until I knew what she was going to ask for.

I paced the room, scratching my belly and farting, letting the piss-hard subside. Malee stayed on the floor where she was. She had been trained well, maybe by an old client, maybe by her strict grandfather, and I made a mental note to ask her about it some time. I stepped up to the sink and took a piss, letting the water run to wash the thick liquid down the drain.

As I peed I watched Malee in the mirror hung over the sink.

She was still kneeling by the bed, with her back to me, and I could see her butt twitching and clenching. I knew she hadn't been out of the room; her sarong was still in the corner where I'd tossed it the night before and none of my things had been moved. She had not gone down the hall to the bathroom yet, and the sink was not made for women's convenience. The cheapest liquor in Malaysia is beer, and I remembered how she'd been tipsy the night before. By now her bladder must be uncomfortably full, I thought, and her knees must be hurting like hell.

I turned from the sink and lit a cigarette without turning off the tap. The first rough smoke of the day abraded my throat, hurt my lungs, and tasted like heaven. I stepped up behind Malee

195

and stroked her knotted and tangled hair. I told her she could drop her hands and they fell to her sides. I reached around and held the filter to her lips and Malee took a long grateful pull off the cigarette. I watched her flanks twitch like a race horse's as the water made a loud noise splashing into the sink.

I turned back to the window and looked out onto Leith Street. Morning vendors of noodles and pancakes, their three-wheel pushcarts sending blue plumes of smoke into the bright morning sky, lined the gutters that had been washed clean by the night's rain. I let the cigarette hang from my lips and unlatched the shutters, letting in the fresh air, then turned abruptly.

"You can go now, Malee."

She looked at me over her shoulder, shock mingled with anxiety on her face. I turned back to the window and took another drag on my cigarette. It tasted especially fine. The water continued to splash in the basin, and when I looked at Malee again, her little brown fists were clenched on her thighs and her butt was shaking with muscle spasms.

"But Noble Lord! Please, I beg you! I wish to stay with My Noble Lord!"

She turned from the bed, but stayed on her knees, and bringing her hands up once again to her forehead bowed to the floor three times. The third time she stayed down, her long hair falling across my feet. I put a foot onto her back and pushed her over onto her side. Malee kept her hands at her forehead and allowed me to roll her onto her back and spread her legs with my foot.

In Asia, the head is the holiest part of the body, and the foot the most profane. To touch another person with your foot is the vilest insult. I planted the sole of my right foot on Malee's vagina and spoke down at her in a right voice.

"Why should I keep you, whore?"

"My Noble Lord, I swear to you, if you keep Malee she will be your willing slave. Every thought will be to your pleasure, every act to your comfort. Malee will refuse her Lord nothing, and My Noble Lord may use Malee in any way he may wish."

The water continued to splash in the sink, and I could tell that it was having its effect on Malee by the way her pubic muscles bunched under my foot. She was in considerable discomfort, and I enjoyed the moment, dragging it out.

"The world is full of willing slaves, whore, and many are younger and more beautiful than you."

As we negotiated I tweaked her pubes with my toes. She remained on her back on the splintered floor, her feet in the air and her legs spread wide open. Under the ball of my foot I could feel the lump of her bladder, like a grapefruit under silk. I have it a gentle nudge and Malee groaned.

"My Noble Lord," she whined, "please, I must enter the water-room quickly!"

"You will go when I say, and not before, whore." I added a lazy yawn for effect. "Soon your old client will awaken, and come looking for you. To deal with him will be a bother. Why should I take the trouble?"

"Please, please, please My Noble Lord!" she wailed. "It is true, Malee is a worthless whore and ugly. My teats are too big and my butt too fat, I have no nose and my lips are too wide. Malee is beneath the notice of My Noble Lord, but if My Lord will take Malee from the chicken-shit foreigner - OW!"

I gave a hard shove on her belly when she used the profanity. It is most rude in Asia and the first slip she'd made in her etiquette with me. When I pushed a small squirt of clear liquid shot out of her snatch onto the dry old boards. Her knees tried to jerk together but I kicked them open again. I picked up her sarong and threw it onto the floor at her crotch. Malee lay on the floor with her hands held over her head now, her feet bobbing around in the air, weeping freely with a tiny squirt of piss coming out on each sob.

"Oh please... uh! My Noble Lord... uh! I beg you... uh! Take me... oh! I'll do what you say, I'll be a good girl, oh, please... o-o-o-oh!"

Finally it all came out together, words and tears and pee in an uncontrolled flood from both ends of her as her feet crashed to the ground and her hands covered her weeping face. I turned off the water at the tap and stood over her savouring my cigarette. When she was finally quiet, sprawled on the floor completely drained emotionally and physically, I reached down and grabbed a handful of her long sweaty hair and pulled her to her feet, where she stood swaying in the centre of the room.

"Pick up your sarong, whore," I said.

Malee bent over in a daze and picked up the sodden stinking cloth with two fingers. I enjoyed her obvious distaste for the soiled garment. It made what I was about to do more delicious.

"Put it on," I said.

She came out of her stupor immediately, looking at me with eyes made wide by revulsion. Asians are a very fastidious people, they taught the Europeans to bathe, after all. "You've made a mess in my room," I said to her. "You're a stinking pig, and if I'm to take you as my property, you must be taught some manners. Put it on, whore."

Slowly, Malee pulled the soggy cotton around her body. It was heavy with urine, and clung to the curves and crevasses of her body. She knotted it between her breasts and then stood in front of me, tears streaming down her beautiful face, breasts shivering with her shamed weeping. She obediently pulled the wet sarong out from the front of her body, and i stubbed out my cigarette on the cloth. It made a hiss and burned a small perfectly round hole in the stinking material.

I threw the cigarette end out of the window and told Malee to drop her hands. When she did, the hole in the sarong fit perfectly over the dark brown puckered bud of one nipple. I took the exposed nipple between thumb and forefinger and twisted it almost 180 degrees. Malee's weeping took on an urgent note, but she kept her eyes on the floor and stood at attention in front of me.

"I should send you back to him now, like this," I said. "How do you think he'll receive you, worthless, stinking, dirty whore that you are?"

Malee shook with her sobbing, and her tears made tiny dark spots on the dry old floorboards next to the bigger ones her piss had made.

Then I went to my bag and got out the old sarong I keep to shine my shoes. I gave it to her with my toilet kit. She looked at the things I gave her and then back at me with wondering eyes, her sobs dissolving into gasps and hiccoughs.

"Go to the bathroom, Malee," I said to her in a gentle voice and using verb forms reserved for intimates and family members. "Bathe, shampoo your hair and brush your teeth. You'll find a razor and cream in the kit, remove the hair from your sex." I licked my thumb and gently massaged the nipple I had twisted so unmercifully.

"Go now," I said, "and if you meet anybody in the hallway, and they ask you what you're doing and where you're going, tell them that you belong to the gentleman in room twenty-four and they can go to hell."

Malee sighed a long breath and dropped to her bruised knees. She put down my kit and brought her clasped hands to her forehead, then she tapped her head three times on the spotted floor. Her voice came up from my feet, choked with emotion.

"Thank you, Most Noble Lord. Thank you one thousand times and into one thousand future lives. You hold Malee's worthless life in your hands, and Malee is happy."

She rose and went to the door, her butt moving with its old perky bounce under the disgusting wet rag, which Malee now wore like a ball gown. I watched her leave, then gabbed my keys and my wallet and threw on a shirt. I had a lot to do before the punk next door woke up, and I wanted to do it before Malee finished her bath.

Mr. Metha gave me his home phone number years ago, but I had never had occasion to use it. I placed a call from the front desk and less than five minutes later Metha came churning into the lobby on his stubby bowed legs. We went into the bar, dark and deserted at this time of morning, and huddled up for a few moments. Pretty soon Metha laughed out loud and we shook hands. I took a couple of hundred dollars out of my wallet and passed it to him. Then I went back to my room and read my book.

After a while there was a tapping on the door, and I called Malee to come in. She looked radiant when she came in the room, her hair wet but well combed, her skin fresh and glowing from a good scrubbing. My old sarong, though it was stained with shoe polish in a hundred places, was clean and carried a faint lingering scent of oil that was not unpleasant. She gave me a big smile and replaced my toilet kit in my bag, then she came and sat on the bed beside me.

I put my book down and lit a cigarette. Malee immediately hunted for the ash tray and brought it to the bed. She held it out to me, waiting, happy, obedient. I reached out and pulled the knot of her sarong, and Malee wiggled a bit to let the cloth fall about her hips. I played with her sweet titties and shared my cigarette with her.

"Malee, did you shave?" I asked, glancing to where the sarong was bunched in her lap.

In answer she stood by the bed, holding the sarong behind her and showing me her smooth pubes. "I can't see all of you, Malee," I said. She turned from the bed and pulled a chair over. She placed one foot on the seat of the chair and bent over its back, so that her ass and cunt were opened and facing me. She stayed that way awaiting my pleasure. "Open you lips for me," I told her, and she reached between her legs with one hand and delicately spread the pink petals of her sex.

At that moment a boy came to pound on the door of room twenty-two, waking the punk and telling him there was an urgent phone call for him downstairs. I saw Malee stiffen when she heard his voice through the wall, and I reached out a hand and patted her butt to quieten her. When she felt my hand she relaxed, and gave me a shy smile over her shoulder. I was seeing more and more honest emotions from Malee, and I liked it.

I caressed her smooth buttocks and the outer rim of her pussy while we listened to the drama next door. The punk could be heard banging around his room, berating the boy for waking him and shouting for Malee.

I was enjoying seeing Malee's cunt close up and in daylight for the first time. Her skin was the colour of creamy caramel, which darkened to chocolate in the crack of her ass and the outer lips of her twat. These outer lips were serrated like the lips of a dog, and the delicate inner lips and asterix of her anus were mottled dark brown and pink like a pair of exotic seashells. The inner throat of her vagina, and the hood over her clitoris, were a bright glistening pink.

I put a finger to the base of her clitoris and pushed, and the tiny head popped out of its hood and showed itself off. I ran the tip of my finger around on the inside of her cunt, gathering some of the abundant juice in there, and Malee gave a little gasp as I rolled her tiny joy bud between a wet thumb and finger. I jammed the finger back inside the warm envelope of her twat and made her rise up onto her toes and gasp again as I found her G-spot. Even though she had been fucked by countless men, her cunt was still tight and snug. Asian genes.

As I'd familiarised myself with Malee's snatch, I'd listened to the punk banging around in his room. When he finally went to the lobby for his phone call, the boy came back and knocked on my door. I gave Malee the pair of shorts and T-shirt I had intended to hand out to her in the hall at the beginning of our relationship, and told her to go fetch her things. The boy opened the door to room twenty-two with his passkey and allowed Malee to move her clothes and passport and return air ticket from that room to mine. I tipped the boy well and after he left told Malee to take off her clothes again.

I laid down on the bed, opened my jeans and told Malee to give me a nice, slow, morning blow job. She started to climb onto the bed but I stopped her. I made her kneel next to the bed, though this time I let her kneel on the crumpled wad of torn mosquito net to save her knees. I had her bend over me, with her hands behind her back, and do the job with lips and tongue alone, while I guided her movements with a firm grip on one earlobe.

A moment later the punk returned, and I listened to him rant and rave about the bogus phone call and Malee's disappearance while she licked lazy circles around my scrotum. A few moments later the police came as I had arranged with Metha and I listened to them arrest the punk for possession of Hashish, a crime that carries the penalty of death in Malaysia, while Malee giggled and slurped up my sperm like a little girl eating tapioca pudding.

3

After the police dragged the punk off to jail I had Malee brush her teeth again at the sink and then stand in the corner. The room was too small for two people to move around comfortably, and I planned to be busy for a few minutes. I was not angry with her, and explained so and let her face into the room instead of putting her face into the corner.

She went obediently into the corner and then asked "My Noble Master, my toy is hot and wet and I haven't 'finished' yet this morning. I ache to play with myself. Please may I, Noble Master?"

I took her hand and put it in her mouth. "Wet one finger, Malee," I said. She chose her middle finger, and when it was good and slick with her spit I said "You have three minutes to 'finish'. If you aren't done in that time you'll be punished."

Her hand shot to her bald snatch and began to rub away at her clit. She leaned back in the corner, throwing her head back and closing her eyes with her concentration to finish in time. She reached down with her free hand to hold her pussy open and I slapped it away. "One hand only." She redoubled her efforts and her breathing turned into a laboured pant.

I checked my watch and began to go through her things. Her worldly possessions, at least all she had brought to Malaysia, consisted of the contents of a single black cotton drawstring bag, made by the Northern Hilltribes of Laos and available for pennies in any Asian airport gift shop. I wanted to make sure that there was nothing in the bag that could make for me the kind of trouble that Metha and I had made for the punk.

I dumped the bag onto the floor and sifted through it with a foot. There were three or four pairs of shorts and a miniskirt of black fake leather. There were some T-shirts and a bikini. I kicked a few pairs of dingy panties and an underwire bra out of the pile and into a corner. If there was time, and she kept my interest, I'd buy her some decent lingerie. Until then it suited me that she go without. There was a plastic bag with some cosmetics which I picked up and threw into the waste basket. I hate make-up on women, I think it looks dirty.

Behind me I could hear a wet slopping noise as Malee rubbed

at her pussy with the edge of an open palm. She was moaning steadily now, long deep breaths that ended in sighs. I took a quick look at her, and saw she was standing on only one foot. The other was raised with the knee almost touching her breast, in order to open her pussy as far as possible. Her free hand was braced against the wall, and her whole body was shaking.

I checked my watch. She had one minute fifteen seconds to finish her business.

The last item in the hilltribe bag was a wallet, and I picked it up and opened it. Inside were Malee's passport and identification card, her return air ticket, an inconsequential amount of cash, and some family photos. I put all these into my own bag and zipped it shut. I was pleased to see that Malee had no drugs, and as the seconds ticked by, I decided to let her have whatever extra time she needed to have her orgasm.

Her hand was a blur at her crotch now, rubbing away at the split in her body, spreading her moisture from clit to asshole. Most bar girls are so desentisied by the constant pounding that their snatches are subjected to that they require enormous stimulation to achieve orgasm. I was surprised to see no vibrator in the pile of cheap clothes on the floor, but then I guess it's the sort of thing that would be pretty embarrassing on an airport security x-ray screen.

I stood in front of her as she shivered her way to her climax, and watched her ample breasts jiggle and quiver, their nipples standing up like tiny soldiers at attention. If I hadn't just had a fantastic blow-job, I would have grabbed her and fucked her senseless, but as it was I was content to smoke a cigarette and enjoy the show. As my watch passed the three minute mark Malee was shaking like a jello in an earthquake and biting her lower lip to keep from screaming. She dug three fingers into her snatch and the warm odour of it came up to me like that of baking bread.

As she came she ground her teeth and growled like a cat, bucking and writhing in the corner. Finally she toppled forward as the leg she was standing on collapsed. I had seen it coming, and, as she had intended me to, I caught her. She hung limp in my arms like a rag doll, gasping for breath, her heart beating so that I could feel it through the fat breast that was crushed against my chest. I supported her over to the bed, then put her on her knees on top of the sheet.

She laid her chest and face onto the mattress and panted like a dog. There were chips of plaster and paint on her shoulders and in her hair and on her big round ass, and she had left sweat stains on the walls of the corner. I liked the smell of her pussy very much, it was clean and warm, and I told her to stay that way, on her knees with her ass in the air, to freshen the air in the stuffy little room while I packed my things.

I put my suitcase on the mattress at her feet and began to remove my shirts from the rickety old cupboard. The first shirt was on a wire hanger, and I brought it with the folded shirt to the suitcase. As I lay the shirt into the case I casually gave Malee a swat on the ass with the wire hanger. I didn't hit her hard, but the wire was thin and left a nice welt. I knew it had to sting.

Malee gasped and jumped a bit. "Stay there, whore," I told her. She began to whimper. "Noble Master, what did I do? I thought I pleased Master with my mouth, and I finished in the time Master gave me..."

"You tried to trick me, whore," I said. I was staring at her bottom, fascinated with the red welt across both buttocks, broken for an inch at the cleavage of her ass, where her little puckered hole would clench and relax each time I thoughtfully dragged the shirt hanger across the wound. "Falling down like that, knowing that I'd catch you. Cheap tricks, whore, and they bore me."

WHACK! This time I laid one on her hard, and she yelped. She put a hand behind her reflexively, and I grabbed it and twisted her arm until she was wailing. I eased off and said "Bite the pillow, whore." Malee did as she was told, and her sobs were muffled. I placed her limp arm back at her head and recommenced caressing her burning ass with the hanger.

"Listen to me, Malee," I said. "I paid a lot of money to remove the insect next door. If you stay with me, I must pay more so that you will look presentable. I cannot go around Penang with someone who is so obviously a cheap whore." On the last word I gave her a little tap with the wire, and she squealed into the pillow more with surprise than pain. "If I take you, you must be honest, Malee. I will tell you how to act and what to say, and if I don't tell you, then you say nothing and do nothing. Do you understand?"

I thought I heard a quiet answer coming from the pillow. Another tap with the hanger produced a muffled squeal, too indistinct to understand as language, but a quick swipe of my thumb up and down the pink furrow of her cunt produced a shiver of her fleshy buns and a lot of wetness.

"Good," I said to myself in English, "now we're communicating!" I set the wire coat hanger on the top of the platform her butt made, and went to the closet for more clothes. I continued to speak as I folded my wardrobe, and as each item went into the bag I casually picked up the hanger and gave Malee another whack on the ass.

I began to whistle tunelessly and Malee turned her head on the pillow, watching me collect clothing through the wet strands of her hair. She had a vested interest in seeing how much clothing I was going to pack. I had three pairs of slacks: Whack, whack, whack! I had a pair of shorts and a pair of bathing trunks: Whack, whack! I had four shirts: Whack, whack, whack, whack! By the time I had put my two pairs of shoes into the bag (Whack-whack! Whack-whack!) Malee's ass looked like a crossword puzzle drawn in red ink on two brown marshmallows. She was sobbing uncontrollably now.

When I pulled my underwear (five pair) and socks (five pair) out of the drawer, Malee began to wail. She fell onto her side, with her butt away from me and against the wall, curled into the foetal position and begging for mercy.

"Please," she blubbered. "Master, please, no more. Malee will be good, oh, Malee will be the best woman you ever had. Malee will pleasure her Master all day and all night and then all day again. Master must stay in Penang until tomorrow, let me show you. Please, master, please..."

I looked into her red and weeping eyes and said "Get back on your knees, Malee. I haven't released you." She climbed once again to her knees, and, sobbing fitfully, laid her head once again on the tear-soaked pillow. I dumped my underwear into the bag and went to the sink. I fitted the rubber stopper into the drain and filled the basin with water. The water in Penang is good and clean and cold, brought into town from the high mountains by aqueducts which are the legacy of British colonial administration.

I poured a few drops of aftershave into the water and soaked a wash cloth in it, then returned to the bed and laid the cold cloth across Malee's whipped ass. She sighed and her crying changed its note. I gently moved the cool damp cloth across her battered cheeks and I knew that the stringent in the aftershave would cleanse the few places I'd actually broken her skin. I made two more trips to the sink, until Malee's beautiful full ass had lost most of its angry red tinge and the welts had lost most of their swelling.

I laid her down on her stomach and I began to wipe the plaster and paint from her shoulders. She spread herself on the mattress and her sobbing died down into gentle sniffles. I made several trips to the sink, rinsing the cloth and wiping Malee's backside to the nape of her neck. I picked all the paint chips out of her hair, the told her to roll over. She obeyed, and once again spread herself on the old teak bed, with her eyes closed and her pussy open to the ceiling.

I cleaned the sweat from her body and the tears from her face with the cool cloth. I had to refresh the water in the sink twice, but after ten minutes Malee lay on the sheets perfectly clean and sweet-smelling. I lifted one arm and let if fall back to the mattress; she was limp and compliant again. I let her rest while I changed into some slacks and a shirt. I picked the fake leather mini—skirt out of the pile of Malee's clothes on the floor, and a T-shirt that looked fairly clean. I put them on the bed and then addressed my new slave.

"Listen to me, Malee," I said.

Her eyes opened and she looked at me. Her eyes were full of trust and something I believe was close to genuine affection.

"I'll keep you for the day, and the night. Tomorrow we both go back to Bangkok. Whether I keep you past tomorrow or not depends on your behaviour today."

"Yes, Master," she replied.

"In a minute we are going to check out of this hotel. It no

longer suits my purposes. Get up and get dressed."

I lit a cigarette and sat on the bed while Malee slid into her skirt and shirt. She looked at the pile of underwear in the corner and then back at me, but I shook my head.

She put the rest of her clothes into the cotton hilltribe bag. She never mentioned that her passport was missing. She had to know that without it she was helpless in Malaysia; as long as I had her passport, ID card and plane ticket, she was mine. She drew the bag shut and looked up at me from where she was squatting on the floor. She was almost on top of the darkened wood where she had soiled herself the night before.

I picked up the room key from an end table and told Malee to take both bags. She did so with a smile. Then I picked up a copy of the Far eastern Economic Review and held it out to her. It was two weeks old and I'd already read it, but put it in her mouth to carry. She stood in front of me, a bag in each hand and the magazine in her mouth, and smiled at me with her eyes.

I did a check of the room; nothing was left behind or in the closet. I held the room key out to her. It was attached by a ring to a small plastic tab, about as wide and long as a box of matches and half as thick, with the name and address of the New Cathay Hotel.

Malee looked at the key with a blank expression. I walked to her, roughly pulled up the front of her skirt, and began to jam the plastic key-tag into her snatch. She gasped and squirmed but didn't drop the bags or the paper, and I managed to fit the plastic rectangle up her cunt all the way to the ring. The key dangled between her legs like a Christmas ornament.

I opened the door and Malee followed me out into the hall. I led the way to the stairs and I went down two steps at a time. Malee followed more slowly, and I turned to watch her from the landing. She had to walk with her knees together, and the skirt was so short that I could catch a glimpse now and then of the key glimmering between her silky thighs. She held her head up so as not to lose the newspaper, and had to feel for each step with the toe of her foot. In this awkward and charming way she descended the stairs.

I took her elbow when she reached the bottom and led her to

the desk. At this hour the lobby was still empty, but there was a sleepy old Chinese woman behind the counter. I brought Malee, with the newspaper still clenched in her teeth, right up to the desk. When we had the old crone's attention, I reached down behind Malee, put my hand under her skirt and dug between the soft yielding domes of her ass. She gasped a bit and spread her legs in a hurry, and when I yanked the rook key out of her snatch she said "OH!" and the week-old Far eastern Economic Review plopped out of her mouth onto the chipped teak counter. Malee's teeth left a semi-circle of indentations on the fold, and there were traces of printer's ink on her lips.

I dropped the key on top of the newspaper, with beads of Malee's cunt juice glistening on the plastic in the clear morning light that flooded the lobby.

"The missus and I will be checking out," I said.

4

The Chinese are a superstitious lot. It doesn't matter if they're peasants planting wheat on the Mongolian border or third generation immigrants with a million US dollars in the bank and a string of Malay minor wives; when a Chinese builds a building he builds it under the guidelines of Shen Fui. Main doors must never face south, and they must be in the middle of the front wall of the building, never to one side or the other. Immediately inside the door must be an ancestor shrine to block marauding ghosts, and since everyone knows that ghosts cannot cross water, immediately outside the door will be a pool, pond or fountain.

The New Cathay Hotel in Penang is set back from Leith Street by a tiny walled courtyard, with a circular driveway running around an ornamental fish pond. The whole place is in such disrepair that taxi drivers grumble about bringing their machines in over the pitted and rusted tarmac, but thee fat carp that float just under the surface of the ghost pool are signs of wealth and bringers of good luck, so they are well cared for by the arthritic, opium-addicted gardener. I sat on the edge of of this pool and tossed cigarette buts to the fish while Malee stood out on the street with the bags, trying to flag down a taxi.

The one she finally got to pull into the courtyard was a dilapidated Holden, an Australian car very popular in Southeast Asia during the Vietnam war. At that time they were cheap and easily imported, since Oz has always had better relations with her Asian neighbours and lower duties imposed on her exports than the rest of the Western world. This one had been ream colour when Saigon became Ho Chi Minh City, but now it was a turgid grey with large patches of red primer paint, like a mutant Dalmation dog. The driver was a young Sikh, with a tight turban coming down to his eyebrows and a hair net wrapped around his head.

He leapt out of the car to help Malee with the bags, and without his foot on the gas the engine immediately coughed and died. He pulled the end of a piece of twine that was hanging out of the boot and the lid popped open; after he'd placed our luggage inside he carefully tied the lid back down. Malee and I climbed in the back seat and I told the Sikh to take us to the Grace Hotel. It was a better place than the Cathay by far, around the other side of Penang island, by a place called Batu Faringi.

It would take us about half an hour to get there. I checked to see that I had plenty of smokes, and as the Sikh pulled out into the traffic I wondered what I could do to pass the time. Georgetown, the main business center of Penang island, is an ugly city and Malee was looking at me with big doe eyes, obviously expecting something. I gave her tits a few playful slaps and watched them swing back and forth, not really intending anything but liking the sight of them. Without really thinking about it, I told Malee to tell me about how she lost her virginity.

She looked at me with surprise, and I said "Tell me, Malee. And tell the truth, I'll know if you're lying." She looked at the back of the Sikh's head and then at me, and I said "Don't worry, he can't understand us. But even if he could, you must obey me, Malee." I looked deep into her eyes and slid one hand up under her T-shirt. It had sixteen pairs of cartoon pigs on it, demonstrating the cardinal positions of the Kama Sutra. I tweaked a nipple furiously and the pigs all danced.

Malee began to speak, quietly and with some self-consciousness at first. "I was born on a rice farm in the Northeast," she said. "I had nine brothers and sisters, some older, some younger. When I was ten my father fell sick and went into hospital. My oldest brother went in the Army, and for a year he sent money home. But then he met a girl and got married, and we never heard from him again. My two eldest sisters went to work in a toy factory in Bangkok. They sent money home to my mother, but it wasn't much. Then they wrote to say that they had been offered work as house maids in Japan, where they could make a fortune just for doing the laundry and looking after babies. We were all very excited when they left, but then they we never heard from them again. Now, of course, I know what happens to poor girls in Japan, but then we all just thought that they had got rich and forgot us. My father died when I was thirteen and Mother began to sell our land, piece by piece. It wasn't very good land, or very much, but it was all we had."

As we drove along, and Malee talked, I kept my hand under her shirt and played with her boobs. They were wonderful boobs, warm and soft and springy, and I kept giving one a slap so that they bobbled back and forth against each other. The Sikh had looked angrily into his rear view mirror when I lit a cigarette, Sikhs hate tobacco, but when he saw Malee's titties jiggling around under her shirt he smiled and slowed down. It was necessary, since he was now watching the mirror more than the road.

"Then a woman came from a big city to the North. She stayed in our village for a couple of days, talking to all the parents who had young girls. She said that she would pay good money for virgins, who would become the minor wives of rich Chinese businessmen in the city. Well, we were ignorant peasants, but we weren't that ignorant. Still, if a family needs money, it was the responsibility of all the daughters, and not the sons, to find it. And the story about being respectable minor wives would save the family face.

"The woman gave my mother some money, I never knew how much, and took me to a shophouse in the city." Malee continued, her eyes gazing off out of the windows at the ugly buildings of Georgetown but seeing a different city in a different country and a different decade. "I stayed a few days in the shophouse with some other girls. There were about ten of us, sleeping together in one big room under the roof. There were girls from Laos, from Burma, China and from the hill-tribes who recognize no border. The doors were locked all day and all night so we wouldn't run away, and after one girl jumped out of a window and broke her legs they took most of our clothes away, too. They fed us once a day, a little rice and soup, and there was a big water jar in the corner that we used for drinking, bathing and washing our shit down a drain."

Malee's eyes were blank now, and she didn't react when I pulled her T-shirt up over her boobs to give the Sikh a real good look. We were stopped at a red light, and he stared into his rear view mirror until the light had changed and the cars behind us were honking madly. He drove on, but I could see that he resented every glance he made at the road.

"Every day men would come to look at us." said Malee. "There we were, ten girls in the room, all of us between thirteen and fifteen years old, all naked or wearing only panties. It was so hot that we were always sweaty, and so weak with hunger that we didn't even try to cover ourselves up when the men came to look at us. Sometimes they were obviously rich men, usually old and breathing heavy from walking up the stairs. Sometimes they were just friends of the man who owned the shop on the ground floor, who was paid by the woman who had purchased us from our families.

"The men would walk through the room, looking us over, and they would sometimes tell a girl to stand up and turn around. Most of us looked pretty bad, with greasy hair and our faces all puffy from crying, but the men didn't seem to care. They would gather around a girl, maybe four or five men at a time, and say the cruelest things about her, about her body and what they'd like to do to her. They would all touch her, everywhere, and if she was wearing panties they'd pull them down to her knees so they could play with her pussy."

Tears were rolling down Malee's face now, and she was oblivious of me or the Sikh or the other drivers who would catch sight of her bare breasts and honk or yell. I had dropped my hand into her lap and pulled up her skirt. She lifted her butt off the seat to free the skirt without appearing to give any thought to her action. I played with the lips of her cunt while she talked, and gradually, they became wet.

"The men that came to look at us never raped us, though. They were afraid of the Mamasan, and she wanted us all to stay virgins until we were sold. Her clients were Bao Boon Chin, which is a kind of cult among Chinese businessmen."

I'd heard of the Bao Boon Chin. These men believed that fucking a virgin is more than just the tightest pussy a man will ever know, they think that there is magic involved. I knew they paid a lot for bona fide virgo intacto, and that they kept the blood on a silk handkerchief which would be taken to a Moh Doo, or soothsayer. This man would read the future from the bloody Rorshack blot, and I had heard that some successful businessmen kept collections of hundreds of these blood stained squares of silk.

"Sometimes one of the rich old men would pick a girl, and then leave. The money always changed hands downstairs, so I also never knew how much I cost the man who paid for me. When my turn came I was taken down to the second floor and put in a bathroom and told to wash. Oh, my God, you don't know how good that hot water and soap felt, and the fresh air. I squatted over the toilet and had my first relaxed bowel movement in days; it was just terrible trying to do it in front of all those girls."

The Sikh wasn't paying enough attention to his driving, and we hit the kerb of the causeway. The cab swung once, twice, and the Sikh found the lane again, but by then my finger had slipped up inside Malee's snatch. It was hot and liquid in there, and flexing like a nervous fist. She moaned and her eyes fluttered shut, and she continued the story without opening them. It was only eight in the morning but it was already hot on the pavements of Georgetown, and all three of us in the Holden were sweating freely. The car was musty and a smell of decades of mildew oozed from the torn upholstery.

"After my bath I was given food and clean clothes, and taken in a taxi across the town to a nice hotel. The Mamasan's driver took me inside and up to a room. He told me to strip and lay down on the bed. I thought he was going to rape me, and I spread my legs to make it finish quicker, but he just laughed and tied a rubber string around my arm. He held my arm very tightly and gave me a shot of something in the inside of my elbow. I immediately felt very sleepy, and I could not move, though I never did actually go to sleep.

"The driver took off the rubber thong and sat in a corner smoking, staring at me lying naked and drugged on the bed. In a while, I have no idea how long I laid there, the fat Chinese who had selected me came in. The driver went out without a word. The Chinese seemed to be in a big hurry, he took off his pants and shirt without ever looking at me. Then he came and slid a square of pure silk under my butt and leaned over my face. 'Can you hear me?' he said.

"It sounded like his voice was coming up through deep water, and I couldn't answer or even nod my head. 'Whatever you do, don't move your ass.' he said. 'You mustn't smear the blood. If you ruin it, I'll kill you.' He said this calmly, like he was saying 'It may rain today.' I was fourteen years old, about to lose my cherry, and he's telling me that if I move my butt while he's ripping me open, he'll kill me."

Malee's voice was shaking and she was crying freely. The Sikh must have thought that I was hurting her to make her cry, but it didn't seem to bother him. He was driving with his left hand, and it occurred to me that I hadn't seen his right hand for a while. Malee was limp, sprawled in the back seat, skirt bunched around her waist and T-shirt shoved up over her chest, exposed completely to the eyes of the truck drivers in their elevated cabs. I had one hand in her snatch and was smoking with the other, and the Sikh didn't seem to mind the smoke at all.

"The Chinese man climbed onto his knees on the bed between my legs." said Malee. "He pulled this very tiny penis out of the opening in his underwear. He spit into his hand and started to masturbate. His eyes were closed, I don't know what he was thinking of, but it wasn't me. His little dick got semi-hard, but it never got truly erect. He flopped down on top of me, nearly crushing me with his weight, and tried to get it in, but it got soft again.

He got back up on his knees and spit into his palm and started over, this time staring up at the ceiling and singing softly. What he was singing sounded like a lullaby.

"He flopped onto me again this time he was able to jam his prick into me. I felt the pain as if it were coming through layers of silk, and it wasn't too bad, I didn't even cry. I concentrated on remaining still, so I wouldn't smear the blood picture, but he was bouncing up and down on me so hard that my legs were flying up in the air. Finally he came, pressing down on me intentionally, and I blacked out from lack of air. I came to when I heard him leave the room, and I laid there on the bed thinking 'I'm not a virgin any more, now no decent man will ever marry me.' Then the Mamasan's driver came back into the room."

At this Malee opened her eyes and sat up. She made as if to push my hand away from her cunt, and there was a wild, hunted look in her face. She seemed to realize where she was, and instead of pushing my hand away she grabbed it and pressed it deeper into her pussy. She huddled against my arm, clutching my finger inside her, and finished her story in a small voice, a little girl's voice.

"The driver came back with three of his friends and a bottle of whisky. The Chinese were allowed to keep girls all night, but never did, so the driver would enjoy the girls until morning. He shared me with his buddies. They all climbed on the bed and started slapping me and pinching me; they didn't want something still and quiet, they wanted something that would feel pain and cry about it. They got the blood going by splashing freezing water on my pussy from an ice bucket that came with the whisky, and when I had a little strength left, they took me... two would hold me down while two fucked me... they fucked my pussy, and my ass, and my mouth... and when they were too tired to get a hard-on, they used the empty whisky bottle..."

Malee dissolved into a gale of sobbing, throwing her head into my lap and crying like a baby. She was clutching at my hard-on, wetting my slacks with her tears. We were only a hundred yards away from the Grace Hotel, and I told the Sikh to go round the block once while I got my pants open and my cock into Malee's eager mouth. She seemed to want it so badly I couldn't say no.

5

We pulled up to the Grace as Malee was wiping my sperm off
her chin with a page torn from my bettered old copy of Frommer's
Guide To Penang. The Sikh was wiping his right hand on a tissue, and when I asked him 'How much' he said 'Never mind'
and grinned at me in the mirror.

I took Malee into the lobby and told her to wait by a potted
palm. The Grace is a nice hotel and doesn't appreciate guests
bringing in foreign whores, and I didn't want a scene at registra-
tion. I booked us into a room and Malee followed me to the
elevator carrying our bags. We were stared at by a few loiterers
in the lobby, but I didn't care. All I was thinking about was air-
conditioning, a cool shower and a drink.

Our room was a standard double: an anonymous cubicle on
the fourth floor with a double bed, small refrigerator, television
set and single window looking out over the red tiled roofs of
Georgetown. Malee dropped the bags and flopped face down on
the bed, heaving a sigh of relief. She wriggled a bit, enjoying the
sensuous feel of the linen bed cover and working her skirt up
over her butt in the process. I turned the knob on the thermostat
as low as it would go and looked at Malee on the bed. Her T-
shirt was stained with sweat and her panties were soaking with
cunt juice.

I said "Stay where you are, whore, I'm going to take a shower"
and went into the bathroom. I took off my sopping shirt and
trousers, wrapped a towel round my hips and turned on the water, then went back into the room to get my medicated anti-fun-
gal soap from my kit. If I use normal soap in the tropics I get
spots on my butt, so I always use the stuff doctors scrub up with.

Malee was standing in front of the TV, watching a game show
broadcast in Malay with Mandarin subtitles. Her T-shirt was in a
lump on the floor and she was pulling her skirt and panties down.
She had them to her ankles when I snapped at her.

"Stop. Stand still."

She froze and looked at me with incomprehension. I stood in front of her and asked "Did I tell you to strip?"

"N-no, Master."

"Then why are you taking your clothes off?"

"I am very hot, Master... I wanted a bath..."

*"You only do what I tell you to do, whore. If I don't tell, don't do anything."

She dropped to her knees and put her clasped hands in front of her face. "I'm sorry, Master." she said. "What will you have me do?" With this she made to reach under the towel for my prick, but I wasn't ready for another blow job yet and slapped her hands away. "Stay as you are." I said. I went back to the bathroom and got a small complimentary bottle of shampoo from the ledge over the sink. I returned to the bedroom where Malee was waiting obediently on her knees and told her to put her head on the carpet. She obeyed immediately, and I reached down and inserted the small, tubular plastic shampoo bottle into her puckered anus.

She grunted but held still, and I stood back to admire my work. She looked very nice that way, on her knees with her head on the floor and her arms stretched out in front of her, her panties and skirt still bunched at her ankles and the pink end of the shampoo bottle peeking out of her asshole. I picked up one of my shoes and gave her a few whacks with it, turning the cheeks of her big round butt a bright red. She whimpered and flinched but didn't drop the bottle. I threw the shoe down and said "Stay like that while I bathe. Then I pulled a cold beer from the small refrigerator under the TV and left her.

I took my time in the shower, enjoying the wonderful Penang water and gulping my beer. When I was finished I dusted myself all over with baby powder and leisurely flossed my teeth. Then I went back to the bedroom.

The TV was still on and Malee was as I had left her, though the shampoo bottle had worked its way a half-inch out of her asshole. With a thumb I shoved it back and told her to stand up. She grunted as she did and I told her to step out of her skirt. She stood in front of the TV totally naked, stooped a little because of the pressure of the little bottle in her rectum, making her tits hang down and sway. She was smiling at me expectantly. I pulled on a pair of shorts and told her to go into the bathroom. I turned off the TV and followed her.

Malee walked into the bathroom with mincing steps, her gait affected by the pressure in her asshole. I told her to stand in the tub, and when she was in it I twisted the blue-labelled knob so that the harsh spray of icy water cascaded over her. She gasped and jumped a bit, putting out her arms against the wall to steady herself on the slick porcelain, but she didn't complain. Her big nipples immediately jumped to attention, standing up in the spray like two wrinkled desert dates.

I let her stand like that under the cold water, enjoying the sight of her lithe brown body against all the white tile and the pink bottle ringed with the dark brown circle of her anus, until her teeth were chattering and her fingertips were wrinkled. I turned off the water and sat down on the toilet seat, taking out my fingernail clippers and watching little shivers run up and down Malee's body. Her knees were knocking together and she had wrapped her arms around her frigid boobs. "Now wash your-self, whore, and do a thorough job of it." I told her, as I began to clip my toenails.

Malee took the bar of scented soap from the side of the tub and began to rub it over her body, working up a thick lather. Her skin was corrugated with goose bumps and her hair hung in wet strands down her back. She was still shaking with the cold.

I examined a toenail on my right foot and said "Tell about how you became a whore, Malee."

"I told you, Master." she answered.

I calmly took a wash cloth from the pile by the sink and ran some water over it until it was wet and heavy. Then I twirled it into a tapered 'rat's tail' and leisurely snapped it at Malee's ass. It cracked like a whip and made her jump. The bottle had slid more than an inch out of her ass when she jumped, and she auto-matically reached back to shove it back in.

"You told me how you gave your cherry to a fat old Chinaman, and how you liked it. Didn't you, Malee?" and snap! went the wash cloth.

"Y-yes, Master... I liked it."

"You loved being fucked by that fat man, and you loved it when the others used you too. You like having men squirt their spunk into you, don't you, whore?" snap!

"Yes, Master," she whimpered from the tub, "I like it."

"Now tell me how you went from giving your pussy away for free to being a whore." I laid the wash cloth on the basin and went back to my pedicure.

Malee continued to rub the small bar of soap over herself, standing in the tub with her knees slightly bent and her legs apart to ease the discomfort in her asshole, and began to speak. Asians don't use toilet paper, and in any hotel in the Orient there will be a hose rigged next to the toilet with a spray attachment. From time to time I would spray Malee with this so that she could get a batch of suds worked up.

"In the morning that the driver took me back to the Mamasan. She bitched at him because I was in pretty bad shape, bruised all over and bleeding from my ass and cunt. But she didn't mean it, she had her money. She put me in another room with some other girls who had also been 'broken' and were waiting to be shipped to Bangkok. The other girls showed me how to put medicine in my ass and pussy to stop infection, and we all waited there for almost a week until she had enough girls to make a shipment."

Malee was rubbing slower and slower with the soap as she got absorbed in her tale, and I enjoyed watching the soap suds slid down her body. Her buttocks were clinched around the pink bottle, trying automatically to reject the foreign object, and now and then she would bend a little at the waist and reach between her legs to push it back in.

"Finally we were loaded into the back of a pick-up truck, fourteen of us in all, and a tarpaulin was tied over us to hide us. It was very cramped and uncomfortable, and when we set out it was just after noon and it soon became like an oven under the canvas. The truck had bad springs and took the back roads to avoid police patrols, and we were bounced around on top of each other.

"Just after dark the drivers stopped for dinner, but they didn't let us out. The chief driver, an ugly man with a scar across the bridge of his nose, stuck a pistol under the tarp and told us if we made a sound while he was away from the truck he'd kill us all. We sat in silence for an hour, the two hours, then three. When the drivers came back, they pulled up one corner of the tarp and yanked out three of the girls who had been sitting there. It turned out that they had gone into a little local restaurant to eat, then got drawn into a card game in a back room. They had lost, and rather than pay with money, had offered to pay with fresh young girls. We waited another hour, and when the three girls came back they were crying. They were shoved into the truck and the tarp was lashed back down and we were off again."

Malee was covered with foam now, and the bar of soap was worn down to a mere sliver. She continued to rub herself, and her hands were rubbing her pussy more often than was necessitated by mere hygienic concerns. She was breathing heavier, too, her boobs rising and falling. "You may touch your cunt, whore." I said casually, and immediately she put one foot on the edge of the tub and began to finger herself. Her other hand went behind her to keep the shampoo bottle from slipping out now that her legs were really spread. Here was a girl who had experience jerking off in the shower.

"Sometime in the night I fell asleep, one girl's foot in my crotch and my face pressed against the ass of another. I woke up when I felt the truck lurch to a stop and heard angry voices outside. The tarp was suddenly whipped back and the glare of several flashlights was in our faces; somebody was shouting at us to tell our names and where we came from. The driver had been stopped by the police, and they were looking for illegal immigrants from Burma. There were five policemen and they pulled five Burmese girls out of the truck, who were screaming and crying their strange language. There were more Burmese girls in the truck, but they only took five of them: five girls for five cops. The driver swore at those of us who were left n the truck and batted at our heads with a rolled up newspaper, then he tied down the tarp and drove on."

The suds had almost slid off Malee now, and she was speaking slowly, in gasps. I knew she was nearing orgasm and so I told her to take the shampoo bottle out of her ass and wash her hair. She looked at me and pouted a bit, but gingerly pulled the bottle out, and gave a little 'ooooh!' when the lid popped out, a sound of half pleasure and half surprise. She opened it and dumped its contents onto her scalp, and as she worked the viscous sperm-coloured liquid into her hair she turned to me and said "Oh, Master, it's so warm!"

I thought 'Yeah, 98.6 degrees Fahrenheit,' but what I said was "Go on with your story, whore, and keep one foot up on the tub, I like you this way."

Malee smiled sweetly and began to talk again. Her hair was long and thick and it took some time to get the shampoo all the way through it. "We got to Bangkok some time after dawn. They let us out at another shophouse, somewhere in the slums, and trooped us all upstairs to a big room with no windows. There was a Chinese man there, who gave the driver hell for coming to Bangkok with five fewer girls than he had taken from the north, but he paid for us anyway."

"I stayed in that room for three days, and during that time more men, and some women, came to inspect us all. The Chinese man fucked each of us at least once, just coming into the room and jumping on a girl and fucking her on the floor while we all watched. I think he only did it when he was bored. When it was my turn I laid still and closed my eyes and thought of home. Some of the people who came to look at us took a few girls, and finally an old woman named Lek selected me and two other girls. She took us to a crib brothel in Thonburi, down by the docks, and that's where I really became a whore."

She used the English word 'crib', though the way she pronounced it it came out sounding like 'clip'. I knew about these places, and thought that I would like to hear that part of her story some place more comfortable than sitting on a hard toilet seat. Her hair was completely saturated with the shampoo now, and she was obviously having difficulty standing on one leg. The air-conditioning had turned the bathroom into an ice box, which I found quite nice, but which was sapping Malee's strength quickly. I told her to shut up while I turned the cold shower on her again, making her stand under it until there wasn't a trace of soap or shampoo anywhere on her sleek, tawny body. When I turned the water off she was supporting herself against the wall, and I could see that she was near collapse.

I helped her out of the tub and made her stand still while I roughly towelled her off. I pushed her against the wall and rubbed the towel across her breasts cruelly, abrading the nipples until she was weeping. Then I wrapped the towel around her wet hair like a turban and supported her into the bedroom. I made her get onto her knees on the bed with her ass in the air and pulled my dick out of my shorts. She was swaying on her knees, and the towel hid her head completely. Her ass looked lovely, big and round and with the marks of the wet wash cloth across it, and without asking permission she began to finger her cunt again. I liked the sight of her slim finger flashing in and out of sight between her thighs, so I let her continue. I lubricated my cock with my own spit; I could have had Malee do it but I wanted a quick fuck and then a nap.

I pressed the swollen purple bulb against her puckered asshole. It was nicely relaxed by the shampoo bottle and I slid inside her easily. I heard her gasp under the towel and watched one tiny fist clench on the bed cover, and felt the other hand brushing against my balls as it was busily plunging in and out of her pussy. With gentle, steady pressure I was inside her to the hilt before I began to pump in and out. Her buttocks were delightfully cold against my thighs, but inside she was warm as toast, and with just two or three strokes I shot a load of jism up her ass while she screamed into the pillow with her own climax. With my last spasm I bucked hard enough to lift her knees off the bed, and then she fell forward, sliding off my rod and collapsing on her face on the bed.

I went back into the bathroom and wash my dick in the sink with warm water and my antiseptic soap. When I returned to the bedroom I could hear Malee's gentle snoring coming through the towel. I pulled the drapes closed, plunging the room into darkness, then climbed onto the bed next to her and pulled the cover over us both. Malee reflectively huddled against my warmth. I nestled my exhausted dick in the crack of her big, soft ass, grabbed a tit and slipped off into a wonderful, dreamless sleep.

6

I awoke to the sound of running water coming from the bathroom. I was alone in the bed and I had a nice stretch and scratched my balls a bit before reaching for my cigarettes. I figured that Malee was washing my sperm. which by now must have become dry and crusty, from her ass.

I listened to the splashing for a minute and then pulled the phone off the nightstand and dialled for room service. I ordered a plate of fried rice for Malee and a hamburger for myself. Then I added a mixed fruit plate to the order.

When Malee came out of the bathroom I had turned the TV back on and was watching a game show. Since Malaysia is a Muslim country, all female contestants were wrapped in howdah, with only their faces and hands uncovered.. I was fantasizing that they were all naked under their ceremonial garb, and had a semi-erection. Malee spotted my thick rod and immediately knelt onto the bed and took it in her mouth.

I let her suck a while, getting harder but not acknowledging her presence in any other way. When there was a sudden knock on the door Malee's head popped up with a surprised look in her eyes, I said "It's some food I ordered, are you hungry, whore?"

"Yes, Master, very hungry!" she replied and I began to gather her clothes. "Don't bother," I said, "just go back into the bathroom and wait."

She did as she was told, and I pulled on y shorts and answered the door. A diminutive Malay boy pushed in the room service cart, with two dishes under stainless steel lids and the fruit wrapped in plastic. I tipped him and sent him away before calling Malee back from the bathroom.

I could see how hungry she was b y the way she stared at the plate of rice, but I told her her "You wait until I've finished, whore, then you may eat."

She was obviously disappointed, but she whimpered "Yes, Master" and sat down on the bed to watch me eat. I put some ketchup on my burger and took a bite; it was just awful. The bad sandwich, probably made from the meat of an old buffalo, put me in a rotten mood. I picked up the plate of fruit and pulled off its plastic wrap. I handed a banana to Malee and said "Start on this, but don't put it in your mouth."

She didn't understand me, and looked from me to the banana and back to me again. "You don't put anything in your mouth until that banana is gone, Malee," I said. She got the idea, and began to peel the fruit. When the meat of the banana was exposed she sat on the edge of the bed and pulled open her cunt lips with one hand.

"I can't see."

Malee climbed up on the bed and turned round, then bent over so that her asshole and pussy were right in front of my eyes. She reached between her legs with one hand and spread her pink twat lips, and with the other reached behind her with the banana and lodged the tip of the fruit in her wet hole. Her anus was tinged red and slightly swollen from being fucked a few hours before, and her big round cheeks were criss-crossed with welts from the wet towel.

She began working the banana inside herself, but it was soft and fell apart. She ended up pushing wads of the pulp into her cunt with her fingers, until it was all gone and her ass and thighs were smeared with the slimy gunk. I put the fruit plate onto the mattress within her reach.

"Now the grapes."

She pulled the white grapes off their stem one by one and slid them up her love canal. With each grape she uttered a little grunt, but they went in easily enough. The fruit was fresh out of the refrigerator, and cold. I kept eating, turning my attention from my food to the TV to Malee's pussy. There were about twenty little white orbs on the grape stem, and by the time Malee had them all inside herself she had to keep a hand over her cunt to keep it all in. All that was left on the plate were some slices of mango and papaya, and as I forked up the last of my coleslaw I told her to finish that too.

By the time she got to the last slice of mango she was obviously uncomfortable, and she stood on the unsteady platform of the bed, with both hands over her crotch and mashed fruit oozing between her fingers. I stood up and pulled out the second chair at the dining table. "Sit, whore," I told her. She gingerly stepped off the bed, and came over to the table, walking bowlegged. I put a napkin on the seat and she sat down, clamping her legs tightly together. I took her hands and tied them behind her back with one of my ties, then pushed her face into the now cold and greasy plate of fried rice.

She gobbled the nasty mess greedily, slurping and sucking the rice into her mouth and swallowing with loud gulps. She probably hadn't eaten since lunch the day before, and I could hear her stomach growling as she ate. I smoked and watched her eating like a pig in a trough, and when she had licked the plate clean she looked up at me with a big grateful smile, grains of rice stuck to her face from hairline to chin.

I pulled her up by her bound wrists and said "Now you can have your dessert." I pushed her backwards until the backs of her knees were against the bed, then pulled her head down so her butt was sticking out over the mattress. Fruit pulp was dribbling down the insides of her thighs, and I put an empty plate on the bed under her ass. I kicked her feet until her legs were spread wide open, and a gush of mashed fruit spilled out onto the plate. She was saying "Oh! Oh! Oh!" with each squirt of pulp, and the more she tried to constrict her cunt muscles to keep it in, the more was forced out.

"Don't get any on the bed, whore, or the floor either," I said, giving her a slap on the back of her head to make my point. I let her stand like that until the stuff stopped coming out, then I roughly dug a finger inside her to scrape out the rest. Most of the grapes had remained intact, but the banana, mango and papaya was pureed; on the whole the plate appeared to be covered with technicolour vomit.

I yanked her up by her hair and spun her around, quickly forcing her to her knees. I pushed her head forward until her nose was in the muck and said "Eat it, whore."

She whimpered a bit, made a few nibbles at the stuff and gagged. "I can't, Master please... please don't make me..."

I reached down for a nipple and gave it a vicious squeeze. "You'll eat it, bitch, or I'll make you put it up your ass and then eat it." She was weeping freely now, but she lowered her face once more and began to slurp up the gunk. In a minute the plate was clean again. pulled her to her feet and propelled her to the door.

"Listen, you worthless cunt," I said, "if I give you an order you obey, understand?"

"Ye-yes,Master... it's just that..."

"Just nothing. If you don't like the deal, fine. You can leave now."

I pulled the door open and made to push her out into the hall. She was terrified. She was stark naked, with her wrists tied behind her, and a mixture of fruit pulp and pussy juice smeared over her face, neck, tits, ass and the inside of her thighs from her cunt to her knees. She looked like hell, smelled like a a combination fish market and fruit stand.

"No, please Master, I'll never disobey again, oh please, Malee is a good girl, Malee will make her Master happy... oh please let me stay!"

I looked at her for a moment, then pushed the door shut. I put her face into the wall and released her wrists. "Go clean yourself," I said, "you look like a pig." She went into the bathroom and sat on the commode, spraying her twat with the douche hose. I leaned in the doorframe and smoked, watching her clean her cunt. She put two fingers inside herself and spread her pussy open, the directed the cold spray inside. She gasped and grimaced, and the water that sluiced out of her snatch looked like fruit cocktail. She kept at it for at least ten minutes, even though she was shivering with the cold; even whores are fastidious in Asia.

When she'd finished rinsing out of cunt and dried herself with a towel, I led her back into the bedroom. I made her stand with her face against the wall while I lifted the double mattress off the bed frame and leaned it against the wall. Like most hotels, the Grace bolts its bed frames to the floor against the wall, the idea being that the guest can't rearrange the furniture and make extra work for the room maid. Without the mattress, the frame was a 6 foot by 8 foot metal rectangle, and 8 inches off the carpet, supported on four short legs. I pulled Malee away from the wall and told her to lie on her back in the middle of the frame.

Using more of my ties I secured each of her ankles and wrists to a corner of the bed frame, and made my knots very tight. I was an eagle scout in my youth, and while I can no longer start a camp fire by rubbing two sticks together, I've never forgotten my knots. She was spread-eagle on the floor, her arms and legs stretched out straight and tense. I pulled her long hair into a twisted braid and tied it to the centre of the part of the bed frame that normally supported the head board. When I was finished she was absolutely immobilized, staring up at the ceiling. She tried wriggling around a bit, but finally gave it up and lay there panting.

I sat down in a chair and considered the picture she made. I turned the TV up as high as it would go; I planned to make Malee scream a bit and wanted no hotel detectives coming to investigate. I lit a cigarette and watched her testing her bonds. No matter how she squirmed, she couldn't move at all. Her boobs were stretched apart, her nipples erect and pointing straight up. Her pussy was wide open and terribly inviting; I had an impulse to fuck her as she was, but a look at my watch told me that I had an hour to kill before the afternoon heat would die down outside. I planned to take Malee on a little shopping trip, since I hated the clothes she wore, but I had some time to kill.

I stubbed out my cigarette and went into the bathroom. I picked up one of the wet bath towels off the floor and soaked it under the sink tap until it was heavy with water. I wrung it out and spun it into a rat's tail, the carried it back into the bedroom.

The TV was blasting out the theme music to a woman's talk show, and the announcer was saying that this week's topic for discussion was 'Men Who Abuse Women, and The Women Who Love Them'. Perfect. I spun the towel round like a plane's propeller and it gave off a whirring sound as drops of water splattered the room's walls. Malee flinched when she heard it, bit her lower lip and squeezed her eyes shut.

She was shivering, so that her boobs were quivering like a jelly, but it was not the air conditioning that made her shake like that!

I stood over her and slapped the towel into my palm with a crack. Malee jumped, as far as she was able trussed up as she was, and I couldn't hear it but I knew that she was whimpering.

I spun the towel once and brought it down sharply on one proud breast; it gave a snap and an angry red welt immediately arose, crossing the dark brown circle around her nipple. She yelped, and tears began to pour down her cheeks. I could see her lips moving, and I knew shed was begging for mercy. Her hands had clasped in fists around the ties securing her arms, and her knuckles were white with the urgency of her grip.

I spun the towel again, and brought it down on the other tit. I missed the nipple this time, but left a beauty of a welt across the soft lower lobe of the boob itself. Her mouth was open, but the only sound in the room was the audience of the chat show applauding for a reformed wife beater, who had come out of prison for one day to explain himself on national TV. His victim/spouse sat opposite him on the stage, weeping into a handkerchief. The moderator, a plump Tamil woman, sat between them looking soulfully into the camera.

I spun the towel like a plane propeller again, and as it spun around and around I lowered it unto Malee could feel the breeze on her belly. Her whole body was shaking. I moved the towel down until the wet end of it was coming within inches of her shaved cunt. I could see the thighs spasming as she instinctively tried to close her bound legs, and her eyes were wide open and trying to stare down at the spinning whip between her legs.

I lowered the towel just a fraction on an inch, and the tip of it went smack along her pussy lips. Malee jumped so that her whole body came off the frame for a moment, then she landed writhing again. I had raised the towel, though I was still spinning it, and now I lowered it again, this time so that she got two good thwacks on her pretty pink twat. Her mouth was moving rapidly, though I couldn't hear a sound over the TV, and she was weeping freely. Her pussy lips were swollen and bruised, I imagined that the pain was fairly intense.

I stood over her, enjoying the sight of her helplessness, knowing that I could hit her anywhere I chose, and on an impulse I reached down and stuck a finger in her twat. Inside she was sopping wet, it was like sticking my finger into a bowl of pudding. As soon as my finger was in her I saw her face relax, and instead of fighting her bonds she relaxed. It pleased me that she was enjoying being beaten as much as I enjoyed beating her.

I left her and went to the TV; the self-accusing apologies of the wimp on stage, and the shrewish complaints of the bitch of a wife, were getting on my nerves. I turned off the TV and dragged a chair over to the bed frame. I sat down and leaned over Malee, running a hand over her tits and belly and cunt. Her body was burning, so I knew that I had been right: it was passion, not chill, that caused her to shiver so.

"Malee," I said gently, "are you horny?"

She looked up at with gratitude and said "Oh yes Master, I want you to fuck me so much! Please fuck me, Master, please fuck me!"

I took her clitoris between my thumb and forefinger and rolled it around gently. It was hard and hot like a ball-bearing in fresh oil. "I'll fuck you, Malee, I'll fuck you nice and hard and long, but first I want you to tell me about how you became a whore."

WE CLOSE WITH THE NEXT INSTALMENT OF OUR RE-VISED AND EXPANDED VERSION OF 'ERICA, PROPERTY OF REX, by Rex Saviour, currently out of print. Previous episodes can be found in Plantation Punishment, Naked Plunder, Selling Stephanie, SM Double Value & Dominating Obsession.

...... I heard them rustling about. "Now, stop where you are." I kept my eyes shut. "Step forward the middle two," I said. "You are chosen." Then I opened my eyes.

One of the two was walking to the door, apparently quite composed. The other had flung herself to the floor and was hugging Turk round the ankles, imploring him to spare her.

"This is interesting," he said. "She who accepts her fate has been whipped many times before. She who has not is more frightened of what is to come, and therefore she shall be spared to sleep with Turk whilst Oi is away." He took hold of her hair and held her up before him. "I think she will be very good to Turk in bed."

"Yes, yes, yes!" wept the girl.

"I like them frightened," said Turk. "It may be she shall watch many times before I have her whipped at last. And now she shall see what this pretty machine machine can do."

"Now, chosen one," he said to the weeping girl, "this time you turn the wheel. When Turk is tired of you, you will be its victim. Now - TURN!"

The girl took the crank in her hands and turned the wheel. It was obviously highly geared, and one turn of the crank became five turns of the wheel, and soon the speed of it made the paddles fly out and slap against Oi's buttocks as they passed. No matter how she wriggled she could not avoid them.

"Faster!" shouted Turk. "Faster! FASTER!"

It was as good a beating as I have ever seen.

"STOP!" he said at last. "REVERSE!" The girl was puzzled. "Idiot!" he said, slapping her cheek, "other way!"

That is when I saw the full beauty of the machine.

*

I sat with my writing pad in front of Oi in her frame, studying the apprehension in her dark eyes as she shivered there with fright. It was not an ideal way to put a person to be interviewed at ease!

"Is it true that your step-brothers burned you with their cigarettes?" I asked.

She nodded. There were tears in her eyes. She was tense all the time, at the mercy of that diabolical machine.

"My step father intended to sell me when I was big enough," she said. "So to stop me from running away he always kept a stick tied between my ankles to hold my legs apart. My step-brothers liked that! At night - I never had a room of my own - at night they would tie my wrists to my ankles and lie me on my back and they thought it manly to smoke cigarettes, which was forbidden, and even more so to stub them out between my legs...

when my step-father found out he was furious, he beat me badly because he couldn't sell me any more and then he took to treating me the same way - oh! oh! oh!"

The machine had snapped into action again, and I got no more of her story that time. But what a story it is! Oh yes, Illustrious King, I know already that her's is a terrible tale that I shall have to write down for you to keep me alive a little longer. It will please you mightily, I have no doubt, when we get round to it.

But first, as to Erica, we are not finished with her:-

2-1

I awoke lazily that morning, to find myself lying on my back with a hard-on. The delicious sensation of warm lips and timid tongue told me that Erica had woken up first - as she still often did on windy nights or when the owls hooted.

But her face down there between my legs - that was quite unusual!

Perhaps she thought it would put me in a good mood for the day?

Well, maybe so, but it was also extremely frustrating, having to deny myself sex because of her youth.

I wound my fists into her glorious long red-gold hair and she reached behind her with both hands and held her shift up to her waist as I pulled her slim body up over my naked one. I was rewarded with the sight of the face that turned me on so, masses of lovely long shining hair, bright mischievous blue eyes, apprehensive now as I brought her lips to mine.

My hands were free to play with her uncovered bottom. How I loved that smooth skin! She squirmed deliciously under my touch and her kisses grew in intensity.

Why?

Then I remembered!

Today, at long last, Erica was nineteen. From today everything would be different. Her total vulnerability tempted me to roll over on her and put my new rights to the test, but just in time I remembered the little ceremony I had planned.

"Out!" I said.

I suffered renewed temptation, seeing her walk to the electric kettle - it was that upright carriage I had taught her and the easy grace that came so naturally. She wore nothing but her shift, the same one I had bought her when she had first come to live with me, many times repaired. It was a pretty pink colour, thin and filmy, by no means as long as she would have liked - it had started hip length but she had grown taller in the two years that she had lived with me, though she was still quite small.

I watched her make the tea and arrange it on a tray. As she came and bent forward to lay the tray in my lap her breasts were fully revealed, high, pert and firm, the tips exceptionally rosy. I saw the usual blush rise in her cheeks as she waited for me to accept the tray.

When I did so, she proceeded to the next stage of our morning routine. This pleasant little interlude in our day is intended to help Erica with her deportment. She wasn't just standing - she was standing at attention, chest out, head up, hands behind the back but held clear of the buttocks. I had taught her never to hide her bottom, because it was the focus of many of her hang-ups and therefore, in the interests of desensitization therapy, I had to warm it up quite often. She wears a broad leather belt at all times, in case I need to use it to correct her behaviour.

Or in case I am bored, or it pleases me to do so for some other reason, or to show my control of her off to friends.

Every ninety seconds she moved smoothly to a different posture in a preplanned sequence. First she went on tiptoe with her hands behind her neck, elbows strained backwards, then it was legs apart hands straight up in the air, clasped above the head. That pose allowed me to check the smoothness of her shaven sex. Her skin is a beautiful light golden brown all over, kind of olive, a legacy from the Argentinian father she so little resembled in any other way. Or more likely some family he had purchased her from.

I beckoned her close, and turned her to admire that spankable little bottom. When I pinched her, just a small one in fun, she flinched a little but did not dare to move away from the harder one she would be expecting.

"Erica!"

She turned back, and I fingered a nipple. "Yes, Uncle?" She still called me Uncle. It sounded better than step-father when I took her into pubs and so on.

"I think I'll have breakfast in bed this morning."

"Yes, Uncle."

"Erica!"

She turned at the door.

"Many happy returns!"

"Thank you, Uncle Rex."

"You can't go downstairs like that, not now you're nineteen, it wouldn't be decent."

"Oh no, no!" There was great relief in her voice. I'll get dressed, then."

"It isn't worth it, you'd only have to undress again. You haven't finished the exercises."

"Oh - but -"

"Put your shoes and socks on."

"Oh!" She sat on a chair and put on her white socks and trainers, then walked reluctantly to the door. "Hold your shift down," I suggested, "it's getting a bit short." By this time I had a small staff - besides the butler there was a chef, a gardener, a stable lad and a chauffeur - loyal, discreet, very highly paid. I think she was worried that they might be in the kitchen gossiping at this time of the morning.

When she came back with the breakfast tray she had fetched from the kitchen she was crying. She was still standing there snuffling when I finished my breakfast.

"You can finish the exercises later," I said, opening the newspaper. "You may come back to bed."

She went to the foot of the bed and raised sheet and blanket to creep in. The timid brush of her hair and breasts, the touch of her hands and the feel of her tongue working its timid way up the inside of my thighs was pleasant.

The appointment with John, my friendly and accommodating solicitor - let us call him Smith - the appointment with John Smith was for 11 am, and he arrived, as always, precisely dressed and precisely on time.

We laid out Rita's statement and the hammer as impressively as possible, then I called for Erica.

John drew in his breath as she entered, as well he might, never having seen her before. Her upright deportment in itself is enough to attract the eye in any gathering, and she filled her clothes to more than perfection: clothes carefully chosen by me, more to display than conceal.

"This is Mr Smith," I said.

"Good morning, Mr Smith."

"Many happy returns, my dear."

"Th-thank you."

"Well," I said, "give him a kiss."

She went into his arms reluctantly, as always with strange men. She has this 'thing' about being touched, a relic of her dreadful childhood. John took his time before releasing her and depositing his considerable bulk at the table.

Erica stood beside him, looking uneasily at the hammer. She looked very small beside him.

"Now," he said, "we have some legal matters to update." He pointed to the Bible he had placed ready. "Put your right hand on that and repeat after me: I swear to tell the truth, the whole truth and nothing but the truth." When she was sworn in, most impressively I thought, he continued: "You are Erica Saviour of this address, formerly Erica Fernandez, born in Buenos Aires on this day nineteen years ago?"

Erica glanced at me. "I - I think so."

"That is so," I said. I produced her birth certificate and handed it to John, along with the amending document. "After I married her step-mother I had her name changed to mine by deed poll."

"Very well, quite in order, yes." He looked sternly at Erica, taking off his glasses and polished them before extracting a document from his brief-case and scrutinising it. Then he handed it to Erica. "Miss Saviour, this is the document we are to update today. Do you recognise it?"

She took it gingerly. "Yes, it's an agreement I made with Uncle Rex - with my step-father, I mean - when I was younger."

"Exactly. It appears that your step-father undertook to cure you of certain phobias by a process known as systematic desensitization, that is, exposing the subject to increasingly strong doses of what she fears until at last the phobia is overcome." He turned to me. "Yes, well, has Erica responded to this treatment?"

Erica and I looked at each other. "Not as yet," I admitted. "I have tried hard in the matters of shyness, being touched and fear of snakes, but with little success."

"Perhaps I had better see for myself. Shyness, then. How shall I test that? I know - take off your knickers, my dear, if you would be so kind."

"I - I can't - I -"

He thumped his fist on the table.

"This is a legal matter. Take them off, I say!"

"But - but - I don't have any!"

"Ah! Yes, I see." He sat back, a little nonplussed, and polished his glasses yet again. "Well, then, I think we must consider the test failed due to excessive blushing. Now, about touch, stand closer, please. A little closer. Yes, but feet apart, and put your hands behind your neck." He ran his hands up and down her bare legs. "My word, she's shaved. See how she flinches from me - another failure, I fear." He paused to make a note on his big pad of ruled paper. "Does she get plenty of punishment?"

"I think so," I said.

"Spanking, for example?"

"Oh yes."

"With a slipper?"

"Yes indeed."

"And the strap? Do you ever strap her?"

"I use her belt, actually. Or my razor strop if we are in the bathroom."

"Frequently?"

"Well, most days."

He licked his lips. "So discipline has been applied, but clearly it has not worked. Perhaps I should test her reaction? Do you think I should do that, Mr Saviour?"

"If you feel it would be helpful, then yes, by all means."

"Very good," said John. He was, as I had suspected, clearly a man who would beat her regardless, given the chance. "I shall test her, then... if you would be so kind as to come over my lap, my dear."

He had her skirt raised and his hand poised before I could speak. "For a proper test," I pointed out, "one needs an instrument."

"I see. Please forgive my inexperience."

"I suggest a hair-brush. Would that be acceptable? Yes? Run and fetch the hair-brush, Erica dear."

The little demonstration seemed to excite him and he carried it out rigorously. He was breathing quite hard when he finished. His comment was harsh: "Quite an unnecessary fuss for nineteen, all that wriggling, quite unnecessary!"

"About the same as usual," I admitted.

"In other words, total failure. This is a grave matter, Mr Saviour. You have quite neglected to cure her. What do you feel, young lady?"

"I - I - well, I think - perhaps -" She glanced at me, afraid to say it.

"Go on," I said. "You are on oath, remember."

"I think I am worse, not better."

"Perhaps he hasn't tried hard enough?"

"Oh God, he has, he has, he's tried terribly hard!"

"Well, he certainly does not appear to have fulfilled his part of the bargain. You are entitled to certain rights in the matter, even though the second part of the agreement now comes into effect." His words, like everything else about him, were very precise. "You remember what that is?"

"Y-yes."

"Speak up, girl, I didn't hear you."

"Yes, I remember. I agreed that I would become his sex slave when I was nineteen. F-for three years. Otherwise he would have sent me home. Or told the police how I killed my father."

"Exactly. The term sex-slave needs to be defined, but first let us deal with the matter of the death of your natural father. We have here certain photographs and statements signed by one Mrs Rita Fernandez. Your step-mother I think?"

Erica shuddered. "Yes."

"Yes. She alleges that you killed your father by striking him on the head with a hammer - this hammer, with his blood upon it. You did that when he was drunk and he fell down some steps into a cellar, causing injuries from which he subsequently died. Is this true?"

"I suppose -"

"Is it or is it not?"

"Yes."

"The man thoroughly deserved it for the disgusting things he did to her," I said. "And besides, he was drunk."

"Nevertheless, she was not tried at the time, therefore she could be now. The law would certainly have her locked up for life." John spoke sternly. He was stretching the truth a bit, a lot as a matter of fact, as I had asked him to do, but Erica didn't know that.

To be continued.........

Our Seven Most Recent Titles

Bush Slave
by Lia Anderssen
ISBN 1897809379

Once again, Lia Anderssen introduces us to a lovely, innocent young heroine to whom pain and humiliation bring ultimate pleasure.
Sold into slavery in Africa, Lisa Carling is kidnapped en route by rebels, and sold to a tribal chief who uses her as a sex slave for his warriors. Finally Lisa realizes that the arousal her treatment brings is what she desires, and slavery is her destiny.

Desert Discipline
by Mark Stewart
ISBN 1897809387

Follow the beautiful Suzanne, as she is kidnapped by pirates and sold into slavery - where she learns to submit herself totally to the cruelty of the whip.

Training Jenny
by Rosetta Stone
ISBN 1897809395

Jenny. Young and beautiful. The wife every man dreams of. Loyal, obedient, submissive, but not a sex slave - or is she?
Three short weeks change Jenny's view of her life forever. Three weeks of total submission to the will of a cold, calculating teacher. Three weeks that plunge her to the heights of passion she never dreamed possible.
Three weeks of pain and pleasure that leave her lusting for more.....

Voyage of Shame
by Nicole Dere
ISBN 1897809409

Commander Arthur Berman's aristocratic features registered incredulous disgust. Thirty years of iron discipline struggled against choking fury and almost lost. It was as thoughthe navy had planned this as one final insult, the last plunge of the knife into his career to which he had devoted his life since the tender age of sixteen

'*A detachment of five WRENS, plus one officer, arriving to join HMS Virago, to form part of seagoing crew.*'

The Admiral grinned suddenly, punched commander Berman lightly on the arm. "Virago's your last seagoing command, so make most of it, eh? Give 'em Hell, what?"

Plantation Punishment
by Rick Adams
ISBN 1897809417

Our dissolute hero progresses from control of a Victorian Poorhouse for destitute young females to the purchase of a Caribbean slave plantation where he indulges his vices of cruelty and rum drinking even more freely - but will the coming og the Voodoo God Exu be his undoing?

Naked Plunder
by J.T. Pearce
ISBN 1897809425

Locked behind thick walls in an exotic location in South America a journalist discovers bonded girls and submissive women, and aquires an alluring sex-slave he must rescue at all costs.

Selling Stephanie
by Rosetta Stone
ISBN 1897809433

Abducted on the orders of an obsessively jealous woman, Stephanie finds herself plunged into a nightmare or revenge, punishment and degradation.

Her youth and beauty and total submission to the desires of her captors are the assets that will ensure a high price when she is eventually sold at auction.

Constant training, total obedience and frequent beatings must be endured for day after day

Out of print Titles

All available on floppy disc
£5/$8 postage inclusive
(PC format unless Mac requested)

ISBN 1-897809-99-9 Balikpan: Ericas arrival *Rex Saviour*
ISBN 1-897809-01-8 Barbary Slavemaster *Allan Aldiss*
ISBN 1-897809-02-6 Erica: Property of Rex *Rex Saviour*
ISBN 1-897809-04-2 Bikers Girl *Lia Anderssen*
ISBN 1-897809-05-1 Bound for Good *Gord, Saviour, Darrener*
ISBN 1-897809-07-7 The Training of Samantha *Lia Anderssen*
ISBN 1-897809-10-7 Circus of Slaves *Janey Jones*

All current titles are also available
on floppy.

This is a mail order only offer !

TITLES IN PRINT

Silver Moon

ISBN 1-897809-03-4 Barbary Slavegirl *Allan Aldiss*
ISBN 1-897809-08-5 Barbary Pasha *Allan Aldiss*
ISBN 1-897809-11-5 The Hunted Aristocrat *Lia Anderssen*
ISBN 1-897809-14-X Barbary Enslavement *Allan Aldiss*
ISBN 1-897809-16-6 Rorigs Dawn *Ray Arneson*
ISBN 1-897809-17-4 Bikers Girl on the Run *Lia Anderssen*
ISBN 1-897809-20-4 Caravan of Slaves *Janey Jones*
ISBN 1-897809-23-9 Slave to the System *Rosetta Stone*
ISBN 1-897809-25-5 Barbary Revenge *Allan Aldiss*
ISBN 1-897809-27-1 White Slavers *Jack Norman*
ISBN 1-897809-29-8 The Drivers *Henry Morgan*
ISBN 1-897809-31-X Slave to the State *Rosetta Stone*
ISBN 1-897809-35-2 Jane and Her Master *Stephen Rawlings*
ISBN 1-897809-36-0 Island of Slavegirls *Mark Slade*
ISBN 1-897809-37-9 Bush Slave *Lia Anderssen*
ISBN 1-897809-38-7 Desert Discipline *Mark Stewart*
ISBN 1-897809-40-9 Voyage of Shame *Nicole Dere*
ISBN 1-897809-41-7 Plantation Punishment *Rick Adams*
ISBN 1-897809-42-5 Naked Plunder *J.T. Pearce*
ISBN 1-897809-43-3 Selling Stephanie *Rosetta Stone*
ISBN 1-897809-44-1 SM Double value (Olivia/Lucy) *Graham/Slade**
*Please add £1/$1.50

Silver Mink

ISBN 1-897809-09-3 When the Master Speaks *Josephine Scott*
ISBN 1-897809-13-1 Amelia *Josephine Oliver*
ISBN 1-897809-15-8 The Darker Side *Larry Stern*
ISBN 1-897809-19-0 The Training of Annie Corran *Terry Smith*
ISBN 1-897809-21-2 Sonia *RD Hall*
ISBN 1-897809-22-0 The Captive *Amber Jameson*
ISBN 1-897809-24-7 Dear Master *Terry Smith*
ISBN 1-897809-26-3 Sisters in Servitude *Nicole Dere*
ISBN 1-897809-28-X Cradle of Pain *Krys Antarakis*
ISBN 1-897809-30-1 Owning Sarah *Nicole Dere*
ISBN 1-897809-32-8 The Contract *Sarah Fisher*
ISBN 1-897809-33-6 Virgin for Sale *Nicole Dere*
ISBN 1-897809-34-4 The Story of Caroline *As told to Barbie*
ISBN 1-897809-39-5 Training Jenny *Rosetta Stone*
ISBN 1-897898-45-X Dominating Obsession *Terry Smith*

All our titles can be ordered from any bookshop in the UK and an
increasing number in the USA and Australia by quoting the title and
ISBN, or directly from us for £5.95 each (UK) or $10.50 (USA) postage
included. Credit Cards read EBS (Electronic Book Services - £
converted to $ and back!)